The

David Coward

© David Coward

David Coward has asserted his rights under the Copyright, Design and Patents Act, 1988, to be identified as the author of this work.

This edition published in 2017 by Endeavour Press Ltd.

Table of Contents

Explanatory Note	5
Chapter 1	7
Chapter 2	15
Chapter 3	23
Chapter 4	32
Chapter 5	42
Chapter 6	55
Chapter 7	64
Chapter 8	81
Chapter 9	98
Chapter 10	108
Chapter 11	119
Chapter 12	138
Chapter 13	149
Chapter 14	162
Chapter 15	175
Chapter 16	186
Chapter 17	198

Chapter 18 209

Chapter 19 222

Explanatory Note

Gaston Leroux's Le Fantôme de l'Opéra *was published in 1910. My translation of the story of Erik's obsessive love for Christine Daaé appeared in 2011, just over a century later.*

A translator develops an intimate relationship with the text during long periods spent turning a book from one language into another. During the winter I spent closeted with Erik, I became curious about him. Leroux tells us little of how he became the murderous Phantom so besotted with Christine that there is no crime he would not commit for love of her. How did he become so hideously disfigured? Where had he been before he became a hermit in his fortress beneath the Paris Opera House? How did he come by his vast knowledge of philosophy, science, engineering, languages and all the arts?

According to the internal chronology of the novel, the tragic climax takes place in the 1880s, when Erik is in his forties. There are references which indicate that he was born in Normandy no later than 1840, that he was the son of a Rouen builder, but no indication is given of his real name, nor why he came to be called Erik. Rejected by his family, he became an exhibit in a touring freak show and lived among gypsies in Northern France. While still in his teens, he left the country and lived for periods in Indochina, the Punjab, Nizhny-Novgorod in imperial Russia, in the Persian province of Mazanderan and in Constantinople before returning to Paris in the early 1860s. Using the comprehensive knowledge of many subjects acquired in the Orient, he bid successfully for a contract to build the foundations of Charles Garnier's new Paris Opera House which finally opened in 1875. By then, he had been living for many years in quarters secretly built beneath the Opera where he had made tunnels and secret passages which allowed him to come and go unseen — except at rare intervals by the persistent Persian, the disgraced daroga (or chief of the police) of Mazanderan who had followed him to France.

These are the pegs on which this story is hung. The rest is speculation.

- David Coward

Chapter 1

The inn of the Golden Cockerel was a watering place held in high regard by carters, tinkers, hawkers and knife-grinders, by lawyers, merchants and doctors of physic, by lords and ladies, in a word, by all who travelled the road that ran from Mantes to Rouen. It was eagerly anticipated not because it was golden, or even welcoming, for it was ugly, dirty and uncomfortable. The reason why weary travellers watched out for it was much simpler: it was the best because it was the only inn on that long, straight, dusty road, the only relief for many miles.

Just now, as on most August afternoons, it was deserted. The potman, cook and stablemen were asleep and the two serving girls were in the fields.

Françoise, the inn-keeper's daughter, black-haired and eighteen years old, with eyes half closed and humming a tune that was old before there was an inn on the road, old before there even was a road, was sitting in the breeze which sidled through an upstairs window, spinning her wool on her wheel.

Maître Amédée Dartigoyte, the landlord, with his moleskin jacket unbuttoned over his vast stomach and his top button of his breeches undone, was taking the air by his front door, with half an eye on the empty ribbon of road which came to his inn and ran away into the wide-skied distance.

On a table beside him was a glass and, beside it, a half-empty jug of white wine. From time to time he sipped from his glass and wiped his brow with a large red handkerchief. He settled back into his chair, rocked by the gentle whirr of the spinning wheel that came from the upstairs window. He began to nod.

His eyes closed, his head dropped, his big face relaxed, his breathing grew more regular, almost overcome by the torpid summer heat. But not for long. The distant sound of horses, coach wheels and the peremptory signal blown on an old bugle made him lift his head again.

The landlord of the Golden Cockerel stirred. He reached for his handkerchief, wiped the sweat from his forehead, got to his feet and shouted for his daughter. But Françoise had heard the sounds of the imminent arrival of the coach and was already rousing the potman, the cook and the stablemen and calling for the maids, urging them to return to their posts immediately. The inn, which had slumbered in the summer silence, was suddenly all bustle.

The two stablemen stood outside, ready to attend to the horses. Maître Dartigoyte took up his position at the door of his establishment, ready to hand down any passengers who looked as if they might have money to spend. His daughter pinched her cheeks to make them rosy, straightened her bodice and patted her hair in the milky-blue mirror that hung at the bottom of the stairs

The carriage swept into the yard. The stable-boys leaped forward and held the horses. They had hardly done so when a tall man with well-to-do bourgeois written all over him leaped out. As his feet touched the ground he staggered and almost fell. Maître Dartigoyte's eyes lit up. A man already in drink was likely to want more. And of the best.

But for once, the landlord was wrong.

'Is there a doctor anywhere near this god-forsaken hole? My wife is about to be brought to bed, she's leaking all over the dammed carriage. I want him sent for at once. I want him here immediately.'

'I'm sorry, your honour, but there's no doctor until you get to Font-au-Vert …'

'And where's that when it's at home? Is it far?'

'Two leagues, your honour, and across country, on a bad road. An hour there and back on a horse but it could take four or five in your coach just to get there.'

'Out of the question. My wife is too far gone. The damned woman wouldn't survive it. Isn't there anyone hereabouts who knows about delivering babies?'

'My wife would have been delighted to help but she's been dead these ten years. She was a pearl.'

'Since she's dead, I couldn't care less if she was worth her weight in ambergris. Are you sure there's no one else?'

'If you've no objection, and I know some gentleman do and their ladies too, there's the man-midwife... Père Lapôtre.'

'Why didn't you say so before, you fool? Send for him at once. And in the meantime, have the lady taken upstairs. Your best room, if you have such a thing. And quick about it. Then send one of your stable-boys to fetch that doctor. If Madame decides to take her time, he might come in useful yet. It's her first, so you never know. But before you do anything, bring me brandy.'

Maître Dartigoyte produced a bottle and a glass as directed then hurried off shouting orders.

The potman improvised a stretcher and under the supervision of Françoise who had a kind way with her and despite her youth, a practical turn of mind, the lady was carried upstairs and put to bed. The patient was very pale and her hair was damp with sweat. Françoise removed her hat and helped her take off her travelling coat. Then she sat her on the bed and removed her shoes. The lady thanked her in an expiring voice and lay back on the pillows with a sigh.

While this was going on, the husband, who Dartigoyte recognised as Prosper Dondedieu, a well-known Rouen builder and man of property, retired to a side room with his bottle and stayed well away from what was happening upstairs.

As Françoise tucked the sheets around Madame Dondedieu, she had an opportunity to examine the patient at close quarters. She could not have been much older than she was herself, but she was very weak and there was no trace of the bloom of youth on her cheeks. Her face was deathly pale, her forehead was cold and clammy, despite the heat of the day, and her breathing was shallow. When Françoise spoke to her, she did not reply. She hardly seemed conscious. Telling one of the maids to stay and watch, she went downstairs.

'Father, the lady is very ill.'

Dartigoyte shrugged: 'I've sent for Lapôtre, he'll know what to do.'

'What! That butcher! You can't let him near a lady like her! He'll kill her!'

Dartigoyte shrugged again.

'It's nothing to do with us. It's what the husband wants.'

At that moment, the maid called down:

'Mademoiselle Françoise, come quickly! The lady is calling for you!'

Françoise ran up the stairs. Dartigoyte went back to his bar.

In the room, Françoise leaned over Madame Dondedieu and felt her brow again.

'Can I get you anything, Madame? Water?'

The woman in the bed nodded weakly, Françoise poured water from a stone jug into a glass, raised her head and held the glass to her mouth. Those deathly pale lips opened and she swallowed a few sips. Françoise let her head return gently to the pillow. The woman opened her eyes and she whispered faintly.

'Thank you.'

Then she closed her eyes and seemed to sleep.

Françoise sat with her. Time passed. At intervals she wiped the woman's brow. She was near her term and from time to time her body tensed and she groaned.

Then she was aware of a change. The woman's breathing came more quickly, her eyes opened wide and were lit by panic. Her hands clutched at the sheet which covered her, twisting the material, cramming it into her mouth to stop the scream which began to build.

From the landing, Dartigoyte, who was growing impatient and had come up to investigate, asked what was going on.

'Come in, father. See, she's near her time. Did you send for Lapôtre?'

The woman on the bed could no longer hold back and released a long howl of pain as the first contraction struck. Françoise pulled back the sheet and put one hand on the woman's stomach. Through the thin cloth of the shift, she could feel movement.

'Oh my God!' she said. 'The baby's coming!'

'You'd better prepare her, girl! She's not likely to give birth as long as she's wearing those travelling clothes! While you're undressing her, I'll send Pascal to tell Lapôtre to get a move on and then I'll let his lordship know what's happening. It's for him to tell us what to do next.'

Five minutes later, Dondedieu the builder lumbered up the stairs and walked into the room wrapped in brandy fumes. He stood over his wife who at intervals writhed under her sheet and howled.

'That's the way, Madame Dondedieu!' he said. 'A few good yells, get it out of your system, a push or two and it'll be over, you mark my words. That's how the first Madame Dondedieu managed it and there's no reason for you to make more of a fuss than she did, God rest her soul and that of the infant who followed her to the grave. So chin up. I'll leave you to it. They'll come and tell me how you get on.'

And so saying, he turned on his heel and disappeared through the door.

Françoise was beginning to feel afraid. She'd seen calves and lambs being born and was well aware that humans were no different from animals in this respect. She'd also been there when her mother had given birth to her twin brothers, Simon and Louis. She knew what was supposed to happen but what was happening to Mme Dondedieu now was different. It was wild and furious and unlike anything she'd seen or heard. It wasn't right that she should be left alone with the woman. How could she be expected to look after her when she didn't know what to do?

'Sir!' she called after the retreating Dondedieu. 'Don't leave me, sir! I can't manage on my own!'

Dondedieu turned on his heel.

'What's the matter, girl? Not up to it? Well, you'd better try harder. It's no good looking to me for help. This is women's business. So pull yourself together and get on with it. There'll be a gold *louis* for you if you take good care of Madame Dondedieu.'

As he reached the foot of the stairs, he almost ran into a thin, elderly, stooping man carrying a battered leather bag. The man bowed and removed his hat.

'Lapôtre, your honour, the man mid-wife ...'

'Good,' growled Dondedieu. 'Just in time. My wife's up there. As you can tell by the row she's making, she has just started and is making a meal of it. The girl will tell you all you need to know. Report to me when you've finished. And don't be long about it. I have to be in Rouen tonight. I've been delayed enough as it is."

And so saying he turned on his heel and went into the side room, back to his bottle.

Lapôtre joined Françoise by the bedside. Mme Dondedieu was thrashing about in the bed, groaning between contractions which were now so urgent that unless the pressures were relieved Françoise was sure she would die and the infant with her.

Lapôtre examined the patient. He frowned. 'Ach! The child is presenting badly. I can feel the shoulder. It must be turned or there will be salvation for neither of them.'

He reached for his bag and from it took an array of instruments which he kept polished and oiled and, especially, sharp. They looked as if they would have been more at home in the torture chambers of the Inquisition than in a sick room. Carefully he laid out knives, scissors, spatulas, pincers, his implements of salvation and deliverance. There were two crotchets, or hooks, which he used to destroy and extract an infant which presented so unfavourably that it had no chance of being born, and a *tire-tête*, which was for gripping the head and hauling on. Françoise shuddered. The sight of them, the thought of them made her feel sick.

Lapôtre pulled back the shift she had put on the patient and set to work to free the child within while Françoise looked on with growing horror. He inserted his tongs, hooks, scalpels and squirts and ... *rummaged* – it was the only word for it – for a hold in the living flesh inside.

'Ah, that's good,' he said. 'The infant has changed its position.'

Mme Dondedieu was by now unconscious, which was fortunate, since it meant that she felt nothing. But Françoise felt for her, felt every horrible twist and push and wrench and tear of Lapôtre's strong wrists. The bed was a mass of blood and he had to keep stopping to wipe his hands so that they did not slip on his implements.

Three times he dried them on his sleeve before Françoise heard a horseman clatter over the cobbles of the yard below.

She looked out of the window and saw the familiar figure of Dr Robert, from Font-au-Vert.

She opened the casement and shouted down:

'Please hurry, sir, for the love of God! There's murder being done here!'

There was the sound of feet on the stairs, the door burst open and a strong man's voice said, 'Get out, Lapôtre, and make yourself scarce. The last time I found you at work butchering a patient, I told you I would flay you alive. Good God, man! What have you been doing? I venture to say you've killed the poor infant and its unfortunate mother with your medieval implements. If you have, I'll see to it that you'll face a charge of murder! Now stand aside!'

'I am trying to save the child. It is my duty, the church orders us to save the child even if it is at the expense of the mother,' said Lapôtre, reaching for a pair of fearsome metal tongs. 'If I can only get a grip ...'

Dr Robert waited no more. With a swing of his fist he knocked the man mid-wife to the floor then yanked him back on his feet by the scruff of his neck and booted him down the stairs. Returning to the room he kicked the charlatan's tools under the bed and examined the patient.

'There's still life here, in both mother and child. But the child will not be born by the usual canal. We must proceed by the caesarean route, but it's a desperate remedy. The poor woman has already lost a great deal of blood and her pulse is weak. Fetch the father. He must know what I propose.'

Dondedieu blanched when he saw the blood

'I doubt,' said the doctor, 'if either mother or child will survive the damage that imbecile Lapôtre has done. But as long as there's a chance we must take it. I assume you agree?'

Dondedieu nodded, clapped one hand over his mouth and fled the room retching.

Dr Robert paid no attention.

'Françoise,' he said, 'get hot water and towels. If we're quick, we'll save the little one. But I fear the mother is gone.'

Half an hour later, Dr Robert held up a squawking baby.

'It's a boy, and alive,' said Françoise. 'Thank God!'

'And the mother still breathes!' said the Doctor. 'The boy's come sideways into the world, and I daresay that's how he'll have to live in it. I doubt that the little mite will thank us when he grows up. See what that fool Lapôtre has done?'

He passed the child to her. Françoise almost dropped him through sheer horror.

The boy's head was a mutilated, torn, bloody mess. It had been repeatedly squeezed by the *tire-tête*. The eyes had been displaced and were now on different levels. The cheekbones had been crushed, the nose and ears and most of the lips had been completely sliced off and the mouth had been ripped at both ends so that what was left of the face appeared to be grinning, like some demon or hobgoblin which had stepped out of the vilest nightmare that was ever dreamed.

When Monsieur Dondedieu was presented with his new son, he stared at it blankly.

'Good God! What do you expect me to do with that?' he said. 'I don't want it.'

'The boy is your son, man' said Dr Robert. 'You cannot just abandon him. It's not natural. Haven't you any feelings?'

'Oh very well,' grumbled Dondedieu. 'Wrap him up. You, girl, get your bonnet on. You're coming with me. You can look after the brat seeing as how you are part responsible for bringing him into the world. Landlord! Harness the horses to my carriage. I've got to be in Rouen tonight,' he said, turning to the doctor. 'Urgent business. I suppose there's no moving Madame Dondedieu? Too weak to travel is she?'

'She would not survive the journey,'

'Damn! Why couldn't the blasted woman wait until we got home, to have her brat? First she holds me up and now I find she's going to give me the extra expense of having her looked after here until she's fit to travel. Mother of God and all the saints, was ever a man so put upon? Talking of which, here's what I owe you and here is an advance to defray the costs of looking after Mme Dondedieu. I'll leave the details to you. But remember she is my wife and must be treated accordingly. I have a position to keep up. Now, where's my coat. Landlord! Is my carriage ready?'

Before the carriage left, the doctor gave Françoise instructions for the care of the infant which he did not expect to live. Then Dondedieu the builder drove off, with Françoise and her bundle and his brandy bottle for company.

Dr Robert ordered Mme Dondedieu to be bathed and moved to a fresh room. He dressed her wounds then sent for his housekeeper. The lady would be looked after at the Golden Cockerel until such time as she was well enough to be moved to his house at Font-au-Vert to convalesce.

He gave as few chances of survival to the mother as he had to the infant.

He also alerted the authorities that near-murder had been committed that afternoon. But by the time the police arrived to take Lapôtre into custody, he had fled and was never heard of again in those parts.

Chapter 2

'So she's not actually dead?'

Marie-Thérèse Dondedieu, builder Dondedieu's spinster sister and housekeeper, crossed her arms under her ample bosom and waited for him to explain. No flicker of human kindness crossed her face, no word of sympathy trembled at her lips.

She was older than Prosper, her only brother, and never held back an opinion on any subject. The family had not allowed her to marry, for if she had taken a husband, they would have had to provide her with a dowry. Napoleon had changed the law that made the oldest son sole heir to his father's property. Instead, all children now had equal claims on the family estate. The building business which had been started by Edme Dondedieu in 1785 would have had to be sold to raise the money to pay her portion, thus leaving each of her brothers with only a share of the capital raised to live on. It was unthinkable. So Marie-Thérèse had surrendered her future for the good of the family. Her temper had not been improved by her sacrifice.

After Prosper bought his brothers out, she had stayed on in the family home where, after the death of the first Madame Dondedieu she had taken charge of the children who had long since fled the nest. Nature had not intended her to be a maiden aunt and her native sour character grew sourer as the years passed. After widower Prosper married again in middle age the previous year, she conceived a bitter hatred for the new, simpering, doll-like wife who had usurped her position as mistress of the house. But now she seemed likely to die. It was the best news Marie-Thérèse had received in years, though, as a good catholic woman, she could not allow herself to think of it in those terms. She felt her heart lighter than it had been for a year and a half, though she could not admit that either. If pressed, however, she would have agreed that the proper order of things had been restored.

Until Prosper had taken charge of the firm, it had limped along under the direction of their well-meaning but ineffectual father who had no head for business. He was weak and allowed himself to be taken advantage of. He was all too easily taken in and would employ a man not because he was a good worker but because he had a family to feed or owed a doctor money for his wife's treatment. He believed all the hard-luck stories his customers told him to delay paying what they owed and in some cases they never paid him at all. In the end, Prosper had bullied his father into retirement and took things in hand. He had sacked most of the employees, hired new men who would work for less, raised prices and made Dondedieu & Son a going concern. Marie-Thérèse admired him for it and said that he was well-named. Had not Prosper made the firm live up to his name?

But it was an article of faith with her that she had been part of his success, for she had encouraged him to take a strong hand and use forceful methods. Nor had she raised objections when he decided to send their parents away. They were an embarrassment, a nuisance. They were packed off to a small cottage in an out-of-the-way village where they would not be seen or heard or remind the public of the firm's reputation for being an easy touch. They had never been much of an advertisement for the business. They lived in the past.

'No, but she is to all intents and purposes,' said Prosper, throwing his hat on the floor for a servant to pick up. 'Blasted woman decided to go into labour when we were so near getting home. Made me late for the Mayor's dinner. I only just made it in time. The result's not a pretty sight. The brat, I mean.'

As a maiden lady, Marie-Thérèse was curious about these matters, but her pride stopped her asking questions. She would find out what she wanted to know later, from the servants. All she said was: 'What is it? Boy or girl?'

'Boy, they said, though you wouldn't know just by looking. It's in the carriage. The girl from the inn's looking after it. Go and make whatever arrangements are necessary. But a word of warning. It's not a pretty sight.'

And Dondedieu turned on his heel and made for his study. He always kept a bottle of brandy on his desk.

Marie-Thérèse stepped purposefully through the front door into the growing dusk.

The coachman and groom were unharnessing the horses. One door of the carriage was open, just as Prosper had left it. In the dark interior,

Marie-Thérèse made out the form of a servant girl holding a bundle in her arms.

'Is that the child?' she said crossly, as any housekeeper would who had unexpectedly been given a distasteful chore to do.

'Yes, mistress,' the girl said in a frightened voice.

'Show me,' barked Marie-Thérèse, though she was suddenly aware that here was Prosper's son, her flesh and blood too, her nephew. There might be a pleasant new role for her in raising the boy without interference from its mother who, it seemed, was not long for this world.

Slowly, gently, Françoise pulled back the shawl she had wrapped round the child. As she peeled away the last layer, Marie-Thérèse leaned forward, curious despite herself. Then she let out a gasp and recoiled in horror.

'What is this, miss? What do you mean by it?'

'It was the man-midwife, mistress! He did it, with his cruel instruments! We thought the lady was dying and he went about it as if he was butchering meat. I told him to stop but he wouldn't.'

'Cover it up this minute. I will not see it. It is an abomination. Is it dead? It's not moving.'

'Not quite dead, mistress. The poor little thing is only a few hours old and is weak. But he breathes.'

'Take it round to the back of the house. Do you have any experience of caring for new-born infants?'

'I looked after a brother and sister when they were born and watched and helped my mother raise four more of us.'

'Then you know more about such matters than anyone else in this house. Tell cook she is to give you whatever you need. Settle it down and then let me know when you've done it.'

'Should not the doctor be sent for, mistress? The infant is very ill and like to die.'

'If it is like to die, no doctor would save it. Do what you're told, and quick about it.'

And Marie-Thérèse strode back into the house. Carefully, Françoise eased herself out of the carriage taking care to avoid any sudden movement that might wake the child which was sleeping the sleep of exhaustion. The coachman directed her where she was to go. She found the door to the kitchen and called out timidly. A large woman with a red face and a white apron appeared and asked her roughly what she wanted.

'Baby? What baby? The mistress at her last gasp ... Oh my lord ... You'd better come in. Fancy a baby! Well I never! There hasn't been one of them in this house in a month of Sundays. Of course, we knew there was one on the way. But there's never been babies in this house as I heard of since the old Mistress lost hers. A girl it was. The croup. Nor did Madame survive it. Dead inside a month. Must be twenty years since. I was just a starting then. Scullery maid. Come in, dear ... Was brought to bed on the way, you say. Well I'm glad the master had you to help out because if it was left to him there'd be no thought given to babies. Boy or girl is it? Boy, you say? Sleeping is he? He's very quiet. Set him down here, that's right, now let's have a look at the poor lamb.'

The next moment, the house was filled with screams of horror loud enough to wake the dead.

The next morning, after a night peopled with nightmarish ghouls, the cook gave her notice.

She said she would not, could not, stay in the house a moment longer.

*

Madame Dondedieu did not die.

Doctor Robert feared for her life, more or less despaired of it. At first he called daily at the Golden Cockerel, then at intervals which grew longer and longer. Her progress was uncertain but, after a certain point, steady. From time to time, he wrote to Maître Dondedieu informing him of his wife's improving state of health. His letters went unanswered. It was over two months before his patient could be moved from Maître Dartigoyte's inn to Font-au-Vert.

Françoise remained at builder Dondedieu's house where she had full charge of the boy. No firm arrangement was made but it was assumed that the infant was her responsibility. She was given a small attic room to sleep in and ate with the other servants in the kitchen. A new cook was engaged.

Since neither the boy's father nor his aunt paid any attention to him and carried on with their lives as normal even though both he and his mother were at death's door, Françoise fell into the habit of calling the baby Jean. For many weeks, he lay whimpering in a poor wicker cot which one of the servants had found in the Monday market. But slowly he gained in strength. The cot was kept in Françoise's room under the eaves. No one saw Jean except her.

When Doctor Robert judged the time was right, he wrote to Dondedieu saying that his wife had asked after her son and wanted to see him. In the doctor's view, it would be beneficial to his wife's health and speed her recovery if the boy could be brought to Font-au-Vert.

The visit was arranged. It was not a success.

When Mme Dondedieu saw Jean, she fainted. The boy was removed from the room and returned to Rouen. Françoise accompanied him.

Before she left, Doctor Robert demanded to know which medical colleague in the fine town of Rouen had so disgracefully neglected the boy's injuries. She told him that no doctor had been employed by Maître Dondedieu. The only treatment Jean had received had been given by her. She said she was sorry but she was only a simple peasant girl with no knowledge of medicines.

'If the man intends to bring the boy up the way he has begun,' Dr Robert snorted, 'then I would not give a green fig for his chances of reaching the age of five.'

And he shook with anger as he spoke the words.

When she returned, Françoise told builder Dondedieu what had happened at Font-au-Vert, he ordered her to bring his son to him, so that he could see for himself what all the fuss was about. Marie-Thérèse, who could not be kept away, was also present for the inspection.

Jean was swaddled in rags which Françoise had rescued from the household linen that was judged beyond repair.

'Well,' snarled Dondedieu, 'show me what you've got.'

Françoise pulled back the cloth protecting his face. Dondedieu gasped.

'Jesus, Mary and all the saints!' he muttered, 'what have we got here?'

What he had was a body which had a head but no face. There were lopsided holes for eyes, though from deep inside them two pupils burned yellow, as innocent and curious as a wild animal's. For a nose there was a red-raw absence and pink gums showed where lips should have been. The skin was dry, like parchment, and, where the flesh was red-raw and still healing, the same putty colour. Both corners of the mouth had been slit and supplied an expression of malignant mockery

Dondedieu recoiled with disgust.

Marie-Thérèse bent over the boy then straightened up when the baby, frightened by the attention he was not used to, began to cry. Her face filled with fury.

'Is this the best you could do, girl?'

'Madame …'

You told me you were experienced in the matter of child-rearing. I now see that you lied.'

'I never lied, mistress …'

'Don't answer back. Now take this … this … monstrosity away. I don't want to see it again until it's more presentable.'

'Will the priest christen him when his wounds have healed, Madame?'

'Christen it?' thundered Maître Dondedieu. 'This … thing will never be sufficiently healed, never presentable enough to be allowed out of this house again. Good God, the family name would not survive the shame. Now do as Madame Marie-Therese says and remove it from my sight. I don't want to see it ever again.'

'But if he is not christened, how will he get a name?'

'Call him what you like,' hissed Marie-Therese, 'as long as he is not called Dondedieu. Now get out!'

Françoise wanted to say that a child that died unchristened had no chance of heaven and would languish in purgatory forever. But she had said enough already and was afraid to say more. As she went, she wondered at the callousness of these people who were surely rich enough to be kind! As she went, she swore to herself that she at least would never abandon Jean.

Builder Dondedieu's wife survived the shock, recovered and eventually returned to Rouen. She did not need Dr Robert to tell her that she would never be able to have more children. But it was only slowly that it dawned on her that she would never walk again. She would spend the rest of her life in her bed from which she would, on fine summer days, be moved to the garden terrace to breathe the air.

But not a day went by when she did not think of the hideous son who, in getting life for himself, had ruined hers.

She never asked to see him again, never enquired after him, never once mentioned him after she was brought back from Font-au-Vert to live the rest of her painful and unhappy life under her husband's roof.

Marie-Thérèse gave orders that the creature was to be kept in a windowless cellar and that Françoise alone would see to its needs. The boy, the whole subject, was never to be mentioned in the house again. Though she was a pious, church-going catholic woman and knew it was wrong, she secretly though that it would be better for all concerned if the creature died. She never seriously considered that the best solution would be for it to be put out of its misery — for its own sake. Yet sometimes, in the quiet watches of the night, she did allow herself to wonder how such a thing might be done.

Builder Dondedieu washed his hands of the matter and left everything to Marie-Thérèse who in turn gave Jean entirely into Françoise's keeping.

*

Three months after Jean Dondedieu, unloved and unwanted son of Prosper Dondedieu, and Laurence-Adelaide, his lawful wedded wife, was consigned to the subterranean darkness of a cellar of the family home, the hand of Marie-Thérèse Dondedieu was sought in marriage by a notary named Gobert newly installed in the town. He had been assured that the lady, no longer in the first flush of youth, would not only jump at the chance but bring a handsome dowry with her and give him the *entrée* into bourgeois society which was indispensable to a man of his profession.

Marie-Thérèse, delighted by the prospect of being mistress of her own establishment, accepted. Her brother tried to discourage her because of the sheer cost to him of such a course of action, but she was not to be moved. To find the money for her settlement, he was forced to mortgage his business. There resulted financial pressures which undermined his health. After the departure of his sister, he grew melancholy and took to the bottle in a serious way.

After her marriage, Marie-Thérèse was too busy making her new husband miserable and persecuting her servants to give any further thought to her nephew in the cellar and exercised her authority as mistress of her own house with great relish.

Madame Dondedieu tried to drive her son out of her thoughts, but failed. She was left only with bitter memories of events which had ruined her life. Meanwhile Jean vanished quickly into the alcoholic haze which filled the mind of Maître Dondedieu.

In his cellar, Jean saw only Françoise who marvelled why heaven should allow such a fate to befall a person whose family name meant 'Gift of God'.

Chapter 3

For the first three months of his life, before his eyes even opened on the world, Jean knew only darkness.

Although builder Dondedieu would not hear of summoning a doctor to treat the baby's injuries which healed very slowly, he grudgingly allowed Françoise to find a wet-nurse for the boy. To do otherwise would have left him vulnerable, should the boy die or the shameful truth come out, to charges of neglect amounting to murder.

When the first applicant saw what a hideous creature she was being asked to feed, she clasped her belly with one hand, covered her mouth with the other and fled the room. She said she wouldn't do it, couldn't do it, no, not for a king's ransom. The second blanched and said that in her view the mere sight of such a monster was enough to stop a person's milk, that he had the mark of the devil on him. She too left in a state of shock but, like her predecessor, mollified by the money she had been paid to buy her silence. In desperation, Françoise hit upon the idea of employing a woman who would agree, for an extra payment, to wear a blindfold. It was an arrangement which suited all parties and, once into a settled routine, Jean began to thrive.

After a few weeks, Françoise started to worry that he was not getting enough air. Plucking up all her courage, she went to builder Dondedieu and told him that infants need light and fresh air and that it wasn't natural for little Jean to be kept a prisoner in his dark cellar. She offered to take him away, to the country, to a cottage her father owned not far from the Golden Cockerel. Permission was refused outright. When a few weeks later, she repeated the proposal, he had come to see the advantage of making Françoise entirely responsible for his problem. Keeping the boy at home was fraught with danger, for the smallest whiff of gossip could turn into a scandal which might well harm his good name and damage his business standing in the community. For reasons he failed to understand, the girl was devoted to the boy and would do nothing to harm his interests. If falling in with what Françoise wanted meant getting the boy out of his sight and sending him far away where he could be forgotten, he saw nothing but advantages in the plan.

For her part, Marie-Thérèse, her mind fixed on the arrangements for her forthcoming marriage, gave her consent at once.

'Do what you like, brother. It's of no consequence to me.'

So he agreed and even made Françoise a small allowance to cover necessary expenses. Françoise never discovered if he had consulted his wife, the bedfast Mme Dondedieu, on the proposal and thought it wise not to ask.

The very next day, she put Jean in a travel handbag, gathered together the few things she had had secretly bought in the market (no serving girl could afford to be seen buying baby-clothes openly) and set out in Maître Dondedieu's own carriage which he had obligingly made available for the occasion.

They quickly settled into their new home where Jean's appetite was quickened by good country air.

He was a contented baby. Of course, when his first teeth came through, he would grow fractious at times. But Françoise could always quiet him with one of the songs which she had learned from her mother. Music always acted on him like a calming draught.

In due course, he learned to say his first words, take his first steps, and opened his eyes to the world under the watchful care of Françoise, his second mother.

She did not allow mirrors in the cottage, she never referred to Jean's disfigurement nor were there any friends or neighbours or strangers to draw attention to it, by accident or design. They lived isolated lives in the small house which lay well off the beaten track. There were no callers though very occasionally a solitary walker who had missed his way knocked on their door to ask for directions or a drink of water. When that happened, Jean had his instructions. He was to climb into the loft and keep very still until the visitor had gone. The loft had no windows. Jean never saw any of the callers and learned to associate other people with caution, darkness and the smell of dust.

But animals were his friends.

By the time he was three, he could talk to chickens and rabbits and their pig, Charles, and birds fed out of his hand. When he was five, a scruffy spaniel strayed into their little vegetable garden. It had big eyes and gentle manners and it attached itself to him and became his inseparable companion. He called it Potage. Together they went exploring. Françoise told him he was not to wander far from the cottage, but sometime he would become engrossed in his adventures and forget. It was on one of these forbidden forays that he found his very own secret place. It was hidden under the low-hanging branches of a beech, near the river, a hole perhaps originally scooped out by a fox which had been widened and deepened by rain and flood. It was big enough for him to stand up in. He liked the dark. It made him feel safe. He kept favourite things there: a knife with a broken blade, a magpie feather and his lucky stone.

He was then seven, a sturdy, adventurous boy. The only humans he had ever set eyes on were Françoise and Maître Dartigoyte (who he called Papy). Papy came once a year, on Easter Monday, to tell Françoise it was time she stopped wasting her life on another woman's child and thought of getting married herself. She was not getting any younger. Anyway, wasn't it time the parents started think about sending the boy to school? He couldn't live his whole life as a hermit. Sooner or later he would come into contact with other people and if it was left too late he wouldn't know how to deal with them. For example, when builder Dondedieu eventually died, he would no doubt make some provision for the boy which would mean that he would have to live in a town and mix with gentry. How would he manage that if all he'd only ever seen were two simple country people? Françoise knew her father was right. But she could not bring herself to take action and kept postponing the decision. Meanwhile, she taught Jean to read and write and count.

One June day, when he was eight, Jean fed the chickens and Charles the pig as he did every morning. Then, calling for Potage, he set out for his secret den. He had got half way when a boy popped out of a bush. He was two or three years older and much bigger.

'Where are you going?' said the boy.

'Hunting,' said Jean. It wasn't true but he didn't know what else to say.

'What, with that mutt?'

'He's the best ratter there's ever been,' said Jean defiantly.

'Come on, I'll race you to that tree!'

The boy reached the tree first but was generous in victory.

'I only beat you because I'm older and bigger than you. You're quite a fast runner, though. What do they call you?'

'Jean,' he said, feeling proud of being a fast runner.

'My name's Isidore. I like it better than Jean. I'm ten and a half and I can fight anyone.'

Jean felt bewildered. His conversations with Françoise and Papy had never been like this. He didn't know what to say. But it didn't matter. Isidore talked for both of them.

'Your face is all funny,' said Isidore.

Jean did not know how to respond to this. So he said: 'You've got a nice face.'

'I know,' said Isidore. 'Want some barley sugar?' he added, popping something in his mouth.

'Yes please,' said Jean.

'Well you can't. That was the last piece. Come on, let's play bandits. You can be a traveller and I'll be a highwayman. Stand and deliver!'

Jean looked at him blankly.

'That means,' said Isidore patiently, 'that you've got to give me the most precious thing you have.'

Jean could only think of his magpie feather and his lucky stone.

'Then you can have a turn at being the highwayman,' Isidore went on, 'and say stand and deliver and I'll give it back to you. We'll play turns. It's only a game,' he said irritably.

'All right,' said Jean. 'But I haven't got my most precious thing with me. I'll have to go and get it.'

'Is it far?'

'I'll show you.'

Jean led the way, Isidore followed and Potage brought up the rear. Five minutes later, they arrived at the low-hanging beech.

'This is my den,' said Jean.

'It's a good den,' said Isidore. 'If I'd been just walking along, I'd never have known it was there.'

He pushed past Jean, removed the branches covering the entrance and tossed them roughly aside. He was too tall to stand upright but made himself at home at once by sitting down on the smooth stone Jean had brought in and used as a seat. From his pocket he produced a pouch and a pipe with a broken stem which he proceeded to fill with tobacco and lit.

The den was soon heavy with acrid smoke which brought tears to Jean's eyes and made him feel so sick that he had to go outside.

When he came back, he noticed that his knife with the broken blade had gone from its place. He remembered their game. He hadn't delivered his most precious thing but that was because he'd had to go outside to be sick. Isidore had taken it. It must be his turn now so he said, in the sort of voice Isidore had used, 'Stand and deliver!'

'What?' said Isidore, knocking the pipe out on his boot and returning it to his pocket.

'Stand and deliver!' Jean said again. 'You've got my most precious thing. Now you have to give me yours.'

'I'm tired of that game,' said Isidore.

'Then I want my knife back. Give me my knife. It's mine!'

'Knife? I ain't seen no knife. What knife are you talking about? Are you calling me a thief? No one calls me a thief!'

'My knife was there when we came in. You took it like the game says. You've got it in your pocket. But if we're not playing any more, I want it back. It's my most precious thing.'

Isidore came up very close and breathed tobacco breath in his face. Potage sensed something was wrong and started barking. Isidore kicked him away. Potage retreated, barked a few time and slunk into the undergrowth outside

'Listen,' he said in a mean voice. 'Just because you got no face it don't mean you scare me!'

Then he moved back and said in a normal voice:

'Anyway, bandits is a kid's game. I don't play kids' games any more. Come on, let's go exploring.'

And he got up and went out into the sunshine.

Jean followed him. Potage brought up the rear, wagging his tail.

Isidore went down to the river bank and started throwing stones into the water. Potage ran after them.

'Know how to swim?' asked Isidore. 'I can swim. Once I swam across a *lake*! I bet you never swam across any lakes.'

'Françoise said I wasn't to go near rivers. Rivers are dangerous. You can slip and fall in and drown! What's drowning?'

'Who's Françoise? Your sister?'

Jean was at a loss what to answer.

'She's the one who's always there.'

'Drowning,' Isidore said patiently, 'is what happens to you if you can't swim. You sink, see, and water goes into your nose and mouth so you can't breathe. How long can you hold your breath? Let's start now and see who lasts longest. Watch me.'

Jean watched as Isidore filled his lungs and held his breath for a moment.

'That's how you do it. We'll start together when I say the word. Now!'

Jean took a deep breath and held it. At first it wasn't a bad feeling. But soon the blood started to throb in his ears. Isidore puffed out his cheeks but his face got steadily redder and redder. He tensed his muscles, put both arms on his hips, fighting the need to breathe. The strain showed in every part of his body which was braced and taut. Pain grew in Jean's chest and he felt as if he was about to burst. He knew he could not keep it in much longer and was about to give up when Isidore snorted, gasped, emptied and refilled his lungs. Jean took this as a signal that the contest was over and did likewise. He felt proud. He had beaten a boy who was older and bigger than him. *And* he could run almost as fast, though he was smaller.

'I won!' he said, vastly pleased with himself.

'Only because I let you. I got fed up with pretending I was drowning.' Isidore scowled unpleasantly. He was glad no one else had been there to see him bested by a boy younger and smaller than him.

'Want me to teach you to swim?' he said.

'All right,' said Jean uncertainly.

But he knew Françoise would not have wanted him to accept the invitation.

'We'll have to go down by that bit of beach.'

When they were by the water's edge, Isidore said, 'First, you got to take all your clothes off.'

Jean did as he was told.

'Now watch me. This is what you do to swim.'

Isidore lay face down on the sand, dog-paddled with his arms and kicked his legs. Then he stood up again. 'Now you do it,' he said.

Jean lay down imitated his movements. Potage ran round him delightedly, barking, his tail sweeping the sand.

'You go in the water and you do that. That's swimming. Go on, let's see you swim.'

Jean walked slowly into the river. The sun was hot and river was cold. But he liked the feel of the sand between his toes and the current plucked agreeably at his legs. When the water reached his waist, Isidore said, 'You can start swimming now.'

After three false starts, Jean bent his legs and pushed himself off into the water. His eyes filled, he felt he was choking. He started sinking, stopped breathing and stood up again immediately.

'That's terrible, you're useless,' sneered Isidore. 'Try again.'

This time, Jean, feeling ashamed of not being able to follow his new friend's instructions, managed a few flaps with his arms before he stood up again.

'You can't come out until you can swim as far as that rock,' said Isidore pointing to a flat stone rising at an angle out of the water.

Jean tried again and again. Soon he was exhausted and started to cry. When he turned to wade back to the beach, Isidore threw stones at him and ordered him to start again.

In the end, he managed to reach the rock and Isidore said he could come out.

Jean stood on the beach and shivered. But the sun was warm and he'd soon be dry.

'About that knife,' said Isidore, 'I got it all right. In my pocket. If you want it, you'll have to take it off me.'

And with one quick move he grabbed Jean by the arm and twisted it hard. Jean lost his balance and fell onto the sand. Isidore was on him in a flash. He straddled his chest and began punching him over and over. Jean tried to defend himself but his arms were too small and thin to ward off the blows. Potage barked and snapped but Isidore went on hitting Jean until his arms were tired. Then he got up, aimed a kick at Potage and threw a stone which caught him on the back leg. The dog retreated to a safe distance and whimpered. Jean didn't move. He could taste blood on his mouth. His head was a mass of cuts and bruises.

'Get up,' said Isidore. He stood over Jean wiping his hands on his shirt and sucking his bruised knuckles.

But Jean didn't move. Isidore bent down and pulled him by one leg to a pool at the river's edge. He gripped him under the arms and forced his head down. The pool was not deep. The mud at the bottom was a drab brown colour. Occasionally, a wavelet from the river lapped into it and ruffled its smooth surface.

Isidore's hands closed round Jean's neck and squeezed. The pain made Jean open his eyes and he found himself looking at the flat surface of the pool which waved and rippled and then grew still. He saw the sky and the clouds reflected in it. And in the water he saw a face staring up at him.

But such a face! It had a hideously leering mouth, black holes for eyes and a gaping pig's snout of a nose.

The sight was so shocking, so horrible that he jerked back convulsively and threw Isidore off his back.

Isidore was on his feet again in a moment. His face was red with rage. He'd landed at the edge of the pool and one sleeve of his shirt dripped river water.

'See what you've gone and done, you ugly pug! I'll pay you back, see if I don't!'

Jean looked up at him and was in time to see the boot start on its short journey to the side of his head.

Isidore kicked him again but it was no fun. It was like kicking a rag doll. He was scarcely out of breath. Then from his pocket he took Jean's knife with the broken blade.

'Here. You wanted it. You can have it. It's a useless thing anyway.'

He threw it on the sand next to where Jean lay still and bleeding. Then turning, he whistled to Potage who had been watching nervously from a patch of showdown. He bent down and picked up a stick.

'Come on, boy! Let's go!'

He threw the stick. Potage ran after it. Then he had second thoughts. He bent down and picked up the knife with the broken blade. He returned it to his pocket and set off after the dog.

The river went on flowing past the little beach and wavelets rippled the surface of the pool. The sun moved across the sky and decided to head for the horizon.

Jean opened his eyes and sat up. He head ached and his neck hurt. After awhile, he reached for his clothes and put them on. Studiously avoiding the pool, he scooped a handful of water out of the river and drank it. Then he walked up the bank and made his way back to his den. He wanted a place to be alone in, where no one could see him.

The branches lay where Isidore had tossed them. Jean went inside. The magpie feather was in pieces, his lucky stone was gone and everything he had arranged so neatly had been pillaged and ripped and scattered.

And in the middle of the floor lay Potage. The knife with the broken blade was sticking out of his right eye and he wasn't breathing.

Jean started to cry.

Chapter 4

Jean was eleven when, towards the end of one airless, hot day in September, Papy Dartigoyte drove his dog-cart into the yard of the cottage in a cloud of dust. Françoise was surprised to see him, for it was not Easter Monday, the day he came every year to urge her to stop mollycoddling the boy and think of marriage. He stepped gratefully into her cool kitchen and sat down. He produced a large handkerchief and mopped his big, shiny-wet face with it.

Françoise brought him a glass and a jug of white wine, sat with her arms folded and waited until he had slaked his thirst.

'There's news,' he said. 'Important news.'

She said nothing and waited for him to continue. She knew from experience that her father was not a man to be hurried. So she was surprised a second time when he came directly to the point.

'Builder Dondedieu is dead. A wall collapsed on him. One of his own walls. Serve him right. They've got the masons who built it on the cheap. There's talk they'll be charged with killing him. But it won't come to that. The family won't let it, they don't want any scandal. Anyway, everybody knows he'd been cheese-paring these last few months. Poor quality materials, unskilled hands, shoddy workmanship. What did he expect? If that wall hadn't fallen on him it would have fallen on somebody else sooner or later. Serves him right …'

'Never mind pontificating and say what you've come to say.'

'There's no money. The man was up to his ears in debt. So that's an end of the pittance he's been paying you for the boy. I thought you'd want to know.'

Françoise said nothing but considered the implications. The allowance builder Dondedieu had made was not generous but it was regular and she had been able to count on it. It had been just enough for them, for she and Jean did not need much to get by. But if that money stopped coming, it would be more difficult to make ends meet.

And so it proved. The winter was hard but they were never cold: Jean gathered more than enough firewood in the form of dead branches from the unguarded woods nearby. They also planted more vegetables. But it was too late in the year to expect a crop until spring. Meantime the price of flour, salt and basic stuffs rose further when the snows came and stayed. There were times when both went to be hungry.

Old Dartigoyte came again one bitterly cold January day. He stood with his back to the fire and without waiting to get properly warm said:

'There's news. Important news. Good news. She wants to see him.'

'Who?' said Françoise.

'The mother, who else? Madame Dondedieu. She wants to see the boy.'

'When?'

'Soon.'

'But I haven't got any clothes good enough to be seen in company,' said Françoise. There was an edge of panic in her voice.

'Oh, she don't want to see you, girl. Just the boy. She's going to send her lawyer to fetch him. He'll dress him up suitable and pay for whatever he needs.'

He sat down and took a gulp of the wine she set before him.

'About time too,' he said, wiping his mouth with the back if his hand. 'It means he's off your hands at last. His mother'll take charge of him. Now perhaps you'll start looking for a man to take you on before it's too late. If you don't you'll be left to grow old and miserable here all by yourself. It's not what your own mother would have wanted, God rest her soul. It's not what I want either, as you know, for I've told you often enough.'

'When's this lawyer supposed to come?'

He came three weeks later, a tall, thin, sour-faced man in tight black clothes.

He looked around the kitchen which was spotlessly clean and refused the glass of wine which Françoise offered.

'Bring me the boy.'

Françoise called up the stairs. Jean came down and, as she had told him to, said: 'Bonjour, Monsieur, my name is …'

'Good God!,' said the lawyer turning pale. 'What do we have here? What is this... this... ? Surely this cannot be the son of Madame Dondedieu?'

'Bonjour, Monsieur,' repeated Jean, cowed by the man's reaction but still on his best behaviour and determined not to let Françoise down, 'my name is Jean Dondedieu.'

'As far as I am aware, my client's son was never formally christened and is therefore not called Jean or indeed anything else. Am I right, my good woman?' he added, turning to Françoise.

'Yes sir. Monsieur Dondedieu and his sister did not want him to be seen in church. Since he needed a name, I called him Jean.'

'And who gave you permission to do so? I must warn you that usurping the prerogatives of the family, of which the right to name children is high on the list, is a serious matter. You do see that?'

'Yes sir, and I'm sure I'm very sorry sir.'

'How old are you, boy?' said the lawyer. The disgust was palpable in his voice.

'Eleven years and six months, sir.'

'And what can you do?'

'I tend the garden, feed the hens ...'

'No, no, I mean can you read and write?'

'Yes sir, and count too.'

'And have you taken your first communion?'

Jean looked puzzled and turned to Françoise.

'We have had little to do with the world outside these four walls, sir, for reasons which you will understand. Jean knows nothing of church-going and has only the knowledge of the faith which I took it on myself to teach him.'

'I see,' said the lawyer. 'Well, I have to tell you that his mother has decided that it is time he saw something of the world he has hidden from hitherto for it is where he will have to live. I fully understand why you have chosen to bring him up far from society, but he is now to go to school. So if you would be so good as to gather up his things — I mean clothes, books and the like — I will take him away and relieve you of the responsibility which Madame Dondedieu wishes to acknowledge.'

He reached into his notecase and extracted eleven gold *louis* which he lined up, one by one, on the table.

'One for each year of the boy's life. Shall I tell Madame Dondedieu that you are suitably grateful for her generosity? You will, of course, never speak to anyone of this service you have rendered the family.'

Then Jean was led out to lawyer Gobert's carriage which promptly sped off.

The novelty of being in a carriage and of travelling faster than he had ever travelled before was not enough to overcome the aching sadness of being separated from Françoise. Lawyer Gobert had not allowed them to say goodbye, saying it was neither necessary nor proper.

Enough had been salvaged from the wreck of her late husband's business to allow Mme Dondedieu to go on living in the family house and enjoy a comfortable, if reduced, income. When Maître Gobert arrived with the boy, it was growing dark (he had planned it so) and the boy was ushered into the house unseen. There, a maid, prepared in advance and primed with money to face the ordeal, put Jean to bed. Next day she made him presentable for the meeting with his mother.

He was pushed into a room where daylight was not welcome and the sun treated like a threatening intruder. The walls were brown, the furniture was heavy and even the deep-red curtains looked black next to the brightness of the windows. As his eyes grew accustomed to the gloom, he made out a heavy-four-poster bed on which lay a whey-faced lady in an invalid's mob-cap and receiving dress. The lady had been looking at him. Now she sobbed and averted her eyes.

Laurence-Adelaide Dondedieu had always known that her son, whom she had never held in her arms nor even seen for more than ten years, had been disfigured beyond the reach of medical art. She had been advised not to see him, for the sight might administer such a shock to her delicate system that she would perhaps never recover. When she insisted, she was told the nature and extent of the mutilation. What she had been told was no preparation for the reality of it. The picture in her mind was a thousand times removed from the apparition she saw before her. Her son, born of her flesh, stared at her out of a hideously misshapen head. She turned her head away with disgust and revulsion.

'Well, child?' said a hearty voice.

Jean now became aware of a second lady standing at the foot of the bed. She was stout and her dress of shot bombazine shimmered purple and red and green in the semi-darkness as she came closer.

'What have you got to say for yourself?' the voice said again.

Jean waited a moment. The lady's dress reminded him of a duck's plumage. He tried to remember what Françoise had told him to say. But his mind was a blank. In the end, feeling the weight of the silence in that oppressive room, he blurted out:

'I don't know!'

'Don't know what?'

How could he tell her what he didn't know? Then light dawned.

'I don't know, *please*!'

'Is the child a fool?' spluttered his tormentor.

Jean tried again.

'I don't know, *thank you*!'

'*Aunt*! I am your father's sister. My name, for your information, is Madame Marie-Thérèse Gobert. Say "Yes, aunt!"'

'Yes, aunt.'

'That's better. Now, this lady is your mother. She is called …' and she slowed her voice, emphasising each word, so that he would have no excuse to forget them, '… Ma-dame Don-de-dieu. Now what do you have to say to your mother?'

Françoise's words came back to him.

'How do you do, Madame. I am happy to make your acquaintance.'

'I have thought of you often,' said the invalid in a halting voice 'Especially on the fifteenth day of each and every August. What is the significance of that day?'

'I don't know, Madame.'

'Dear God!' burst out the Aunt, 'the child doesn't know anything. It's the feast of the Virgin, you ignorant ninny!'

'Also the day you were born and the day my living death began, the day that ruined my life forever. I would never have been confined to bed, too weak to stand, too frail to go out into the fresh air, too unhappy to smile, if you had not been born!'

The words were spoken quietly but with all the pent-up venom and loathing which Madame Dondedieu's bitterness had kept alive and tended, like sickly flowers in a sunless garden, for eleven long years.

Transfixed by those hate-filled eyes, Jean said nothing but started to tremble.

'Sister-in-law, bring me my looking-glass,' said the woman in the bed. 'They tell me,' she went on, 'that there were no mirrors in the place where you have lived these last eleven years. Is that true?'

'I don't know, Madame,' said Jean in a barely audible voice. So much was happening so fast that he could take none of it in. 'Please, what's a mirror?'

'So you never saw your reflection?' his mother said with grim satisfaction.

'Don't know,' said Jean, almost paralysed by fear.

'Then you shall see it now.'

She took the mirror Aunt Gobert handed to her and peered into it for a moment. Then she said: 'Make the boy stand close to me.'

Aunt Gobert pushed him roughly in the back until he was brought up short by the bed. The woman who said she was his mother gave off a fragrance of musk and violets mixed with something else which he did not recognise but was the smell of hate.

'Hold his head fast,' she hissed.

Aunt Gobert took his head in a vice-like grip. He tried to wriggle free but she was far too strong for him. Mme Dondedieu held the glass close to his face.

Although Aunt Gobert was so much stronger she could not prevent the convulsive jerk provoked by the sight of his monstrous, grotesque, sickening self, a gross and horrible travesty of all the other faces he had ever seen. Only then did he remember Isidore and the pool in which he had seen a spectre so horrible that he had blotted it from his mind. But if Aunt Gobert's grip slipped momentarily she tightened it again and imprisoned him in front of the picture of himself he would never forget.

'Oh,' said the women in the bed, 'if you had been a pretty child, with golden curls or thick black hair, eyes of blue or brown, and cheeks with the bloom of a ripe peach, I might have forgiven you. I might even with time have taken a sincere interest in your welfare. I have searched my heart many times to discover what sin I had committed to have deserved such a punishment. Finding none, I conclude that I am blameless. Yet I have given birth to the progeny of the devil. The fault must therefore lie with you, in your wicked, evil nature which, as I can see for myself today, is written on your misbegotten face!'

Jean did not take in everything his mother said. But he understood enough for him to feel the words like a serpent's strike and the venom made him flinch and tremble.

'Well may you shake in your boots,' snapped his Aunt.

'I shall never acknowledge you,' the woman in the bed went on. 'Yet it is my Christian duty to make some provision for your future. I first thought you should be kept confined in an attic in this house and never leave it for as long as I live. Yet I doubt now if that is a sufficient punishment for the misery you have inflicted on me.'

Aunt Gobert broke in, speaking as if Jean was not in the room:

'According to Gobert, the boy has his basic letters but is a stranger to even the rudiments of religion. A sorry state of affairs.'

'Then,' said Mme Dondedieu with a gleam of satisfaction in her eyes, 'he must have them beaten into him. It is the only way. You shall be sent to school, child, where you shall mingle with other boys who may play with you and be your friends, Or not,' she added after a grim pause,' as the case may be.'

'Shall you like that?' asked the Aunt.

'Whether he likes it or not is immaterial,' said Mme Dondedieu tartly.

'But first he must be given a name,' said the Aunt. 'Even an ignoramus must have a name. A priest has been sent for. Since your sainted mother cannot travel to church, he will perform the rite of baptism here. When he has done that, you will have a name.'

'But I have a name already,' Jean cried. 'My name is Jean.'

'From this day on,' said Mme Dondedieu, 'you shall be Gustave.'

'I won't!' cried Jean.

'But not Gustave Dondedieu,' said Aunt Gobert, relaxing her grip. 'You cannot be allowed to go into the world a Dondedieu. It would bring perpetual disgrace on the family. In your school, you shall be Gustave Flon. It is decided.'

'And in addition to a name, you shall also have this,' said his mother, holding up a square of rough calico. 'You shall wear it at all times. Sister-in-law, would you…?'

'Gladly,'

And so saying, she told Jean to stand still and, with the strings attached to the cloth, pulled it over his face and tied it at the back of his head. The mask had two holes for his eyes and another for his mouth. Jean struggled but Aunt Gobert was again too strong for him. When she had finished, she released him.

'Ah!' his mother said spitefully. 'Such a handsome sight! What mother would not want a child as beautiful as you, Gustave! Now get out!!'

Marie-Thérèse locked him in a broom cupboard until the priest came.

The priest was old and bored. He muttered the requirement to the few witnesses – Gobert who stood as godfather had requisitioned his clerk and the family's physician – who had gathered round Madame Dondedieu's bed to renounce the world, the flesh and the devil and they devoutly agreed to do so. Father Thomas slopped water onto the mask covering Gustave's head signed the certificate of baptism, pocketed his money and retired to the vestry of St Saviour's to make the necessary entry in the parish record of births. He filled a dirty glass with wine, drank it off, and poured more. Soon he was snoring gently.

The same afternoon, Jean, wearing his mask, was taken away by carriage and left, with a trunk containing a change of clothes, outside the Académie Gordas, a boarding school for sons of gentlemen. The tall building, of smoke-blackened sandstone, glowered down at him. The porter arrived with a handcart to carry his trunk. He stared at the new boy.

'What are you doing with a bag on yer head for?' he said.

'Please, sir, I've got to wear it.'

The porter shrugged and told him to report to Monsieur Havelsen, the headmaster's assistant. Jean didn't know where to go but was afraid to ask. He set off nervously. He climbed stairs and walked along empty corridors, past classroom where choirs of boys chanted Latin verbs and their times tables. Then a bell was rung for the end of class, the chanting stopped and boys burst through doors into the corridors, pushing, jostling and shouting.

One of the boys, stopped and looked him up and down.

'Oh my,' he said, 'what do we have here?'

He looked down his long nose and saw a boy in a green jacket which was much too large for him, pale blue breeches hitched higher than nature or the tailor who made them had intended, a pair of heavy brown boots and a grey cloth cap with a shiny peak. Under the cap, in place of a head, was what could have been a plum pudding wrapped in a cloth.

'Please sir,' said Jean, 'I have to report to Monsieur Havelsen. But I don't know where to find him. Which way should I go, sir?'

'Got any cake?' the older boy said.

Just then a portly middle-aged man with a furious expression on his face strode past.

'Excuse me, sir. This is a new boy. He's lost. He says he's been looking for you.'

'What's your name?' the man said crossly.

'Jean,' he stammered and then added: 'Aunt.'

Monsieur Havelsen narrowed his eyes and hissed:

'Don't you be funny with me, boy. Try again. Surname first, then baptismal name. And say sir.'

'Dondedieu, sir, Gustave. No, I mean Flon.'

'The boy's an imbecile,' said Monsieur Havelsen. 'I haven't got time for this now. Chabeaud, you'll have to look after him until supper.'

'Well?' said Chabeaud, when the master had gone.

Jean looked at him uncomprehendingly.

'Have you got any cake or not?'

'No, sir.'

'"Nom-de-dieu." That's a funny name.'

'My name's Jean Dartigoyte!' he said angrily.

So much had happened in such a short time that he no longer knew where or who he was or what he was saying. But speaking his name brought him back to reality. He clung to it. It drove out all the confusion and made him aware that he had had enough of being called an imbecile, of being treated like a parcel, of the antagonism and hatred that awaited him at every turn.

'And if I did I wouldn't give you any!' he said, backing away.

'Keep your hair on,' said Chabeaud, 'that is, if you've got any. Let's have a look. Come on, show me what you got under that pudding cloth.'

And he raised his right hand to pull the mask off.

Jean lashed out and caught Chabeaud a solid blow on the mouth. Chabeaud went down, blood already oozing over his lips.

Then Jean turned and ran. He ran blindly down corridors, around corners, past more classrooms and finally out through the gate by which he had come in. He stopped, not knowing which way to turn.

Behind him the porter came out of his lodge, shouted that boys weren't allowed to go out once they'd come in.

Jean looked over his shoulder, saw the man bearing down angrily on him. He sped off along the empty street into the dusk.

As he ran, the face of his mother floated unbidden into his mind. But it was not the face he had seen that morning, bitter and twisted with disgust. It glowed sweet and tender and loving. A gentle smile played on her lips.

What he remembered especially was the moment when, called upon by the priest to do so, she had declared before God and the assembled company that she was Laurence-Adelaide Dondedieu, mother of the child to be baptised.

Laurence-Adelaide!

It was the most beautiful name he'd ever heard.

Chapter 5

In the days that followed, sightings of fearsome apparitions were reported by the *Gazette de Rouen*. Persons of both sexes, all ages and classes claimed to have been confronted by a hideous, squat ghoul with burning eyes, yellow fangs, a long tail and the ability to vanish into thin air. The anticlerical *Courier moderne* dismissed the claims which it attributed to the 'black crows of the church' who kept the people 'in the thrall medieval superstitions'. The clergy fought back, denouncing the irreligious, godless influence of the so-called 'progressive' press.

The fact that citizens suddenly stopped coming forward with accounts of traumatic experiences did not prevent the battle for minds and souls from being vehemently engaged. But much bitterness would have been avoided had due consideration been given to one encounter with a ghoul which was unreported in the press.

The very day the *Courier* published its thunderous editorial declaring war on the enemy of reason, Father Jacquemart, a teacher and choir-master of St Benedict's hospice for foundlings situated in a pleasant suburb of the town, was on his way to see the bishop to discuss the possibility of sending his two best boys to join the cathedral choir, which had recently been depleted by the departure of several choristers whose voices had broken. The day was warm and Father Jacquemart was in no hurry. He sat for a moment on one of the benches in the market-place and thought of how best to make his case to the bishop.

And then he became aware of the sound of a voice so smooth, so lovely, so touching that he was transported.

Rising to his feet, he followed the sound to its source and discovered the diminutive figure of, he guessed, a boy. He could not be sure, for the figure was swathed in an old shawl and around the head was a bag made of whitish stuff, with holes for eyes.

Father Jacquemart paused and watched. Passers-by seemed as deeply affected as he by the boy's singing voice – yes, a boy, definitely, for the soprano sound, though untrained, was unwavering in its purity. Persons of both sexes and all ages stopped to listen and even scurrying men of business slowed as they walked by. But more listened than dropped a coin in the singer's cap.

The beggar-boy was in the middle of a country song which had been old before the great cathedrals were built, when two other boys, bigger and very determined, appeared as if from nowhere, snatched the cap, took the money it contained and aimed hefty kicks at their victim. Then they ran off as quickly as they had come.

Father Jacquemart crossed the street to the beggar who had stopped singing and was rubbing his injuries but seemed otherwise unhurt.

'They don't like me, sir,' the singer said resignedly. 'They say I spoil their pitch and take their trade. But most of them have a place to sleep and some have families. It's not fair.'

'And you have no family or home to go to?'

'I did once, sir. Françoise looked after me and Papy came sometimes.'

'Why don't you go to them?'

'I don't know where they are.'

'Who taught you to sing?'

'I never learned, sir. But Françoise used to sing to me.'

Making up his mind, Father Jacquemart took the boy by the hand. Such a gift was meant to be used for the service of God.

'Come with me,' he said.

*

'What do you mean, Father, by bringing this ... this ... ill-begotten creature to me?'

The Abbot of St Benedict's home for foundlings, a man of austere appearance and strict views, looked at Jean with horror.

'It may well be that the boy is an unfortunate, that he is to be pitied, that his appearance is no fault of his own,' he went on with distaste. 'But I tell you, if sin had a face, it would surely be the face of this child. If the Antichrist himself walked the earth, his countenance would not be more hideous!'

'Maybe so, Reverend father,' said Father Jacquemart, 'but is it not unkind to say so in the poor boy's hearing?'

'Pray let me be the judge of what is kind and what is not,' said the Abbot crossly. 'Let me also remind you that our mission here is the welfare of *all* the orphaned and abandoned infants who are placed in our charge. I must consider what the unsettling effect of placing this child in their midst would have on them …'

Jean stood silent while the two men of God argued. He did not know what the words Sin and Antichrist meant, but he sensed they were not nice things.

'But does not service to God take many forms?' asked Father Jacquemart.

'Indeed it does,' said the Abbot firmly.

'This boy has the purest, sweetest voice I have ever heard,' said Father Jacquemart earnestly. 'It is a rare gift and it was given to him so that he might glorify and magnify the Lord through music. If only you heard him sing, Father, you would know at once that he possesses an instrument of exceptional beauty.'

'The boy may be the vocal marvel you say he is. But think a moment. What would sitting the boy in the front row of the choir achieve except to make the faithful shudder at the sight and question, first, God's goodness in allowing such a specimen to exist and, second, our wisdom in making a public display of him. I remind you that we are dependent on the generosity of our congregation and I will do nothing to jeopardize our work it by alienating them. No, I cannot, I will not have this … this … boy here. He is an affront and a threat to everything we stand for. Make arrangements for him to be taken to Mourthe at once.'

Mourthe was a town in a distant part of the diocese. It was the location of a charity school for boys which taught the rudiments of education to the Sons of the Deserving Poor. Jean was taken there the same day. Father Jacquemart wished him well and gave him a few small coins. When he arrived, Monsieur Mardy the bursar read the note written by the Abbot which the carter handed him. He swore under his breath. The boy was not to be a pupil, for there was no money to pay for his studies. But a bed had to be provided for the boy, food put in his belly and a use to be found for him. Find him a bed? Where? The school was full to the rafters with the ill-begotten sons of the deserving poor. Fill his plate? That was easier; there were always leftovers in the kitchen even if it meant robbing the pigs. Put him to work? That was easier still; there was always room for another pair of hands to light fires, chop and carry firewood, sweep the yard, scrub the floors and help out and much more in that line.

'Very well,' said Monsieur Mardy with bad grace. 'He can sleep in the wood store. But what's that bag over your head for, boy? Been naughty, have we? Had to wear it as a punishment, is that it? Well, we know how to knock naughtiness out of a boy here. We've had a lot of practice. Off with it!'

And so saying, he pulled the cloth off roughly.

Although the sun had set and twilight was gathering, there was enough light to illuminate Jean's face with a livid glow, throwing it into horrible relief and making it glare and grin like a malicious fiend.

'Good God!' gasped Monsieur Mardy, taking a step back. 'Whatever's happened to you, lad? The Devil's spawn don't come anywhere near it! You'd better cover yourself up again — and don't you ever let the other boys catch sight of that ugly face of yours. They won't take kindly to it.'

That night Jean had somewhere to sleep. The wood store was dry. But he got no supper. It was too late.

And that was why, from that night on, the good people of Rouen saw no more phantoms and spectres of evil walking the streets of their town.

Jean remained at the Charity School for the sons of the Deserving Poor at Mourthe for a year. In that time, he slept in the wood store and ate scraps from the kitchen. He was worked unsparingly. When not carrying water, sweeping the yard, or cleaning the stables, he hid from the pupils. They had been told not to approach him, for the school authorities feared the disruptive effect of such monstrous ugliness on the order and routine on the rest of the pupils. So they were told he had a horrible, unspecified infectious disease. The ones with imagination said it was leprosy; others said plague. But there were always boys who broke the rules. They missed no opportunity to hunt Jean down, taunt him, throw stones and generally make his life a misery. Most nights he cried himself to sleep, wondering why everyone hated him and yearning to see Françoise again.

In time, however, he stopped asking the same question over and over because the answer was clear: everyone hated him because his face frightened them. Once he realised this, he stopped waiting for the day to dawn when someone would like him. He began devising plans to escape from his tormentors. Running away was not the answer: he had tried it once and he had been caught and ended up closely confined and worse off than he had been before. He had managed to keep the few coins kind Father Jacquemart had given him and had even managed to earn a few more from tips from delivery men and such like. But his meagre savings would not take him far. But however hard he racked his brains, there seemed to be no way out. But every time a new carter appeared, or when the postman or a new gardener appeared, he asked them if they knew where Françoise and Papy lived.

One man, a haulier whose breath had wine on it, said there'd been a Dartigoyte who ran an inn on the Mantes road. But he thought the old man must be dead, for there was a new *patron* in charge of the Golden Cockerel now. He also remembered old Dartigoyte's daughter, a good-looking piece, he said with a leer. But she'd gone too and he didn't know where. Still, Jean thought, if I could go to the inn the people there might know in which direction Françoise and Papy had gone.

And thinking of Françoise also reminded him of how important she said the reading lessons she'd given him had been. So, whenever the opportunity arose, he would crouch outside the schoolroom windows while the boys inside were taught to read and write and count. He had almost forgotten everything Françoise had taught him. But it soon came back. He decided he would look for Françoise and once he found out where she was, he would write her a letter and maybe she would come to take him away from Mourthe.

*

One evening, he was sitting in a corner of the stables reading a battered, almost illegible copy of a primer he had rescued from the furnace flames (nothing that could be used was ever wasted at Mourthe). He felt safe there. No one knew about his little bolt hole, he thought. But he was wrong. Suddenly a voice said, 'Why, it's the skivvy! So this is where you hide yourself!'

It was Bastingard, fifteen years old and cock of the walk. He was big for his age and handy with his fists. He led a gang of older boys who terrorised the young ones and made them hand over all the money or food their parents sent them. If they refused, they tasted Bastingard's fist.

Before Jean knew what was happening, a hand swooped down and snatched the book from his hands.

'What's this? Skivvy learning himself to read? We'll see about that.' And slowly, he tore the pages out of the battered volume. As they fell to the ground, the wind took them and scattered them over the yard.

'If you want to read, skivvy' said Bastingard, 'you'd better look sharp before all them pages blow away.'

Jean did not move.

'Go on!' said Bastingard. 'Get up and scramble for them like I said. Or do you want to feel the toe of my boot?'

Jean sat and looked up at him. His life with Françoise and Papy was a distant, fading memory. Sometimes he wondered if it had not been real, a dream. All he seemed to remember now was that almost everyone he had met behaved cruelly to him. Oh, he knew why, there was no mystery about that: he was ugly. Toads were less ugly than he was, lepers were more handsome and monsters in dreams were not as terrifying. He knew this because people had told him so many times in words, by their reactions and the expressions on their faces. He had become accustomed to the hatred of grown-ups and the vicious treatment he got at the hands of the sons of the Deserving Poor, just as he was inured to summer heat, winter cold and perpetual hunger. They were the furniture of his life.

But it was not just the experience of cruelty and rejection that gave him a measure of stoical resignation. His voice had broken and was now deeper and firmer. He had grown taller, sturdier, and his muscles had developed. He had acquired a natural assertiveness which replaced the timidity of childhood. He was no longer a little boy. In the year he had spent at Mourthe, hard work had toughened him and made him strong.

Jean kept staring at Bastingard. Then he stood up and faced his tormentor.

'Don't you stare at me like that, baghead, or you'll catch it,' said Bastingard. But his voice was a little uncertain now. For he was disconcerted by those two eyes which glared yellow, like a big cat's, a tiger's maybe, from the two holes cut in Jean's mask.

'I'll teach you to stare ...' he started, raised his fists and then stopped.

For Jean reached up with one hand and tore the cloth away from his face.

*

Like all the other boys at the school, Bastingard had never seen Jean unmasked before. The good fathers laid down the strictest punishment for anyone who tormented their skivvy. He gasped with terror and took two steps back.

'It's the Devil himself!' he said, more to himself than to Jean.

Jean advanced a few steps. Bastingard retreated.

'No, the Devil's spawn!' said Jean with a leer that sent shivers down Bastingard's spine. 'The Devil is my father. So if you don't do what I say, I'll ask him to send ghosts and ghouls dripping with blood to visit you when you're sleeping. I'll make you go mad with fear. You'll be sorry you were born. If you don't believe me, you can see my tail if you want. Well?'

Without a word, Bastingard turned and fled.

*

Jean replaced his mask and sat down again.

He felt exhilarated. He had made a great discovery. He had been made to suffer because he was a repulsive sight. How many times had he wanted to look like other boys? At that moment he knew he would never be like them, that he would always be an outcast. But today he had learned that his ugly face could be his salvation, if he chose. It was a weapon. He could use it to frighten people into doing what he wanted. If he couldn't make other people love him, he could at least make them fear him!

He waited for a chance to put his discovery to good use.

Bastingard, who had never missed an opportunity to trip him up, punch or mock him, now gave him a wide berth. But two evenings later, as he walked back from the latrines across the school yard, he heard a whispery voice ordering him to step into the shadows. He didn't have to think twice about whose voice it was.

'Bastingard,' it hissed. 'Got any money?'

Bastingard said he had a few francs.

'Give,' said the voice.

He reached into his pockets for the coins and held them out. He shuddered when his fingers brushed against a hand which felt cold and scaly to the touch.

'It's not enough. Bring more. Tomorrow. Or else!'

As Bastingard's hurrying footsteps faded, Jean laughed to himself. He was no longer afraid!

Over the next few weeks, Bastingard brought Jean all the money he and his cronies extracted from the younger boys. The bully now cringed and wheedled, pleading with Jean to ask his father, the Devil, to stop sending him nightmares full of terrifying hobgoblins. He grew pale and drawn, for he was afraid to go to sleep, for then he was visited by fiends and semi-human spectres who reached out with clammy, scaly hands. Whenever his eyes did close with exhaustion, his rest was fitful, interrupted by garish visions of monsters with tails and eyes like yellow saucers. Jean was as much amused as amazed, for it struck him as laughable that a hulking brute like Bastingard could fill his own dreams with the things he most feared. And to see and hear him whine and beg made Jean feel good.

He had discovered the pleasures of power!

He had no compunction about taking money stolen from little boys. It was normal, a rite of passage, that they should be bullied as he had been. One day, when they were old enough and if they were made of the right stuff, they too would get the upper hand over their enemies. Jean was learning the way of the world. He never thought that if Françoise knew what he was doing, she might not have approved.

When he had amassed 50 francs, he decided it was time to leave Mourthe. Spring was turning into summer and the weather was becoming warm. It would be pleasant to sleep in hedges as he walked the road to Mantes where the carter had told him he would find the Golden Cockerel.

*

He wore his hood at all times. For food, he stopped in villages and bought bread, and sometimes a pie. If he saw a chicken coop, he raided it for eggs which he swallowed raw. He stopped occasionally to ask his way but otherwise he avoided people. But one day, he walked into a village decked with flags. A crowd had gathered in the main square. Jean joined it though he stayed on the fringes, hearing what the people said, seeing how they behaved. He would have liked to mingle with them, to be like a pebble on a pebble beach or a drop of water in the sea. But he knew he could never be as anonymous as the least of them.

Suddenly, there was the sound of a bugle. The crowd parted and let through half a dozen soldiers on their best parade-ground dress, all looking fit and well-fed. They marched into the square in battle order, preceded by two drummers. They cleared a space and into it stepped a tall man, with sergeant's stripes and a bristling military moustache. He was wearing shiny black boots, white trousers and a bright red tunic with green facings and gold trimmings. A long sword hung at his side. He stood surveying the crowd with haughty eyes. He was flanked by two privates holding, not muskets or halberds, but long poles from which dangled hams, sausages, bottles of wine and golden, crusty loaves of bread.

Pulling his hood well down. Jean said to the man standing next to him: 'Who are they?'

'A recruiting sergeant and his gang of thugs, that's what they are,' was the reply.

'What's a recruiting Sergeant?'

'A man who signs men up to be soldiers in the army, to fight for France. Everyone knows that. Where have you been that you don't?'

Jean moved away to another part of the crowd.

When the Sergeant felt he had the attention of the spectators, he gave the order for his drummers to stop and in a powerful voice that rose above the noise of the crowd, he bawled:

'In the name of his royal Majesty hear this! His Majesty's regiments have room for well-set-up lads from good families. Qualifications: must be over fifteen, able to drink and chase skirts. Make the most of your chance, me hearties. It's a good life. All you can eat and drink and all the adventure you ever wanted.

'Just turn your nose this way. Can you smell that ham, so tender and full of flavour? Or them Toulouse sausages? They'd go down nicely with a hunk of that fresh, soft bread and that bottle of red wine which is just crying out to be drunk! Listen carefully and you'll hear it begging for it. So look lively, lads! Never let it be said that the young men of – (under his breath he growled at the Corporal: what's the name of this hole-in-the-middle-of-nowhere?) – valiant young lads of the famous village of Saint-Paul-les-Champs were backwards in coming forwards. Take another look at what's dangling from them poles. There's all sorts here to suit all tastes. That's the sort of grub you get every day in the army. Just ask these men here, they'll tell you. You'll be billeted in palaces and you'll all become generals. When they see all your medals, you'll have the girls throwing themselves at you! So what are you waiting for?'

Times were hard and there was great unemployment in the country. Three young farmhands, one no more than a boy who looked as if he'd hadn't seen a square meal in a fortnight, stepped forward sheepishly.

'That's the stuff. Don't be shy,' said the Sergeant.

He asked the first candidate for his name and age, family if any and education if any. He wrote the details down in a ledger. At his signal, the drummers gave a loud roll on their drums, and he announced that the first volunteer had been successfully enrolled into His Majesty's Royal Infantry. Then he bawled 'Next!' in a loud voice and proceeded to deal with the other two recruits. As the third man was led away by the Corporal, to be given his ham and sausage and bread and wine, a fourth volunteer stepped up.

'And what do we have here?'

'I want to be in the army, sir,' said Jean.

The Sergeant looked down at him from a great height.

'Age?'

Jean hesitated. 'Fifteen.'

The Sergeant looked him up and down.

'You're too small for fifteen but you make a decent thirteen. Come back when you're fifteen and we'll see.

'I'm very brave, I'd be a good fighter,' said Jean in a gruff, manly voice.

'What's that bag on your head for?'

'Cut it, sir. The bag's to keep the sun off the wound.'

'Well you tell your mother the sun is just the thing for drying up wounds. Take it from me. I've seen action in Algeria and I know what I'm talking about. Let the air get to it.'

And he reached out and whipped off Jean's mask.

Shocked at the ghastly leering face he saw, the Sergeant stepped back and dropped the ledger in which he had written down the particulars of the new recruits. The crowd let out a collective gasp of horror when they saw Jean' naked face.

Before anyone could do or say anything, Jean darted through the spectators and was gone, leaving the village wondering what horror it was that they had seen.

As he ran, he felt very afraid. What had he been thinking of, stepping up like that and volunteering? He'd succeeded only in drawing attention to himself. It was the last thing he should have done. Maybe it was the excitement of the market-place, the Sergeant's red tunic and his salesman's patter. Whatever it was, he had made a dangerous mistake and he'd had a lucky escape. Pulling the wool over Bastingard's eyes was one thing. Thinking all his troubles were over, that he could behave as if he was just like everyone else, was another. His blood ran cold. He could have been caught. They'd have locked him up.

That night, he cried himself to sleep again, knowing that the victory he'd won over Bastingard had been hollow.

Next morning, he continued his way along the road he'd been told led towards Mantes. Fearing that men might have been sent out to look for him, he hid in ditches and clumps of trees whenever he heard the sound of horses or saw the dust of approaching travellers. He gave every village he came to a wide berth.

On the evening of the third day, he found a deserted barn to sleep in. He climbed up into the loft and, feeling fatigued, settled down to sleep without having any supper. It was a dark in the barn. There was a hole in the roof and the stars that filled it made him feel very small. But he was soon asleep. He had not been sleeping long when he was awakened by the sound of a pipe playing a merry tune.

He looked through a space which had once been a window at the back of the building. Outside, the land was silvered by the moon. Below him a fire burned. Around it he made out three caravans. Either they had been there when he'd reached the barn and he had not seen them, or else they had turned in off the road for the night after he'd fallen asleep.

There was a smell of stew cooking in a pot over the fire. Lit by the flames, children played and shrieked with laughter in the moonlight. Men sat around, smoking and talking while the women busied themselves with preparing the meal. After they'd eaten, there was dancing and more music and laughing. A pretty girl went among the men filling their earthenware mugs from a jug. It was very late when the fire was allowed to die down and everyone climbed into the caravans to sleep.

Jean was entranced. He would have given anything to be part of the magical sight he'd seen, to join in, to dance and play and laugh. He was too excited to sleep. He kept remembering what he'd seen. He chuckled at the games the little ones had played. He was reassured by the sober way the men had behaved and the charm of the pretty girl who had gone among them. The stars were dimming in the lightening sky when he finally slept, only to dream of what he'd seen. In his dream, he was part of the fun and the pretty girl asked him to dance. He would have liked to say yes, but he didn't know how and felt foolish and embarrassed. He woke with a start. The sun was already high in the sky. He sat up and looked eagerly through the hole in the wall. He was in time to see the last caravan turning onto the road.

Gathering his few possessions together, Jean climbed quickly down the ladder and set off in pursuit.

He kept the caravans in sight all day, but was careful not to be seen. He felt slightly guilty because following them now seemed more important than finding Françoise. But he managed to silence his qualms with the thought that the convoy was going the way he would have gone anyway.

There was still an hour before the sun set when the caravans again stopped in a field not far off the road. He watched them make camp, light a fire and settle down for the night. The children played, the women set about preparing supper, the men talked around the fire. He looked out for the pretty girl but did not see her. He remembered her fair hair and the way she laughed. But then she was there and, at a word of command from one of the men who played a pipe, her father probably, she danced. Jean had never seen anything as graceful and captivating. Finally, everyone disappeared into the caravans as they had the night before.

Again, it was late when Jean finally fell asleep.

The next day and the day after that, he followed their slow progress through the green Normandy countryside. They were irresistible. Just being near their happiness made him feel happy too. He could not imagine that there could possibly be a more perfect way of living: trundling slowly over roads which constantly opened new and interesting landscapes, stopping when tired, eating, making music and dancing. This was surely what the homesick boys at Mourthe had meant when he'd heard them talk about their families. He felt part of it. When one of the little ones fell over and grazed a knee or elbow, he felt the hurt. When they screamed because they were about to be caught in a chasing game, he held his breath anxiously. When the pipe played, he followed the tune. And when the pretty girl danced – the man he imagined was her father called her Marie – he clapped his hands (silently, of course) with delight.

On the fifth night, he watched his new friends set up camp again. He found himself a vantage point in a hedge bordering the field and settled down to watch.

First the fire was made, then there was a rattle of pots and pans. Meanwhile, as usual, the children chased each other, screaming and laughing. All present and correct – no, one, the small boy with the red hair was missing. Ah, there he was, sulking in a corner. There were the men sat around talking earnestly and the pretty girl going among them with her jug. Soon she would dance. But the man he thought must be her father was nowhere to be seen.

He raised his head to get a clearer view. Suddenly a hand gripped his collar and a voice said:

'What are you up to?'

Against the setting sun, he saw the outline of one of the travelling men.

'Please, sir, I'm not doing anything wrong.'

'Spying on us are you? Who sent you?'

Jean was suddenly struck by something very odd. The man had his back to the sun and Jean could not see his face. But by the same token, the man must be looking at him, must be seeing his face clearly, the face which terrified everybody who saw it, But unlike them this man, who he recognised as Marie's father, did not recoil in horror. He had not even flinched!

Though thoroughly frightened, Jean managed to stammer that he was making for the Golden Cockerel to look for Françoise.

'Who's Françoise and what do you want with her?' the man asked, a little less gruffly.

Jean explained.

The man relaxed his grip.

'The inn's gone,' he said. 'Burned down last year. Nobody there.'

Jean felt as if the bottom had fallen out his world. Now he'd never find Françoise! He went very quiet. Then he began to cry.

'No need for that,' said the man. 'Things are never as bad as they seem.' Then he added in a different voice: 'Hungry? You can have supper with us. But if you'd rather, you can stay here and watch. I don't mind. It's up to you.'

Jean said he would like to have supper with them.

His tears dried. He was being invited to walk into his dream. He was about to meet his new family.

Chapter 6

Every year, a great fair was held in the market town of Arnouville in the Ardennes during the first week of August. It was always eagerly anticipated by the population roundabout, for its bustle and noise brought a whiff of urban excitement into country lives which had gone on in much the same way for centuries. And this despite talk that the new-fangled railways, with their noise and smoke, were poised to shatter their rustic isolation and send them hurtling into a new age of progress, a prospect which thrilled some but filled most with apprehension.

But on the great day, the perils and promises of the future were forgotten. The weather was fine and crowds thronged the streets. A piano-organ played on one corner and a hurdy-gurdy man stood at another. Amid the hubbub, a queue formed outside a fortune teller's tent and hawkers went about selling slim books and pamphlets with blue covers and crude woodcuts of which most were devoted to religious topics, the rest being seditious or scurrilous or frankly obscene. These last, though the most expensive, sold best. Women, the hems of their dresses muddied from being dragged through the unpaved, still-damp early morning streets, sold flowers from baskets, wafers filled with jam and cakes in paper cornets shaped like nuns' coifs. Men with wicker cages strapped to their backs offered birds of various species for sale. But the cocks of the walk were the charlatans.

There were quacks of every sort and description, all with fantastic names. Baron Pètefort, Count Cantorbéry, Signor Abrupto, doctor of the University of Rome, advertised panaceas, nostrums and physics for every ailment. Testimonials from distinguished members of Academies of Medicine at home and abroad and assorted European crowned heads spoke glowingly of their universal efficacy. Their patter was relentless and their lies barefaced.

'Step up ladees'n'gemman, and buy Count Cantorbéry's elixir, two *sous* a bottle, and Count Cantorbéry's pomade, three *sous* a jar. Don't be shy. If it's good enough to go on the crowned heads of Europe, it's good enough for the good folk of Arnouville.'

A little further on an officer of the watch grabbed a thin man with a lantern jaw who had been seen trying to steal a lady's purse. He was struggling, shouting his innocence for all his worth. But the policeman refused to listen and dragged him away past the try-your-strength booth and a merry-go-round turned by two bored-looking donkeys.

Next to the merry-go-round was a large platform formed of three flatbed carts over which a brightly coloured awning had been stretched on a frame to form a closed tent. There was a short set of steps at each end. The one on the right was for entering the tent and the other for coming out again. A pretty young woman with fair hair and a dazzling smile stood at the foot of the first set of steps and gave out tickets in exchange for the two *sous* it cost to see the marvels inside. In front of the booth, stood a barker in a top-hat and frock coat, like a circus ringmaster. He juggled with coloured balls and did tricks like a clown to attract the attention of the passersby.

'Roll up, roll up! See Monecq's World-famous House of Horrors! See the baby with two heads! That's right, two! He's in a bottle, poor mite. But you will also gaze on living, breathing horrors, including the Bearded Lady and the world's tallest man and tiny Princess Men Lai, all the way from Peking, China!'

'And what's so special about her then?' shouted a man from the crowd which had formed to see Monsieur Monecq and hear his patter.

'What's special about the Princess, my friend, is that she's just three feet tall and as beautiful as a lotus flower! A veritable living doll that moves and breathes!'

'What can she do?' said the same man.

'She don't *do* anything,' said Monecq. 'But if you smile at her she'll smile back at you.'

'Is that all you got in your tent? Haven't you got anything else you didn't have last year when you was here?'

'Now that you mention it, I have got a novelty to place before the discerning public of Arnouville,' said Monecq imperturbably. 'A hexhibit never before displayed anywhere. I been keeping this particular item for you, ladees'n'gemman, for your special de-lectuation. I have for you, wait for it, a novelty the like of which the world has never seen. And you, the good people of Arnouville, shall be the first to see it! Not

Kings and Queens in their palaces, but you! So roll up to see The Living Corpse!'

''Ere,' said the same man, 'he wouldn't be the same one as was The Living Dead last year and Devil Boy the year before? If so, I seen him already. Twice. Has he learned to do any tricks?'

'He don't need to do tricks,' said Monecq, sidestepping the question of whether his new exhibit was an old exhibit with a new name. But at the same time, he gave an imperceptible nod to a large man with one eye, a former wrestler, who worked as the travelling freak show's scene-shifter and roustabout. Before the Awkward Customer could ask any more awkward questions, he was bundled into a side street and sent on his way.

Monecq carried on smoothly, as if nothing had happened ...

Inside the tent, Jean sat in the last of a row of cubicles waiting for the first customers of the day to arrive. Before reaching him, they stopped in front of a series of glass jars containing the baby with two heads, a hand with seven fingers and an unrecognisable organ said to be the heart of Joan of Arc. Also on display were Galileo's own glasses, the very musket ball that smashed Robespierre's jaw in 1794 and the uniform worn by Napoleon at the battle of Marengo. They would then move on and pause to stare at Dolly Vercourt, the Bearded Lady. Dolly ignored the ribald remarks aimed at her (she had heard them all before) and passed the time knitting. She had got used to the indignity of her fate and accepted that being a freak at least meant that she didn't have to work for a living, unlike the stupid, gawping rabble who handed over their hard-earned money to see her. In the oriental decor of the next cell the diminutive Princess Men Lai usually started the day by nodding and smiling sweetly. But she was prouder than Dolly and soon was scowling back. Claude, the Human Beanpole, always read a book but looked up pleasantly each time he turned a page. Jean stared back at the starers. He had a vague hope that one day Françoise or old Papy might just have heard that a hideously disfigured boy was on display in Monecq's travelling freak show and come to see for themselves.

But in the three years he had been with Monecq's travelling show they had not come.

Jean was the last exhibit. From time to time, for different venues, Monecq dressed him in different clothes. As the Awkward Customer had said, he had started as Devil Boy. Monecq had fitted a pair of horns on his forehead, pinned a long tail made out of an old piece of rope on him and made him hold a satanic trident. When he was the Living Death, he wore a long robe and leaned on the grim reaper's scythe. As the Living Corpse he now sat upright in a coffin. Monecq, a man with a keen nose for business, was always looking for a new incarnation for him. At one moment, he'd toyed with the idea of giving Jean a metal helmet to wear and billing him as the Original Man in the Iron Mask 'as made famous by Alexander Dumas's celebrated novel of the same name'. But then he realised that it made no sense covering up the very thing that was his star exhibit's main attraction. Anyone could wear an Iron Mask. What was the point in hiding a face which did good business as Devil Boy or the Living Death? He was currently wondering how a tableau vivant of Beauty and the Beast would go down. His daughter Marie was pretty enough for the role. He wondered how much it would cost to devise a fetching costume for her. A loincloth would do for Jean.

Few customers lingered in front of Jean's gloomy cell. Nearly all were horrified by the sight of him and hurried away as quickly as they could. The women gasped, even the men fell silent. Persons of a delicate disposition were known to have fainted, but while some of these 'sensitive' casualties had been paid to pass out by Monecq, it was quite true that on one occasion a pregnant woman had gone into labour on the spot. By any standard, Jean was the star of Monecq's touring freak show.

Monecq had seen the boy's potential the night he had caught him loitering around the camp. He lived with freaks, made his living out of them and was not in the least shocked by Jean's horrifically devastated face. On the contrary, he was intrigued and immediately saw an opportunity who no man of business could afford to pass up. Nor had Jean produced the usual horrifying effect on the other exhibits who merely felt curious, though it drew a degree of professional rivalry from the sour-faced Fattest Man in the World and the dyspeptic Boneless Wonder, both since deceased. Even Marie, Monecq's daughter, the one who had asked him to dance in his dream, had made him welcome. Jean was happy. For the first time since he had been taken away from Françoise by lawyer Gobert, he was treated like a normal person. At last he had friends.

It had not taken much persuasion for Jean to join Monecq's touring show. He was guaranteed food, lodging and employment. He was also won over by thoughts of a life of adventure and travel and the prospect of making his fortune which Monecq said was virtually certain. Jean swore that when he was rich, he would return and give all his money to Françoise to repay her for her kindness. Meanwhile, he felt at home and the hunted feeling left him.

Everyone made him welcome. Dolly Vercourt gave him a pair of socks she had knitted, Princess Men Lai offered him her sweetest smiles and Beanpole lent him books. He just looked at them and turned the pages, for they were mostly about politics and too difficult for him. But the kindest of all was Marie — Marie la Belle as Jean secretly called her.

When he first saw her she was fourteen and very pretty. Her fair hair, blue eyes and teasing smile delighted him and he was never happier than when she was near. She taught him to dance and encouraged him to sing. She said she loved his singing voice. She called the deep notes 'thrilling' and 'poetic' and the high notes were 'manly'. For weeks after she told him this, Jean hummed one or other of Françoise's old songs whenever she was near. Monecq was also impressed and a few times let him sing as part of the preliminary, free entertainment he put on to bring the public in. But despite a wig and an eye-shade which hid most of his face, his appearance still put the customers off.

By the time Marie la Belle was seventeen, she was a full-blown, ravishing beauty. Jean would have gone to the ends of the earth for her. He lived for her. Hearing her voice was the greatest pleasure he knew, second only to seeing her smile. He followed her like a dog. He did whatever she told him, fetching and carrying, unable to refuse her anything. He never thought where it all might lead. Being with her every day was enough for him. She was always so kind.

*

Of course, as she grew older, Marie became aware of the power she had over men. Monecq saw it too and realised that her pretty face and flirtatious ways were money in the bank. He dressed her in a ballet skirt and pink tights and while he urged the crowd to roll up and see the show he allowed her to dance to popular tunes played on a penny-whistle by Beanpole behind the curtain. When she had finished dancing, she sat at a small table under which her legs were displayed to good advantage.

There she took the entrance money and issued tickets. Many men stepped forward and paid up just to get a close up view of those deep blue eyes and plump red lips. Marie's secret hope was that one fine day, a gentleman would come along and take her away from her travelling life with her father and his disgusting collection of freaks.

But at seventeen she was growing impatient. She was no longer willing to wait until her gentleman came along in his own good time. In any case, not many gentlemen came to country fairs. Instead of waiting for one to come to her, she was going to have to go out and catch one herself. She'd heard that there were plenty of such well-to-do men in Paris. So she would go there. She'd easily find work at one or other of the capital's permanent fairs or along the Boulevard du Crime where blood-thirsty melodramas pulled in the crowds every night. With her looks, she couldn't fail. She could juggle and dance and sing and, she was sure, act. But she knew her big eyes, long legs and a low-cut bodice were her best assets, for they amounted to much more than all her other skills put together. One night, after attracting a particularly thin crowd in a dull town in a dismal, distant part of Picardy, she told her father she was leaving.

'You can't do that, girl' he snapped. 'I need you here, with me.'

'Listen, Pa, I'm seventeen. I've got my future to think of. As it is, I'm going round in circles and getting nowhere.'

'You're not leaving, girl,' said Monecq furiously. 'You're obligated. I raised you and I fed you …'

'So that makes me an investment and you want your money's worth?'

Monecq looked at his daughter in surprise.

'Who's been putting ideas in your head? Listen, you're staying with me, and that's final.'

But it wasn't.

*

Two nights later, Marie brought the subject up again. Tempers flared on both sides and voices were raised. Jean happened to be passing Monecq's caravan and could not help overhearing them quarrelling. He could scarcely believe his ears. Marie, his lovely girl was intending to go away, a long way away, to Paris! He'd never see her again! He felt weak and could not breathe.

'I know who put you up to this!'

'Who?'

'Beanpole! He's always got his head stuck in a book. All he thinks about is these modern ideas that's causing a lot of trouble He's getting far too political for my liking. It's dangerous. What's he been telling you? I'll wring his damned neck!'

'Beanpole hasn't said anything.'

'It's not Princess Lai, is it? I always knew she was a sly one. I wouldn't put anything past her. Calls herself Chinese but she was born in Paris. She's never been further east than Strasburg. Was it her?'

'No.'

'It can't be Dolly. She's dimmer than an unlit candle. That leaves Jean. He's always following you about like a puppy dog. And I've seen you encouraging him. Here,' he said suddenly, 'you're not thinking of taking him with you? It would be the end of your old father, you heartless girl. He's the best exhibit I ever had.'

Marie laughed. 'What a thought! No, Pa, I'm not planning to run away with him. Oh I let him run and around and do things for me. But I only put up with him because he's useful. I hate him. The very sight of him makes me feel sick. He's grotesque! He's a *gargoyle!*'

The word struck Jean like a blow from a fist.

She *hated* him! In that instant, his world fell apart. His legs were just strong enough to let him creep away into the darkness. His first thought was to blame himself for thinking that someone as lovely as Marie could ever love him, or even like him or even look at him without feeling disgust. Why should she? She was perfect and he was ugly as sin. Everywhere he had been rejected. His family, even his own mother, had repudiated him. The Church did not want him, he was not welcome in any school, and the army had turned him away. Wherever he went, people could not bear to see him. He was an outcast and he had been deluded to believe that someone as beautiful as Marie could ever feel anything for him.

And then his thoughts turned to his own stupidity. How could he have been so blind? Even those who did not hate him had their reasons for tolerating him: Monecq, because Jean was his prize exhibit, and Dolly and Beanpole and the Princess because they were gargoyles too — do not birds of a feather flock together? But Marie had deceived him, she had had disguised her feelings, encouraged him the better to use him. All night he thought about her, and the more he thought the lower she fell in his estimation until the last scale dropped from his eyes: she was false, heartless and cruel. By the time the sun came up and the camp was stirring, the spell she had cast was broken. He now despised her far more than she hated him. She had revealed her true self and it was as ugly as his face!

Yet she had at least done one thing for him: she had shown him the only identity he could ever have. People fear what is unusual, they feel most comfortable when they are surrounded by the familiar and the ordinary. A man's face is not always his fortune. To live a happy life he does not need to be handsome, just more or less like everyone else. The man with average looks passes unnoticed in a crowd, has friends, and is accepted into the company of human beings.

But he, Jean Dartigoyte, the Living Death, could not go among other people unnoticed. Everywhere he would always be met with hostility and fear. Well then, since he was an outcast from the human race, why should he try to behave like a human being? He was doomed to be different, an outsider, everyone's worst nightmare, the face of evil. Very well. Since he could not be human, he would become what his face proclaimed him to be. He had been born under the sign of Evil. Evil was his destiny, a dark sun which hung over his life and lit his path.

It was war!

His uncertainties and doubts vanished. Knowledge of his secret power made him strong. No obstacles, no opponents could resist him now! How easily had Isidore got the better of him! And yet how little it had taken to turn Bastingard from a bully into a quivering wretch.

His immediate target was, of course, Marie. He continued to behave with her as if nothing had changed. As he sat displayed in his coffin, he thought of ways of taking his revenge. What would hurt her most was obviously to have her looks spoiled. A splash of vitriol would do it. It was easy to arrange and made to look like an accident ... Or he could spread rumours. He'd send the authorities an anonymous letter saying that she performed spells and took part in witches' Sabbaths...

He was still meditating on what he would do when Monecq returned late one evening and called Marie, Dolly, the Princess, Beanpole, Jean and the roustabout to a meeting in his caravan. As they all climbed in and settled down, he looked at them ashen-faced.

'I got news. Bad news. I won't beat about the bush, I'm not that sort of man, as you know. So I'll come straight out with it. Tonight I had too much to drink and got into a card game. I lost. And what I lost was Monecq's travelling show. It's no longer mine.'

There was a stunned silence.

'What does it mean,' asked Dolly?

'It means the show now belongs to a man named Vincent Vinh Duc. Some sort of Chinaman. From now on you belong to him.'

'What if we don't want to?'

'You got no choice. When you joined you all signed a legal paper saying you got to do what the owner of the company tells you to or pay to have the paper cancelled. So either you go on as you are or else you buy yourselves out. Like in the army.'

Beanpole spoke up: 'What's he like, this Vincent ... er ...'

'Vinh Duc,' said a silky voice through the flap of the curtain at the rear of the caravan. 'At your service.'

A face appeared through the gap. It had black, almond eyes, a flat nose, hair in a centre parting, long plaits and a thin drooping moustache. Next they saw a green silk robe held around the middle by a matching sash as Vincent Vinh Duc climbed the steps and joined the members of what was now his company.

'I have plans. Good plans. I will make your fortunes,' he said with a thin smile. 'Stay with me and you will see the world and grow rich!'

Of all those present, only Jean was not dismayed at the prospect.

Chapter 7

The next day Marie packed her bags and left for Paris without saying goodbye to her father or giving Jean time to contrive a suitable revenge. At first he felt cheated. But on reflexion he decided that she had taught him a useful lesson. So perhaps he owed her something after all. Then he dismissed her from his thoughts.

Dolly, Beanpole and the Princess were not risk-takers. They borrowed the money to buy themselves out of their contracts and joined other travelling shows: better the world they knew than face an uncertain future with a mysterious Oriental. But to Jean, it seemed that fate was offering him a way out, new start, the chance to live up to the face he wore.

In reality he was about to take merely the first, faltering steps on what would prove to be a long, hard road.

Monsieur Vincent did not try to resurrect Monaco's freak show and pocketed the buy-out money he got from Dolly, Beanpole and the Princess without comment. But he seemed set on making something of Jean. He bought him a new suit of clothes, a wig and a pair of dark eyeglasses which modified his appearance and allowed him to walk through the streets without attracting anything more than curious looks. The next day, they travelled to Le Havre and the same evening boarded the schooner *Espérance*, bound for Shanghai. Jean did what he was told, but not out of meekness. His new employer was a man of the world, seemingly rich and successful, who gave orders and was obeyed. He did not answer questions directly and never spoke of his business. Such a man was worth observing and learning from.

Monsieur Vincent was only too happy to instruct him. During the long voyage, he told him about the Orient, for that is where his new life would start. He taught Jean to speak Vietnamese (Monsieur Vincent was a native of Tonkin, in Indochina) and found that his pupil had a remarkable flair for languages. Jean missed no opportunity for self-improvement and put the tedium of many months at sea to good use.

The other passengers paid him little attention. Monsieur Vincent let it be known that his young protégé wore a broad-brimmed hat on medical advice, to protect his weak eyes from strong light, while his silk face mask was designed to shield his delicate skin against the elements. Thus equipped, Jean was able to move freely among passengers and crew.

They had left a grey, rainy France. It was high summer when, after many tedious months, they finally sailed into the South China Sea, making for the port of Hai-Phong where they were due to deliver cargo and take on board new merchandise for Shanghai

The typhoon season was early that year. On the third day of May, the Master of the *Espérance* looked up at the sky, saw danger in the angry clouds and ordered a change of course. They made good speed into the Gulf of Tonkin and were within sight of the coast when the storm burst upon them. The Captain took the ship closer to the shore where he hoped to find a lee of land to shelter in But the swell which had rocked the ship violently turned into mountainous waves. Passengers were advised to stay in their cabins and strap themselves in their bunks to prevent being tossed about and injured.

Monsieur Vincent came to Jean:

'Tonight,' he shouted, against the din of the storm, 'we will be in great danger for some hours. If I succumb, there is something you must do for me. Take this ring. Come, put it on your finger. Now, the land you saw before the storm broke was the delta of the Song Koy, the Red River. If you live, you must take the ring to a man named Hong Boa. He is a person of importance and well known. He will not be hard to find. Show him the ring and say that you are The One and that I, Vincent Vinh Duc, sent you. To find Hong Boa, you must travel up the Red River to Hanoi. If you do not locate him on the way, you will ask his whereabouts when you get to the city.'

Jean wanted to ask questions, but the noise was so overpowering that nothing further could be spoken. He felt he had been shut up inside a tin drum which giants were rolling down a steep, rocky slope. The whole world vibrated, the air shuddered and the ship's timbers creaked as if they were being tortured by cruel sea fiends. Then the groaning suddenly gave way to an agonised screech. The ship gave a sudden lurch and stopped moving, his cabin door burst open and sea-water poured through it. He untied himself and climbed out on to the deck. The raging wind pulled at his hair and tore at clothes. He narrowed his eyes against the stinging spray and saw that the ship was aground. It lay at a drunken angle, the bows rearing high on a pile of jagged rocks and its stern, where his cabin and that of Monsieur Vincent had been, almost submerged.

There was no one else in sight. Were passengers and crew trapped below or had the order to abandon ship been given and he had not heard it? The question ceased to matter when a gigantic wave poured over the taffrail and washed him off the deck. Engulfed by tons of raging water, he was carried along helplessly until it seemed his chest would burst. Just as he felt he could hold out no longer, he sensed that the wave lose its power and in a matter of moments, finally spent, it deposited all it had swept before it on a wide sandy beach.

He coughed the sea-water from his lungs and sat up. Lightning suddenly illuminated the reef on which the *Espérance* had foundered. It lit part of the bow, which was all that remained of it, and, behind it a monstrous, white-capped wall of water was bearing down on him. Not waiting to see more, he turned and scampered as far up the beach as he could before the new, hungry wave could reclaim him and drag him back into the wildly thrashing sea.

He found a refuge under the trunk of a fallen palm-tree. There he cowered from the storm which, by dawn, had lessened in intensity and, within the hour, had blown itself out. Under the freshly laundered blue sky of the new day the world looked bright and clean, as if the passing fit had purged a sickness of the elements. Exhausted by his ordeal, Jean slept.

He woke suddenly and sat up, fully alert.

Squatting not more than three feet away was a lean, semi-naked Oriental of uncertain age.

Jean was suddenly afraid. Monsieur Vincent had told him that much of the eastern seaboard of Indochina was home to a floating population of blood-thirsty cut-throats. There was a pirate village at regular intervals, and they had harbours of their own on many of the islands scattered along the coast. They attacked ships, robbed travellers and kidnapped members of wealthy families for ransom. But there were also gangs of opium smugglers who, as they made their way from one safe haven to the next, might take it into their heads to loot a village or take a military post and steal its arms.

Or murder castaways.

But the man now looking at him seemed harmless enough. He wore his hair in a top-knot and a faded blue *sampot* around his loins. He was not armed and looked far from hostile. How long he had been there, Jean could not say. In his hands he held a bowl of what proved to be a dish of rice and cooked chicken. The man motioned to the bowl and said, in the Vietnamese language Monsieur Vincent had taught him: 'Eat, lord.'

Jean took the bowl and fell on the food. As he did so, he heard a low murmur of approval. He glanced up and saw a number of men and women in a circle, all squatting like the first man. They were not repulsed by his face. If they stared, it was out of curiosity. Then Jean understood and almost laughed aloud.

They thought he was a god!

The people of the Delta believed that all the forms of nature were inhabited by spirits, that fox-devils and tiger-demons walked the land and that all living things had been created by *ma-koui* – sea-gods and river-deities. Neither they nor their ancestors had ever seen one of the many spirits of sea, river and storm. But since the strange creature on the shore looked so little like a human being, they supposed it must be *a ma-koui* It was an anxious time. Would the demon bring peace and blessings, or pain and misery? When it accepted their offering they had made, they were greatly relieved. It was the sign that it would bring good joss, not bad.

Jean surveyed the crowd impassively but inside he exulted. He had been granted his wish. His face, no longer a curse, was his salvation. His monstrous ugliness was a mark of distinction: it had made him a God!

He wondered how gods behaved.

He decided that gods spoke little and insisted on being obeyed.

When he had eaten the gift of food, Jean looked out to the reef. The view was empty. Even the spars of wood had disappeared, either washed away by the sea or salvaged by the silent peasants who had made him welcome.

'Have you seen others of the storm?' he asked in the language Monsieur Vincent had taught him.

No one replied. No one dared.

'Where is the Song Koy, the Red River? Will you take me to it?'

The villagers looked blankly at him. The question made no sense. The Red River was there, all around them, moving slowly through the Delta, a vast marshy area created by the silting of Tonkin's great river, a mosaic of lagoons and dykes.

The old man said: 'Lord, we do not know where the Song Koy runs. But Phât Quang will surely know. He is a student, a scholar, and knows many things. Shall we take you to him?'

Jean knew 'Phât Quang' meant 'light of the Buddha' and hoped the student was as enlightened as his name suggested. He agreed to the proposal and was led in a procession through a wetland of flooded paddy fields whose embankments served as roads which converged on Doc Ngu, a village made up of wooden houses on stilts. Dogs barked and the feet of the crowd raised a cloud of dust. The procession halted outside one of the thatched dwellings and the name of Phât Quang was called.

When he learned that a *ma-koui* had appeared in visible form and had come to ask his help, he turned pale. He was a keen student of the acts and deeds of divinities, but he had never read anywhere of the manner in which mortals should behave towards them face to face. Hoping for the best, he lowered his eyes, bowed reverently and spoke meekly of the honour the occasion did him. Jean, who was no more used to dealing with disciples than the student was to meeting gods, decided it would not do to kow-tow to a low-ranking priestling. He accepted the homage with a curt nod, which was greeted by a murmur of approval from the entire population of Doc Ngu, and then stood in silence.

Phât Quang, his eyes humbly lowered, listened while Da Trang, the old man who had first found the god, repeated Jean's question. Relieved to be set no harder task, he replied that in the Delta the Red River was not one, but many, it was all around them. He said it was their mother, that it fed and nurtured them and that the great city of Hanoi stood on its banks some 20 *li*, or twenty leagues, to the west.

'Take me there,' said Jean.

'The Lord from the Sea should know,' said Phât Quang, 'that the way there by land is arduous. It lies through a jungle thick with vines, ferns and sugar palms. The way by water is smoother,'

'Then we shall take the way by water.'

Da Trang offered to prepare and provision a *sampan* for the journey. Jean said they must start at once, for he had business with the deity of the Song Koy at Hanoi. But the village elders were quietly insistent. His coming must be marked by a celebration, a feast worthy of the occasion. It was clear that they had no intention of allowing him to leave until the rites of hospitality had been observed.

Sweetmeats were set before him to eat and, to drink, green tea and wine flavoured with cinnamon. After the meal there was entertainment. A man in a green silk robe recited a poem telling how a marsh nymph once gave a pearl to a poor farmer and told him to put it under his tongue. He would then be able to talk to the animals, birds and fish. But the farmer grew careless and dropped it in a pool and thus lost the gift which would have permitted men to live at peace with the Great Lord's creation. This was followed by dancing to the music of drum and flute. When the dancing was finished, the village elders approached Jean and complained of the gangs of Chinese smugglers and bandits who roamed the delta flats and asked for his protection. Jean nodded sagely and replied that, in return for the welcome they had given him, he would attend to the matter in due course. The elders bowed and withdrew, well satisfied with the favour they had been shown.

Their departure was the signal for an end to the ceremony. The villagers went to their homes leaving the warmth of the night to Jean and Phât Quang. But once the clamour of humanity had been stilled, the night was far from silent. Faint splashings came from the banks of reeds and bamboo which grew everywhere and the surface of the placid water was sometimes broken by widening circles of gentle ripples. It was the time of the nocturnal inhabitants of the place, the rats, snakes and lizards.

'Tell me,' Eric said to Phât Quang, 'what you know of Hong Boa.'

The student gave a start.

'I am but a poor student, Lord. I know as much of politics as it is wise for a humble seeker after truth, such as myself, should know.'

Jean repeated his request. He was told that it was not wise to speak of such high persons even in a place as isolated as Doc Ngu, for there were always ears open to hear. Jean reassured him, saying that was doubtless true in the normal way of things. But surely even the humblest seeker after enlightenment must know that what was communicated in private to a spirit of the river could not be overheard by other mortals.

Hong Boa, said Phât Quang, was the older brother of Tu Duc, the Great Emperor of all Vietnam.

'Why does the younger brother rule and not the older?' asked Jean. 'Does not custom say that the first-born should take precedence over all who come after him?'

'That indeed is the custom, Lord. But court intriguers have plotted against Hong Boa and forced him into exile. Many believe that Hong Boa is better fitted to rule, for he is strong and wise, while Tu Duc is sickly and weak and his people do not respect him. He fears *ta dao*, the infidel, and wages cruel war against them and their religion. Those of his subjects who pay attention to the men in black have *ta dao* branded on their cheeks. Foreign priests are merely drowned but any Vietnamese who wear the black and preach the infidel religion are sawn in half.

'It is said that Tu Duc fears that his brother will rise against him and usurp his golden throne in Saigon. But there are many in every province who long for the hand of Hong Boa to be raised against his brother. Hong Boa has strong support here in the north... But I have said too much, for who am I, an insignificant particle, to concern myself with the affairs of the great?'

Jean said nothing but thought: 'Monsieur Vincent, into what dangerous waters would you lead me?'

He retired to the quarters which had been prepared for him, lay down on a straw mat with his hands cupped at the back of his head and was instantly asleep.

He was awakened by bloodthirsty cries. Four young men rushed into his quarters, pulled him to his feet and bundled him outside. The night was dark, with clouds scudding past the full moon which, at intervals, covered the land with cold mother-of-pearl. They manhandled him along the street and did not stop until they reached a low building made of mud bricks. A door opened and he was flung inside. The door closed after him.

Jean was bewildered and not a little alarmed. Had he been found out to be an impostor? Were there plans afoot for another ceremony in which he, a *ta dao* who had abused their beliefs and hospitality, would be put to a protracted and agonising death?

An oil lamp gave sufficient light for him to see that he was in a small shrine. Incense sticks perfumed the air and the lamp flame burned on an altar before the statue of a big-bellied, smiling Buddha.

Then the door opened again and Phât Quang entered quickly.

'You are safe, Lord!' the student gasped. 'We were in time!'

'Safe?' said Jean. 'Explain yourself!'

'Lord, the sounds you heard as we sat by the water's edge were not made by snakes or rats or any nocturnal creatures, but by men, Chinese bandits, who are even now attacking the village!'

'But how did they manage to get so near without being detected?'

'They came under the surface of the water.'

'Are they then fish that they do not need to breathe the air that mortal men must have if they are to live in water? Explain.'

'No, Lord, they are not fish. They entered the river at some distance away and waded. The water is not deep. When they were near enough to be heard, they each took a hollow reed, sank beneath the surface and used the reed to breathe without being seen or heard. In this way they made their approach. Then, at a given signal, the rose up and took the village by surprise.

'They must be stopped!' cried Jean, rising to his feet.

'They are too many, Lord. The elders instructed the young men to hide you here, in the shrine, which is the strongest building in the village. Here you are safe.'

But at that moment, they heard the sound of approaching voices which were excited, loud and threatening. The village had provided poor plunder. The bandits clearly hoped the shrine would prove more profitable.

'They have seen the light and are coming to steal the Buddha!' hissed Phât Quang.

'They will not succeed,' said Jean and, reaching for the lamp, he told the student to open the door.

Drawing himself up to his full height, he held the lamp at chest height so that it would light his face and went out to confront the attackers who, as they approached, waving gleaming weapons and flaming torches.

As he stepped outside, the moon emerged from behind a cloud and shone full on him, making it seem for all the world as if he had materialised suddenly out of the darkness. He was cloaked in cold, blue light. From below, the lamp threw his eye sockets into deep shadow and made them appear blind, enormous, all-seeing. His twisted mouth was a vicious snarl.

In his deepest voice, he cried: 'Be gone from this place!'

The attackers stopped dead in their tracks, awed by the apparition.

After a moment's hesitation, their leader cried: ''Tis a demon!' and turned to flee. With howls of terror, his men followed.

Throwing down their weapons, they scattered in disarray. The place before the shrine was suddenly empty. The sounds of the routed bandits as they splashed through water and crashed through the reeds finally died away, leaving absolute silence.

Jean exulted. Here was confirmation that his face was a great gift which gave him a power few other mortals possessed. Half a world away from his native land, he had ceased to be a ghoul, a fiend in human shape; he had indeed become an object of veneration, and dread: a god!

Phât Quang emerged from the shrine and fell at Jean's feet. Moments later, the villagers arrived. eager to revere the god of the river who had so promptly answered their prayers. Some showed their wounds from the recent battle.

Jean was escorted in triumph to his quarters. There, the poet who had told the story of the farmer and the magic pearl, improvised a poem to commemorate the occasion. The celebrations lasted until dawn.

When the village was finally asleep, Jean roused Phât Quang and said it was time to leave. His business in Hanoi was urgent. They woke Da Trang who, plying the *yu-lu*, the great oar which propelled the *sampan*, took them past low-lying banks into widening channels which brought them at last to the great highway of the Red River. From time to time a pagoda or some private *yamen* surrounded by trees stood out white against the cloudless blue sky. There were temples everywhere. An easterly wind rose and filled their sail as they mingled with every kind of native craft.

Jean fingered the ring given to him by Monsieur Vincent who was therefore not merely a person of some importance but an agent of Hong Boa and therefore part of the conspiracy to oust the Emperor. So what had he been doing travelling in provincial France? Why had he acquired Monecq's freak show when he clearly had no interest in touring from one fair to another? What role had he cast Jean for? What had he meant by saying that he was 'The One'?

Jean leaned back in the boat and watched the land slowly slip by. Here the jungle did not grow, as woods do in Europe, in an orderly fashion, with tree trunks springing out of the ferns and bushes of the forest floor and daylight reaching down into the undergrowth. Here, all was furious, unrestrained, savage life and everywhere a sense of danger and menace hung heavily in the air.

The waterfront at Hanoi was long, busy and crowded. Da Trang found a berth and Jean, preceded by Phât Quang as his guide, prepared to venture into the city. Before leaving the *sampan*, he donned Da Trang's conical coolie's hat and wound a scarf around his face leaving only a small gap to see through.

'Take me to where I shall find Hong Boa or to persons who know where he is.'

They walked through, narrow, twisting streets, through a labyrinth of gesticulating, noisy sellers and buyers of goods which ranged from enamelware to live animals and spices. The noise and bustle had a familiar, fairground quality which put Jean at his ease. Gradually the crowd thinned and he found himself in a wealthy, residential part of the town. He saw ladies dressed in silks with their heads decorated with jewels and pearls, a few gentlemen in European clothes, and Chinese ladies who, on the way to call on friends, were carried on a servant's shoulder because their small feet made it difficult for them to walk.

At last, Phât Quang halted outside a kind of citadel defended by high walls punctuated by watch towers. It was surrounded by a moat covered with large, brilliantly coloured lotus flowers. A two-arched marble bridge brought him to the gatehouse. He asked, no, demanded, to see his Excellency Hong Boa. The guard looked at him suspiciously and asked why he hid his face. Jean told him imperiously that such matters were not his affair. Without waiting for a reaction, he removed the ring Monsieur Vincent had given him from his finger and ordered the man to take it to his master. While he waited for him to return, Jean had ample time to look through the gate at Hong Boa's palace of marble. He was still admiring the house and its shady walks and fountains when armed guards marched in good order to the gatehouse. Jean and the student were instantly surrounded. Spears were pointed at them and an officer announced that they were under arrest. As they were led away, Jean tried to protest but he was silenced with the flat of a sword that was not designed for ceremonial use. They were pushed roughly into a small cell-like room and left there. The blank white walls were relieved by one high window which let in in just enough light to see by.

Phât Quang was terrified, but he was also angry. He knocked Jean's coolie hat to the floor and tore the scarf from his face.

'You are no *ma-koui!*' he cried. 'No deity would allow himself to be treated so! You have deceived me and my people, abused our good faith. You are *ta dao*, a foreigner, and untruthful like all foreigners.'

Before Jean could respond, the door opened and an amused voice said:

'A deity? My, we have been riding high!'

Jean took a step forward: 'Monsieur Vincent!' he cried, 'thank God you're here! There's been a terrible mistake!'

'The man you knew as Monsieur Vincent was a convenient invention to enable me move freely among your people. I am Ngoc Lu Sinh, chief adviser to his Excellency Hong Boa.'

He clapped his hands and ordered the two guards who flanked him to seize Phât Quang and take him away.

'Where are you taking him?' cried Jean. He felt suddenly afraid. The man before him was not the mild-mannered 'Monsieur Vincent' who had sailed with him on the *Espérance*, but a man of authority, as his manner and clothes proclaimed. He wore a richly brocaded tunic over loose silk trousers, slippers embroidered with dragons and studded with precious stones and, on his head, a wide-brimmed black silk hat.

'All in good time,' said Ngoc Lu Sinh. 'But first I want to know how you lived through the storm and reached Hanoi without causing a stir. Spectacular ugliness such as yours is rare and here news travels fast.'

When Jean finished his tale, Jean in turn asked how his former mentor had survived the wreck.

But Ngoc shrugged and said: 'Oh, I always survive. But you have done well so far. It was a stroke of good fortune to be taken for a god from the sea. But, you made the most of the opportunity. Of course no one here will be taken in by such tomfoolery. So you're going to have to do better than that. Your business here has hardly begun.'

'What business?'

'What reason do you suppose took me to France?'

'I assumed you were in the same business as Monecq. I thought you were looking for exhibits for a show you intended to put on here or in China.'

Ngoc Lu Sinh smiled deprecatingly.

'You are far from the truth. I was entrusted with a secret mission. For some years, France has been showing great interest in our poor country. You now have an emperor and an emperor needs an empire. That is why the French are casting covetous glances at us. I was sent to discover what view your government would take if his Excellency Hong Boa were to succeed in mounting a coup d'état. Would they welcome it? They said they would, for they do not like the war Tu Duc is waging against the Catholic Church and see Hong Boa as more sympathetic to their plans.'

Jean recalled enough of Beanpole's political lessons to follow the argument.

'What has that to do with me?'

'I had completed my business in Paris and was travelling to Le Havre to take ship. On the way was a town and in the town was a fair. I saw you and in you I saw a monster. At that moment, I knew I had found a way of eliminating Tu Duc! The charade of bankrupting Monecq at cards and releasing the rest of the freaks from their contracts was a distraction. It was you I wanted and I did not even have to buy you: you fell into my hands. But now you are here, and your work can begin.'

'What work?'

'You are going to kill Tu Duc and put Hong Boa on the throne. I assure you he will be suitably grateful.'

Jean could not believe his ears.

'I am no murderer,' he cried.

'Jean, you are fascinatingly repulsive to look at. Tu Duc is a man of feeble mind and easily amused. You will be a novelty for him, a curiosity. He will be fascinated until he wearies of you. But until then he will be grateful to his brother and not harm the gift he will see as a peace offering.'

'I am not a thing to be given and received …'

'You will be,' said Monsieur Ngoc silkily, 'exactly what I want you to be. Your face makes you unique and perfect for the task. And now we shall speak of arrangements.'

'What arrangements?'

'To send you as a gift to Tu Duc in his golden palace in Saigon. You will have free access to him. He will be off his guard. You will poison him. Never fear, we will tell you how and when the deed is to be done.'

Then Ngoc Lu Sinh bowed.

'Now you must excuse me. I have matters to attend to.'

He left Jean alone with his thoughts in a whirl. If he refused to do what was expected of him, he would be killed, for he could not be allowed to live and reveal what he knew about the plot to murder the Emperor. But if he agreed, he would surely be killed by Tu Duc's guards, for he did not believe for one moment that a safe means of escape would be arranged for him. Why should it? Life here was cheap and once he had served his purpose, he would be discarded.

Ngoc was right. His time in Tonkin thus far had been charmed. His success in fooling the peasants of Doc Ngu had been a matter of luck. He had not saved himself. He had been saved by the superstition of the ignorant people who had found him on the beach. The time had come to take charge and become a real demon.

'Well?' said Ngoc Lu Sin next morning. 'You've had a night to think about my proposition. Are you still virtuously outraged?'

'I shall expect to be paid handsomely for the risk I shall be taking.'

'Of course,' said Ngoc Lu Sinh, surprised by his cool tone. 'You are being sensible. But now, come with me. Hong Boa wishes to meet you. He wants to see your face.'

Escorted by two guards, Ngoc Lu Sinh led Jean through the gardens to a room in the main palace. A tall, fleshy man in gorgeous robes was writing at a desk carved with representations of dragons and serpents.

He paid no attention to the newcomers.

Eventually he looked up and stared at Jean for a moment.

Then he said in excellent French, 'Yes, he will do very well. I never saw a more loathsome creature. Truly the stuff of nightmares. My brother will be delighted.'

Hong Boa had spoken of him as though he had not been there.

'Now leave me.'

Ngoc bowed and, taking Jean by the arm, led him out of the presence of Hong Boa.

'You pleased him,' he said, once they were outside. 'Do as you are told and you will be a rich man.'

As they walked, Ngoc Lu Sinh outlined the plan. He would be taken to Saigon by boat and given to Tu Duc as a gift to seal the rift between the brothers. He would be the Emperor's toy, his fool. He would choose his own moment to slip poison into the Emperor's drink. He need not fear for his own safety, for Hong Boa could not afford to let anything happen to him before or after the deed was done because he could not be allowed to be captured. Any whiff of the truth would be politically fatal. Jean would come to no harm. He would escape from the golden palace, receive the fortune that would buy his silence and be returned to Europe. His escape had been arranged. A spy inside the palace would unlock a door and a party of Ngoc Lu Sinh's men would escort him to safety. There was nothing to fear.

Jean did not believe this for one moment. It would be easier for the inside man to cut his throat and drop his body down a well than to arrange for him to escape. And why should Hong Boa buy his silence when a dagger through his heart would be cheaper and leave no room for doubt?

'However,' said Ngoc Lu Sinh, 'in case you are not entirely convinced, let me show you what happens to those who try to meddle with Hong Boa's plans.'

Escorted by a man-at-arms, they crossed a courtyard where Hong Boa's personal bodyguard were drilling. Ignoring them, Ngoc Lu Sinh led the way to a decorated pagoda in a remote part of the palace. Ngoc nodded to the guard who opened a door.

Jean found himself in a windowless, featureless room. After the brightness of the day, it took his eyes a few moments to adjust to the gloom. When they did, he could hardly believe what he was seeing.

Phât Quang was hanging from a beam by a meat-hook which entered his throat beneath his chin and pulled his head backward until he was staring vertically at the ceiling. One forearm and a foot were missing. They lay on the floor where they had been thrown after removal. The body had been ravaged by multiple cuts, as though it had been whipped by a sharp blade. Blood had collected in a sticky pool under the corpse. Phât Quang had died a slow, agonising death. The instruments which had been used by his torturers had been set out neatly on a low table against one wall. They had been cleaned and gleamed in the half-light

Jean had heard of the 'Death by a Thousand Cuts'. It had featured among the more lurid attractions of the fairs where he had been exhibited. But nothing had prepared him for the horror of what he saw now.

Slices of the fleshier parts of the living body of the victim had been had been removed, some to the bone, but in such a way that he did not bleed quickly to death. Then ears, nose, lips, fingers and toes had been taken before the large limbs were taken away ... in stages.

Ngoc nodded casually to the hanging remains of Phât Quang and said:

'He told us nothing because he knew nothing, If he had known anything, he would have told it.'

'You did this to a human being?' Jean said in a horrified whisper.

'Ach, he was dispensable. An idealist. You must not be sentimental about such people. Besides, he was not butchered. He was given his quietus according to the ancient rules of the art: there was more skill, care, artistry and beauty lavished on him than he deserved. But you are incapable of appreciating what a triumph of the art of torment hangs there ...'

At that moment there was the noise of an explosion. Through the open door Jean saw uniformed men began running towards a plume of smoke that rose into the air. As it started to drift slowly towards them, Ngoc Lu Sinh swore and said, 'This is Tu Duc's doing!'

He snapped an order to the guard who ran off to find out what was happening. Ordering Jean to follow him, Ngoc Lu Sinh turned to leave. In that split second, Jean acted as the owner of such a face as his should act.

Two steps took him to the low table. He seized the first weapon that came to hand, a heavy hammer, and clubbed Ngoc Lu Sinh to the floor. He made sure that he was dead then removed the clothes from his body. He put on the tunic and trousers and managed to get his feet into the dead man's slippers. He made a point of retrieving the wide-brimmed hat which had fallen off during the attack. With one last look at Phât Quang and Ngoc Lu Sinh, he left the room, closing and the door behind him.

Smoke, black and choking, swirled around him. He pulled the hat down over his eyes and held a cloth over his mouth as if warding off the billowing fumes. He began retracing his footsteps and, as he crossed the drill-ground, wished he had paid more attention to the way he had come.

But when he reached a magnolia which he remembered he turned and made out the fountain straight ahead and, beyond it, the gatehouse. When he reached it, still holding the cloth in front of his face, he barked an order to the gatekeeper who, deferring to Ngoc Lu Sinh's clothes, swung open the heavy gates. A moment later, Jean was in the street outside.

He pushed his way through the crowds which were fleeing the explosion. He had to get away from the vicinity of Hong Boa's palace. He set off to return to the waterfront, the only place he knew in all Hanoi.

His only chance was to go back by the way Phât Quang had brought him. Without breaking step, he searched for clues. He recalled a gaudy shop-front then a street-corner which seemed familiar as did a cook shop exuding the same aroma of roasting pork ... Soon, he had left the residential quarter and began to thread his way through the narrow streets of the market. People stepped back when they saw him coming, deceived by his clothes which marked him out as a person of importance. Partly by using his eyes to guide him and partly by luck, he finally reached the quayside. He paused and looked up and down its length.

There, not fifty yards away, was Da Trang sitting patiently in his *sampan*.

Jean stepped into the boat and ordered him to cast off.

Soon, they were gliding through the flotilla of small vessels and moving easily down river, heading east, toward the port of Hai-Phong where Jean hoped to find a ship, bound for any destination, which would take him away from this hellish place.

There was no sign of pursuit. Jean had vanished into thin air.

For the next two days as they drifted with the current down the broad river to the sea Jean considered his options. He could not stay in a country where he had found only danger and horror. He must find a ship. When they reached Hai-Phong he thanked Da Trang and told him he could return home. The old man asked for a blessing and kissed his robe when he was given two of the small gems sewn onto Ngoc Lu Sinh's slippers. Jean stepped ashore, careful as ever to keep his face hidden, and sold the rest of the jewels. He scoured the Hai-Phong waterfront for a berth on a ship.

Captain Vidal, master of the cargo vessel *La Golconde* bound for Marseilles, agreed to carry him as a passenger. He insisted on being paid in advance.

La Golconde set sail for France the very next day.

Jean Dartigoyte did not know that it would be ten years before he saw his homeland again.

Chapter 8

The coast of Tonkin was not yet out of sight when Captain Vidal's suspicions were first aroused. A passenger who did not come up on deck to watch the mainland disappear below the horizon was, in his experience, a rare exception. But he shrugged and put aside his doubts. The man was probably ill or had not yet found his sea legs. After ten days at sea, the passenger, carefully muffled with silk scarves and a cap with a visor, appeared briefly on deck. But he had not been seen since and took all his meals in his cabin. Captain Vidal put such behaviour down to an unsociable temperament and shrugged his shoulders again. But by the time they were into the Arabian Sea and heading for the port where *La Golconde* was to land silks and woven cloths and pick up a cargo of spice, Captain Vidal had reached the conclusion that the man was deliberately avoiding drawing attention to himself: he was hiding his identity.

He thought such a man would pay good money to protect his secret.

The night before they reached port, he called on his mysterious passenger with a proposal.

The following day, the master of the vessel could not be found and the first officer was left to berth the ship.

A full search of the vessel was instituted. A steward discovered Captain Vidal lying on the floor of the cabin of the mysterious passenger. He had been stabbed in the heart. There was no sign of the occupant of the cabin, but his belongings were still there, except for a small case he had insisted on carrying on board himself when he embarked at Hai-Phong.

The local representative of the ship's owners confirmed the first officer as the new master of *La Golconde*. The authorities allowed him to proceed on his journey when they had completed their enquiries. Since no one had witnessed the murder or had any useful information to give, it was concluded that it was likely, though not certain, that the Captain had been murdered by the mysterious passenger who had disappeared under cover of darkness.

All that was known of him was that he was European.

It was not enough to justify further investigation.

And so the murderer, jumping from one frying pan into another, left the safety of his cabin and escaped into a world of new dangers.

*

Nine days later, a lone traveller heading north towards the Punjab through Sind province was set upon by robbers. He was later discovered in a ditch by the side of the road. His attackers had taken all he had, even his clothes, and left him with barely enough to cover his nakedness.

Such occurrences were frequent and no note would have been taken of it if the victim had not been a devout and holy man, as was clear from the mortification of the flesh to which he had evidently subjected himself.

Few had not seen holy men who bore the marks of horrible self-mutilation undertaken to demonstrate the depth of their faith. There were Fakirs who had bound their hands together with cord in prayer for so long that their finger nails had penetrated their flesh. Others, having taken a vow of silence, had sewn their lips together, leaving only a small hole for a straw through which they fed themselves a liquid gruel made of rice. Those who had seen the robbers' latest victim with their own eyes believed they had received a great blessing. They told marvelling friends that the saint looked like a living corpse. They said he had put out his own eyes, cut off nose, ears, lips and part of his cheeks, so that the teeth were exposed. But such reports were considered, exaggerated, even by local standards.

The man never spoke, either because he could not or would not. Accordingly, no one knew his name or where he had come from.

His wounds were tended and he was cared for until he was able to go on his way.

Wherever he went, the faithful were impressed by his piety, which was writ large for all to see on that ravaged face which he made no effort to hide. When he passed with his begging bowl. Few people did not put a small amount of cooked rice or a handful of nuts into it.

*

'They say there's a European in town, gone native. I keep hearing rumours. Know anything about him?'

George Marling, the East India Company representative in Lahore, scowled at the *punkah-wallah* who was dozing in a corner of the office of the District Superintendent of Lahore's police force. The DSP, Charles Hutchinson, caught his glance and barked an order at the Indian who woke and resumed his rhythmic wafting of the great fan which swung to and fro. It was too hot for this sort of conversation, Marling thought.

'Not much,' he said in reply to the DSP's question. 'He made contact with our office here a month or six weeks back. Said his name was Domson. No passport. Some tale about being robbed which was probably true. Wanted a job. There was nothing for him. Well there was, actually, but Harris who saw him didn't think it right to give it to a Frenchman. And I agree. My God, it's only three years since we were fighting Sikh infantry trained by French army officers!'

Marling, a thickset man of forty with a florid face, leaned forward, steepling his fingers.

'One other thing,' he went on. 'He kept his face covered the whole time. Could have been a wound, even a skin rash, possibly contagious. But maybe he didn't want to be recognised. Anyhow, Harris thought it all very rum.'

'Did this Domson give any indication that he might be working for the French?' asked Hutchinson.

.'Not really. Why? In what way working for them? You mean spying?'

'What did he do when Harris turned him down?'

'What can Europeans do in this country when they're on their uppers? They put their hand out in one way or another. Or go to the bad. I've no idea.'

'Did Domson, if that's really his name, go round with his hand out?' asked Hutchinson.

'Not that I heard. He disappeared.'

'Well he seems to have done well for himself since. Gone into business, it seems. Has money to burn. Lives in the native quarter.'

'Must have gone to the bad, then,' said Marling.

The DSP paused again.

'Do you think he's mixed up in the opium trade?' he asked.

'I suppose it's possible. Is it important?'

'Perhaps. If he is, he must know Afghanistan.. There's trouble brewing with the hill tribes there. Dalhousie is worried. If Domson has been doing business with the Afghans, the chief would like to know. Keep this to yourself, but there's talk of a *jihad* against the *feringhees* which would be bad news for us. Any information about the mood in the streets of Kabul and the surrounding hills might be helpful and save a great deal of trouble later on.'

Hutchinson lit a cigarette and inhaled deeply.

'Be a good fellow and keep an eye open for him. Let me know if you hear anything. I'd like to see him.'

*

Hutchinson did not have to wait long to meet the man called Domson. Within days, a routine patrol reported that a European had been involved in an altercation in a bazaar in the native quarter which had turned nasty. The man was outnumbered and had been taken into custody for his own protection. The DSP sent for him.

'Seems a lot younger than I'd imagined,' thought Hutchinson when Domson was standing in front of his desk. But it was hard to tell. The prisoner was dressed in western clothes but his face was swathed in a *puggarree*, a turban cloth which obscured his features. The DSP assumed it was there to hide the marks of the fight he'd been in. Or maybe his rash hadn't cleared up.

'Well, Mr Domson, perhaps you'd care to explain what happened last night?'

'A small disagreement about business,' the man replied in passable English. 'Even the best of friends fall out sometimes.'

'What sort of business?'

'Oh, just business. Buying and selling.'

'My sergeant says the men you call your friends don't like the way you buy and sell. Seems you undercut their prices and steal their customers.'

'These people are very backward. They do not understand modern business.'

'Perhaps. But they have a simple way of dealing with any outsider whose face doesn't fit.'

Domson gave a curious, hollow laugh, as if there was unintentional humour in the remark..

'It's no laughing matter,' said the DSP sharply. 'If I let you go, you'll be dead by tonight.'

'I'll have to take my chances,' said Domson.

'There might be another way. Does opium figure in your business activities?'

'Perhaps. I deal in many kinds of goods.'

'No need to be cagey. I'm not looking for opium smugglers today. I'm more interested in where you get your supplies. Afghanistan, I suppose?'

After a moment's hesitation, Domson nodded.

'You have been there?'

'No. All my dealings have been with Afghan traders here, in Lahore. But I'm due to leave with a caravan for Kabul tomorrow, which is why my current predicament is... inconvenient.'

'Then perhaps we can come to an arrangement. I will be frank. It is likely that there will soon be trouble in the border provinces. It would help us to know more about where the hill tribes stand and in particular whether there is any truth in rumours that Dost Mohammad is planning to send his Afghans to join forces with the Sikhs here in the Punjab. In your trade, you'll have your ear to the ground. Business prefers peace to war.'

'War is another name for business. But, Monsieur, you want me, a Frenchman, to spy for Britain?' said Domson in an amused voice.

'You can spy for us with our protection or walk out of here without it and wait for that knife in the back. How do you say?'

*

From Lahore, the road west rolled out across the plains and great rivers of the Punjab towards Peshawar and the North West frontier where India ended. The caravan which Jean had joined made slow progress under a scorching sun.

At first it was a dry plains heat which burned hands and feet and drew every drop of moisture from the body, leaving eyes sore, lungs on fire and skin rough and irritable. Before they had gone half a day, Jean was regretting the humidity of the Red River delta. To pass the time, he talked to any Afghan who would listen and made good progress in acquiring their Pashtu language. They were lean men, armed to the teeth and ready to use their weapons at any hint of profit to be made. They also taught Jean to use a sling and an efficient way of garrotting enemies by means of the Punjabi bowstring, a deadly noose of catgut or silk. They were good-humoured enough, but they could turn from friend to mortal foe without warning. Jean learned to watch for the tilting point.

Later, as the land rose towards the great Khyber Pass, the heat moderated slightly and they saw villages and unexpected oases of lush growth. But the landscape also turned scrubbier and stonier, and rangy warriors in *puggarrees* and long coats appeared at intervals along the road. Evil knives like pointed cleavers hung from their belts and long rifles, the Afghan *jezzails*, were slung over their shoulders.

Their road now led them over a series of passes, gorges and narrow valleys which had been scooped out of the rocky terrain. The caravan managed the low passes without difficulty but struggled at others where the going was hard and often very hard. Even the sure-footed animals could not avoid slipping on the rocky trail and the drovers remained in a state of screaming rage and frustration until the way became easier again. And as they toiled over the next pass, hauling the carts up on ropes and braking the wheels on way down, the process was repeated. Gupta, the leader of the caravan, stayed cheerful, and with every delay confidently declared that the next pass was the last, that on the other side a smooth, broad highway awaited them. It did not take long for his optimism to become a bad joke among the travellers, though they preferred his exaggerations to the truth.

But the terrain was not the only danger. Like the rest of the company, Jean was aware that they were being followed on the heights by hill men who had a terrible reputation for savagery. They held life so cheap, the drovers told him, that they would kill a man as easily as they would shoot a stray dog or cat. Despite Gupta's warning that they should stay together for safety, the more impatient travellers would at times move on ahead and gain a quarter of a mile on the main body of the caravan. Others, with Jean among them, dropped behind, confident that they would be able to catch up quickly.

The caravan was at that moment struggling along a narrow stretch of the trail which clung to the almost sheer wall of a narrow valley. Jean, well to the rear of even the last elements of the caravan, was sitting on a rock watching great birds of prey circling on the air current or looking down at the valley floor which was bisected by a river that he could see but not hear. Suddenly he felt a reverberation beneath his feet and his rock seemed to sway The tremor lasted for five seconds and culminated in a violent lurch. Jean leaped into the lee of the boulder he had been sitting on while rocks and stone from higher up the slope rained down on him.

The air filled with their noise but did not drown the shouts of alarm and panic. Jean lifted his head in time to see a length of the trail lose its moorings and slide gently into the void, taking about half the caravan with it in a great cloud of dust. Donkeys and horses squealed and men and women screamed with terror, but long before the last of dust had blown away on the wind, the carts, travellers and animals which had formed the rear section of Gupta's waggon train had vanished, as had a number of the stragglers of whom, he realised, he was the sole survivor. The narrow trail had gone too, so that he was separated by an impassable stretch of sheer rock from what remained of the expedition.

He watched and heard Gupta, who had been at the head of the line, urging his drovers to beat their animals on in a mad scramble to reach safe ground. The shouting grew fainter and, as the last of the men animals and carts vanished round a corner, finally fell silent.

Jean felt very alone. He was cut off, with no supplies, and it was about three hours before sunset. He could not return the way Gupta had brought them, for it had taken them four days to cover the distance, four days therefore to the nearest human habitation. He had no choice. He would have to climb up the slope above him, pass over the highest point of the scar gouged out by the earthquake, and hope to rejoin the rest of the party further along the trail. He felt a cool breeze blow across his face. If he did not catch the caravan before dark, he would spend a cold, hungry and very uncomfortable night on the mountain.

How long he climbed he could not tell, but he neither reached the top of the scar nor found, in the fading light, a way of traversing it. He stumbled across a faint trail made by animals and followed it. When it was too dark to see, he sat down by the side of the trail and considered what to do

The heat had gone from the day and was replaced by bitter cold. The wind howled around him. A wolf called in the distance.

He found shelter under an overhang of rock and slept the fitful sleep of exhaustion.

He woke before the dawn had begun to fill the wide, wide sky. His whole body was frozen and his teeth chattered uncontrollably.

He stood up, stretched and took stock.

He was high in rugged country, surrounded by jagged peaks, south of the Khyber Pass, and winter had already shown him its teeth. His possessions amounted to a flannel shirt, a pair of torn nankeen trousers and boots whose condition had not been improved by the battering they had taken during his climb. He had, no water, no food and no weapon.

Stumbling over the loose stones, he picked a way up a long stony slope until he found a snaking goat trail, probably the one he had seen the night before. There was no vegetation and no sign of life.

Yet at intervals, much to his surprise, he encountered a few springs where bushes bearing nuts and berries grew. He drank and ate his fill and loaded his pockets with the fruit and continued on his way.

Soon he realised he could no longer see the marks of the scar and, thinking he had reached the point where the earth had begun to slide, he took hope. If he cut across to his right and then started climbing down, surely he would soon remake contact with Gupta's band of travellers. But cold, hunger and exhaustion added to the effects of altitude, made him light-headed so that later, he could not remember the moment when he first saw, in a deep, steep-sided bowl in the hills, the white walls of a temple. Its bulbous domes and the delicate columns of its minarets rose out of an unexpected growth of palms, magnolias and bamboo. A gate interrupted thick tall ramparts decorated with sculptures. It was open.

Inside was a broad avenue flanked by a row of stone elephants carrying divinities on their backs, like the virgin of Vanagui or Kristna as a child, through a forest of exquisitely carved columns. The way led through carefully tended gardens to a palace of white and black marble. Men in green robes with shaven heads were visible at intervals. Some were working in flower beds, others in vegetable patches and orchards. They paid no attention to him. He kept walking until he reached the palace. Its door stood wide open too.

The interior was sparely but elegantly furnished in the Oriental style. Tapestries hung on the walls, richly patterned carpets covered the polished floors and intricately carved wooden screens filled the archways.

Jean paused a moment, enjoying the coolness and waiting for his eyes to get used to the gloom of a vaulted hall which was deep enough for torches to be burned. They filled the space with sweet-smelling resin.

'Welcome to Lakya-Pore. I am Phara-Padh.'

The voice, though not loud, filled the hall, though it seemed not to come from any one direction. It took Jean several moments to locate its source, a tall figure in a red robe standing in the middle of the room.

'Come,' said Phara-Padh, 'let me offer you refreshment. You must be hungry and tired. When you have eaten and rested, I will come again. You shall tell me your name and later we shall talk.'

The man said no more but led him through an arch into an alcove and left him there. Though his mind teemed with questions — how could there be such a place with its own temperate climate in these harsh mountains? was it a palace or a monastery? who was Phara-Padh? — Jean fell on the food which was set out for him. There were dishes of rice, curries of venison and fish and a variety of fruits in glass bowls. When he had eaten, he was overcome by fatigue. The cushion-covered couch beneath a latticed window was irresistible. He lay on it and slept.

When he woke, he found water to wash in and a robe of green silk which had been laid out for him. He bathed, put on the robe and waited. Then Phara-Padh entered the room.

Jean thanked him for the hospitality he had shown a stranger. He explained that he had been separated from the caravan but said nothing of his business or the spying mission he had undertaken for the British authorities.

'And now, it is essential for me to go on my way …'

'And which way is that?'

'To where my duty lies …'

Phara-Padh frowned.

'So you eat my food but reject my welcome?'

'On the contrary, Excellency. I revere and honour it. Your generosity has saved my life. But I must leave. I have urgent business in Kabul.'

'But you cannot leave. The winter has already come to the mountains and the high passes are already blocked by snow. You must wait until spring opens them again.'

'But if winter has set in, why is this place still warm and green?'

'There is also question of payment,' said Phara-Padh, ignoring the question.

'Payment?'

'A man who has urgent business in Kabul is a man of wealth. Such a man can afford to pay.'

'Of course. But you should know that I have no money, nor will I have any means of getting any until the spring, if what you say is true.'

Phara-Padh's face darkened with anger, his eyes grew larger and he clenched his fists so hard that they showed white against the red of his tunic.

'You doubt my word?' he said in a menacing whisper.

As he spoke, the torches in their wall-sconces dimmed and went out, though there were no servants in the now semi-dark chamber who could have extinguished them. Phara-Padh suddenly produced a walking-stick from nowhere. He pushed down on it with his left hand and slowly crossed his legs as he rose two feet above the ground where he hovered, without any other support than his cane. Jean's amazement turned to alarm when a dozen snakes materialised from nowhere and formed a ring around him. They raised their heads and darted their tongues at him. He tried to move his arms and legs but they seemed paralysed. He knew beyond question that the serpents were only waiting for a signal to attack. But the signal was not given. Imperceptibly, Phara-Padh descended to the ground, the snakes faded, the torches began to burn bright again and life returned to Jean's body.

But his mind was reeling. What exactly had he seen? Phara-Padh was surely no cheap illusionist nor a fakir. Was he, then, a master Magician, a powerful practitioner of Black Arts? If so he was very dangerous.

Then, as if nothing had happened, Phara-Padh smiled and said pleasantly: 'We have almost everything we need here at Lakya-Pore. What we lack we send for to the world of men. The last supply expedition of the year returned with all we need for the winter only three days ago. There will not be another for four or five months.'

'Then I am trapped here?' said Jean.

'Not trapped at all. You may leave at any time,' said Phara-Padh with a smile.

The next day Jean walked through the open gate and headed north, only to be driven back by the blizzards which raged beyond the ring of great mountains that sheltered Lakya-Pore. He retraced his steps, feeling like an escaped prisoner returning to his cell..

In time, he discovered that the other inmates were bound by the same invisible chains: all were free to go but none dared brave the elements. At first, he had believed they were members of a religious community, there by choice. Instead, he discovered that they too had wandered by accident into Lakya-Pore. Since the alternative to remaining was dying in the lethal winter snows, they stayed and spent their days working in Phara-Padh's gardens and workshops on the endless task of embellishing his mountain palace. They lived in hopes that some day they could buy their freedom with money raised by friends and families in the world below. Occasionally, one did so, and the hopes of all were raised with his departure.

Their every need was catered for and on the surface their lives seemed filled with peace, quietude and useful employment. But there was hardly one among them who did not feel a prisoner.

At first they were wary of Jean. Most were ignorant herders and tribesmen only too ready to believe that such a malformed creature was an evil sprite conjured by the Magician they called *Huzoor*, or Lord, to spy on them. They were guarded in what they said to him. Their fear was palpable, though what they feared he could not discover.

One afternoon, as he cleared dead leaves that had collected on the avenue of the elephants, he heard a shout and looked up. On the opposite side of a pool covered with bright lotus flowers, a section of wall was being rebuilt. Part of it had collapsed on a mason. Jean was first on the scene. The man was trapped beneath a stone slab which had come to rest precariously on a pile of rubble. Before it could slip and crush him, Jean gripped the slab and heaved, but it was too heavy. He looked around for a tool and found an iron bar. Using it as a lever, he raised the slab high enough for the trapped man to struggle free. He was not young and looked dazed by his ordeal but apart from minor bruises he was unhurt. Several other workmen who had been hurrying to the scene, their green robes flapping, suddenly stopped when half a dozen others, dressed in black from head to foot, appeared from nowhere. The old man was seized and dragged away protesting. He tried to resist but the guards were too strong. There was a look of terror on his face.

'Who are they?' said Jean to a thin-faced man who had been working nearby and had also come to help. 'Where are they taking him?'

'To the House of Pain, for punishment. He was careless. It is not the first time that he has attracted attention to himself.'

'The men in black robes are guards? I thought all here was harmony and peace.'

The man looked carefully around him:

'Such talk is dangerous,' he said. 'You are new here. You must go back to your work now and carry on as if nothing had happened. If you do not, you too will draw attention to yourself. Meet me here tonight, after supper, and I will explain.'

He walked unhurriedly away and left Jean to his thoughts.

He did not know what to make of Lakya-Pore. It had the air of a monastery and the residents looked like monks. Yet Phara-Padh was patently far more interested in material things than was consistent with true piety. Moreover, his manner and methods smacked more of tyranny than religion. The gate was always open and there were no bars, yet the place was a prison.

When it was dark, Jean strolled casually through the gardens. The night was calm and warm and the moon shone hard and bright out of a starry sky. He found a seat by a cypress tree and waited.

He had not been there five minutes when a voice said:

'Don't turn round. It's best if we are not seen. Phara-Padh does not like his slaves to associate in secret. Now, tell me who you are and how you came to be here.'

Jean gave his new friend a brief account of his life from his childhood to his survival after the earthquake, omitting his part in the death of Vincent Vinh Duc and his involvement with the British imperial police.

'And your face?'

The question was direct but not brutal.

'I was told I was born with it. But my mother said it was carved for me at birth by the leech who dug me out of her belly.'

'She sounds a bitter woman. With such a face you must have suffered deeply.'

Jean did not reply. Few people had talked to him like this, on an equal footing, with human sympathy and respect.

'My name is Verhoven,' said the voice. 'I was born in Belgium. The story of my life is quickly told. I was ordained a priest in the catholic church and was a missionary in Pondicherry before I was abducted and brought to this place. I have been rotting here for nearly twenty years.'

Twenty years! A life sentence! Jean swore that no one would keep him locked up once the passes were open again in the spring

'But why have you let twenty springs go by and twenty opportunities to leave when twenty winters have opened the passes and left you free to go?'

'My friend, you will learn that such freedom as we have here is given to us by Phara-Padh and that freedom that is given is not freedom at all.'

'Who is Phara-Padh?' he asked.

'A madman,' said Father Verhoven, 'but a remarkable one. He stumbled into Lakya-Pore by accident thirty or forty years ago. It was a monastery then. They say he ousted the community's leader and got rid of the Buddhist monks one by one. But he needed hands to keep his kingdom gorgeous and replaced them with travellers. He pays men of the Giza tribes to bring them here by force. Women too, though they are kept in purdah and are never seen. He has absolute power. It is his mania. It is what sustains him. It is also what makes him cruel and very dangerous.'

'And what is this House of Pain?'

'It is a building without windows and it contains every man's worst nightmare.'

'How can that be?' said Jean, 'It's not possible.'

'How little you know, Jean,' said Father Verhoven. 'Thus far I have avoided being taken there, so I have no direct experience of what goes on inside. But men who have been there say it contains wild beasts, snake-filled pits, deep pools to drown in, swarms of biting insects, it is a living chamber of all the horrors.'

Jean said nothing, but remembered his own first meeting with Phara-Padh when he too had seen things which terrified him.

'But let us talk of other things,' the priest said. 'You saved Haman Fazio's life. That will not have gone unremarked. But Archimedes would have approved.'

'Archimedes?'

'You used an iron bar to raise a heavy stone exactly as Archimedes recommended.

'Never heard of him.'

'He was a famous Greek scientist who discovered the power of a lever. He said that if he had one long enough and a fixed point on which to rest it, he could move the earth on its axis.'

Father Verhoven explained the reasoning behind the principle. Jean understood at once: it was a revelation. It was the first time he'd discovered that mathematics meant more than adding up and taking away. Forgetting Phara-Padh and the House of Pain, he asked Father Verhoven if mathematics also explained why they were enjoying a warm, pleasant evening when by rights they should be shivering with cold.

'No. For that you need the science of geology. A ring of mountains, the Seven Sisters, keeps the winter storms away and warmth is supplied by heat which rises directly from the volcanic fire which burns beneath the earth's crust. There is no mystery. It is the result of the physical configuration of the land.'

Jean marvelled at the ease with which the priest explained things which were incomprehensible to him. He tried to think of something else to ask, but Father Verhoven forestalled him.

'The passes will stay blocked for some months, so whatever you think of Phara-Padh and his paradise on earth you are going to have to spend at least one winter here,' he said. 'A wise man uses his time wisely. You must do likewise. You must decide what it is you want from Lakya-Pore.'.

'I came here by accident. I was seeking nothing but a way off the mountain. I still am. I want nothing from this place.'

'We do not always know what we want,' said Father Verhoven with a smile, 'and do not always want what is best for us. The key to life is thought. Have you read Descartes?'

'Was he a Greek scientist too?'

'No, Descartes was a countryman of yours, a philosopher who said that we exist because we think. Not because we feel or desire or have needs but because understanding the world is what makes us human. It sets us apart. Listen, Jean. If you want to learn, I will teach you. It will make our time pass more quickly. What do you say?'

But before Jean could answer, the priest whispered: 'Someone's coming. Be here tomorrow night.'

The next moment, he was gone.

Jean sat on for a while, reflecting on what he had been told. He was excited but he was not sure if he could trust a man who seemed to know everything except how to escape from Phara-Padh's prison. Yet the weeks that followed ended Jean's resistance and he at last knew what it was to have a friend. And more than a friend: Father Verhoven became his mentor.

Although the inmates of Lakya-Pore were carefully watched, the gardens were large enough for master and pupil to meet safe from prying eyes. Jean had a quick mind but it was empty, unacquainted with the learning built up over the centuries by scientists, philosophers and scholars.

'Knowledge is its own reward,' said Father Verhoven. 'But it is also power. It is what makes Phara-Padh master of Lakya-Pore. But just as knowledge enables him to enslave us, knowledge will help you to escape from the weakness that is ignorance. I will teach you what you do not know, but on one condition: that the knowledge you acquire must be used for good, not evil.'

Jean nodded his agreement.

'You will accept my guidance and you will work hard. We will begin with philosophy, which will teach you how to think clearly; ancient tongues, which will show the importance of words; and modern languages which will teach you how to express exactly what you think. Physiology and medicine will explain the body, and psychology will explain the mind. Chemistry, biology and physics will reveal the workings of nature. Economics and political science will give you an understanding of how societies organise their affairs while literature will show the best that has been thought and written about the choices which humans make. Mathematics will help you to understand arts such as music, which is numbers expressed as sound, and architecture which is harmony in stone. But you will also learn that there are deep mysteries that lie beyond the reach of reason.'

During his years as a missionary in India, he said, he had witnessed many impossible marvels. He had seen fakirs mutilate themselves, then heal their wounds leaving no scars. He had observed yogis who caused grapes to ripen by the sheer force of their will or hypnotised serpents and made them as rigid as a tree-branch.

'European science has never been able to reproduce or explain such phenomena. But the secrets of marvels have been revealed to me, and then they have ceased to be marvels and lost their mystery. Shall I demonstrate?'

Jean nodded.

Father Verhoven stared into his eyes for a moment, then said:

'Get up.'

Jean made an effort to stand but try as he might he could not move. It was as if his body had turned into lead. He ached all over and could not even raise one arm. Then Father Verhoven smiled and Jean felt the weight lift and he was free again.

'A simple trick,,' said Father Verhoven with a smile.

It was some time before Jean appreciated that his mentor was a marvel in his own right, a comprehensive, living encyclopaedia. But Father Verhoven was in turn astonished by Jean's quick and supple mind.

Each having a purpose, one to teach and the other to learn, discovered that time passed quickly and neither found confinement in their open prison unduly irksome.

*

By day, Jean worked in Lakya-Pore's Gardens of Harmony and by night he plied his Master with questions and absorbed the answers. He did nothing that might attract the attention of the Gilzai guards in black robes and spoke no careless word that might reach the ears of Phara-Padh. At intervals, usually for minor misdemeanours, fellow prisoners were seized and taken to the House of Pain. What they said on their return, confirmed what Father Verhoven had told him: it was a place where minds, rarely bodies, were tortured by horrible visitations of what every man most feared.

Jean's urge to leave was dispelled by his eagerness to learn. He applied himself diligently to his studies. But by the spring of his third year of captivity, he began to grow restive.

One day, Father Verhoven told him he could teach him nothing more. Jean now knew as much as he, from the pure and applied knowledge of European learning to the mysterious powers and arts of the east: hypnosis, ventriloquism and those self-induced states which enabled a man to subject body and mind to extremes of self-control. But whether Jean had grown wise as well as educated was another matter. He was able to contend now with his master on more or less equal terms. The only difference between them was that he had a young man's impatience. Where the master was tolerant and measured, the pupil strained at the leash. He regarded Father Verhoven's optimism about human affairs as an error, for did not history show that men never change, that a small number of them, self-obsessed and ruthless, always enslave the majority? Was not Phara-Padh, who ruled Lakya-Pore by fear, one such despot and living proof of his argument? Unless tyrants are challenged, nothing will ever change.

It was not long before he was to have an opportunity to put his views to the test.

Father Verhoven was no longer young and age had taken its toll. One afternoon, Phara-Padh appeared in the garden where he was working and accused him of idling. Moments later, black-robed guards appeared. Jean tried to stop them but could not prevent his friend being taken to the House of Pain.

He returned two days later on a litter. Usually, those who been punished for two days were physically unharmed but mentally wrecks. Father Verhoven was serene in mind, but weakened in body.

'Phara-Padh plays games with the mind, Jean, he is a fakir, a master of the art of suggestion. He filled my head with horrors and tried to make me believe I saw what I merely imagined. But I was too strong for him and his illusions. But he has won all the same. I resisted but did not overcome. When he saw he could not control my mind, he reverted to the less sophisticated and more direct methods of the poisoner.'

Jean set to work finding an antidote which would save his mentor's life. But his symptoms were not consistent with any vegetable or mineral poison he knew of through his studies. The patient grew confused and was unable to give an account of his symptoms. He threw his head back and rubbed his throat. He shook, broke into a cold sweat and his pupils were dilated, yet his pulse remained strong and there was no vomiting.

Before night fell, Father Verhoven was dead.

An hour later, Phara-Padh's guards seized Jean and marched him off to the House of Pain.

Chapter 9

The House of Pain was located in a distant corner of the grounds known as the Garden of Eternity and largely obscured by cedars and flowering bushes. Jean had never seen it before: only black-robed guards prisoners were allowed anywhere near it. The air of secrecy was deliberate, for being imagined rather than seen, it acquired a mystical aura as a place of unspeakable dread. It was smaller than Jean had expected, but imposing nonetheless, an elegant, dazzlingly white building which might have been mistaken for a shrine to one of the many deities which had been worshipped over the centuries at Lakya-Pore. Fountains crooned nearby and the scented air was cool. The façade was decorated with bas reliefs of gods and fearsome, snarling, coiled creatures of fable and legend.

Jean was marched through the main door and pushed roughly to the floor at the feet of Phara-Padh who stood, arms folded, under the looming figure of a fierce, luridly painted stone dragon. He saw no instruments of torture. There were no windows and the walls were featureless save for a gilded latticework gallery which ran round it a dozen feet above his head. The *Huzoor* of Lakya-Pore was dressed in his usual red robes to which he had added a close-fitting ceremonial silk cap of peacock blue. He did not speak.

'Why was I brought here?' said Jean into the silence.

'Because I wished it. I cannot allow the peace of Lakya-Pore to be troubled as you have troubled it with your seditious talk with the priest. But this is no time for words.'

At his order, one guard seized Jean by the hair, yanked his head back and held it in a grip of iron. From a commanding height, Phara-Padh's eyes bore down on him, magnetic, metallic, irresistible. They had a demonic power which thrust images into his mind which bloomed there like flowers of evil. At first, he saw, really saw —for he knew they were not imaginings but real and all too-horribly alive — crawling creatures with darting tongues, vile, hissing things which lurked in dark, shadowy places. Soon the age-old night creatures which slither and slide in the bilges of our minds and rear up on hind legs into all our nightmares evolved and metamorphosed. As those inescapable eyes bored deeper, they sought out Jean's buried memories. Visions of his past crowded round him, but horribly changed and twisted into new shapes of cruelty and horror: Françoise with a knife in her eye, his mother holding a bag of slithery slime to put on his head, Aunt Marie-Thérèse's jagged-toothed jaws ready to bite his neck, Bastingard shouting silently through lips from which venomous, scaly creatures issued by the dozen and swam, as in water, towards him. Oh yes, it was real! He heard them! Smelled them! They were so unbearably real that he stopped breathing, for he knew beyond all doubt that his smallest movement would enrage the creatures to the point when they would attack, biting, tearing his flesh, crawling all over and, worse, into his body! Then he gulped and the rush of air that filled his lungs momentarily cleared his head

Jean stopped struggling for in that instant he understood what Phara-Padh was doing. He was reaching into the innermost workings of his mind and tearing out painful experiences to torment him with. His panic subsided. The things he saw were *not* real: Phara-Padh was mesmerising him, taking over his mind. The guard had no need now to hold his head in a vice for he was staring back with steely intentness into Phara-Padh's eyes. Had not Father Verhoven taught him the secret arts of fakir mystifications?

He saw Phara-Padh's fixed gaze waver for a moment and an expression of annoyance flash across his high-cheek-boned face. He was not accustomed to resistance. Jean narrowed his eyes to slits, increased his concentration and commanded the creatures which had been propelled into his mind to return whence they had come. Phara-Padh turned pale, for they had returned to him who had sent them, and with interest. He took one step back, furrowing his brow as he raised the power of his own hypnotic stare.

Jean clenched both hands, dug his nails into his palms so that the pain would keep him in the real world. He emptied his mind of everything but the titanic struggle which he must win if he was to survive. Veins stood out on Phara-Padh's forehead, his jaw tightened and his knuckles showed white with strain. Two master magicians were locked in battle. They launched flying lizards and fire-breathing dragons at each other, conjured up racks, burning sulphur and gallows, and scenes of torture which reached deep fears and phobias.

How long the struggle of wills lasted neither contestant could measure. But the end came suddenly. Jean showed his antagonist an *oubliette*, a deep well inhabited by toads and snakes and leathery-winged bats and immediately sensed a weakness. He forced Phara-Padh to look into its depths, at the blades of swords, sabres and scimitars which projected from the sides of the pit. Then he saw and felt what his enemy was seeing and feeling, an agonising sensation of falling: an arm sliced off by a sword, a leg lacerated on an Arab blade, the casual slash of a sabre, and blood, blood, oh the blood, the pain! And the horror of landing among all that teeming, squirming life!

Phara-Padh's resistance ceased abruptly and he fell to his knees, broken, crooning to himself, jumping at sounds that only he could hear, looking round him warily as if he expected starving rats to materialize and leap for his throat.

The black-robed guards watched in bewilderment as their once almighty *Huzoor* collapsed, moaning, gibbering words that made no sense, a broken man.

They stepped back, respectful now of Jean.

'Look at me, Phara-Padh,' he said, glaring at his fallen enemy, maintaining the intensity of his staring eyes, 'and behold your nemesis! LOOK AT ME!'

Phara-Padh raised his head and looked up, wild-eyed and lost.

'Remember this face, gaze on it. It is the face of your nightmares. It is the face of Terror! On your knees and call me *Huzoor*!''

Phara-Padh struggled to his knees, laid his forehead on the marble floor and breathed in a hushed, awed voice:

'*Huzoor*!'

'Take him away,' said Jean to the slack-mouthed guards. 'I am master here now.'

Bowing low, they did as they were ordered, observing a deep, shocked silence. But as Phara-Padh was unceremoniously dragged away, Jean heard whispering and rustling and looked up seeking the source of the sounds. They came from the gallery above his head. The whisperings changed into ululations and cries of rejoicing, descended to ground level and as Jean watched impassively the whole company of Phara-Padh's veiled women in robes of pastel shades burst through a door, shamelessly breaking their purdah. Ignoring Jean, they bore down on Phara-Padh. The guards in black robes dropped him and withdrew hurriedly, for even they were not prepared to face the wrath of these women who had been abused and enslaved by the man they had been forced to call lord and master.

Some used their iron-heeled slippers as clubs, others blades of different shapes and lengths but of uniform sharpness. Together, they set about Phara-Padh who raised his arms across his face to ward off the blows that rained down on him. But he was overwhelmed and disappeared under the heaving regiment of screaming women who had succumbed to the blood-lust of revenge. One of them, her face and hands crimson, emerged laughing from the melée holding up Phara-Padh's severed head by the hair. Another brandished a stick on the end of which was skewered a gory gobbet of flesh.

A ghastly screech of delight went up: it was Phara-Padh's manhood.

Jean, drained by his mental combat, walked slowly past them through the door and out into the sunshine. His fellow prisoners, drawn by the shrieking of the women, had left their work and were waiting, agog with curiosity.

'Phara-Padh is dead,' he told them. 'He was no Lord, no magician, merely a charlatan. He ruled by terror and by terror he died.

'But what of us, *huzoor*?' they asked. 'What is to become of us?'

'Do not call me *huzoor*, for you are free men. Leave this place if you wish, or stay and make Lakya-Pore once more a haven of religious peace. The choice is yours'

Jean returned to his quarters and slept the sleep of exhaustion.

He woke refreshed and made arrangements for the burial of Father Verhoven. Phara-Padh's remains were left at the gate for wild animals to devour. When his friend had been laid to rest, Jean received a deputation of his now liberated companions petitioning him to stay and be their leader.

'Exercising the same freedom as I gave you, I have decided to leave this place as soon as the passes are open. Find another head man, if you must have one, or better, have no chief at all and choose the wisest among you to form a council of governors. I ask only two things. First, that you deal honourably with the women and, second, that you raise a monument to my teacher, Father Verhoven, a saintly man and your true liberator.'

They thanked him for his advice and withdrew.

Jean disbanded the guards but said that those who wished should be allowed to don the green robe and join the ranks of those they had guarded. Most opted to stay but a small number, six or seven, decided to leave at once.

'But how is it possible,' asked Erik, 'for anyone to leave Lakya-Pore while the high mountain trails are impassable?'

'Phara-Padh, God roast his soul, was wicked and a liar,' said one of the guards. 'The passes are not closed, *huzoor*. They are never closed and there is always a way through.'

The man was a Ghilzai named Afzul who, though respectful of the new master of Lakya-Pore, showed no fear and made himself useful in many ways. It was he who helped Jean to make a thorough search of Phara-Padh's apartments. They found several chests filled with gold coins and jewels, ransom booty accumulated over the years. This treasure Jean gave into the keeping of the newly formed council of wise men, for their servitude had lasted longer than his and their sufferings had been the greater. But he accepted a gift of money for his journey plus a few items of value which would be useful as presents to buy his safe passage from unfriendly warlords. A crowd gathered to mark his departure for Kabul with Afzul and his escort of Ghilzai guards.

The road from Lakya-Pore was rough and hazardous and the passes, though not blocked, were full of snow which made the ponies slip and stumble. On the third day Afzul sighted a Barustani scout.

'But do not fear, Captain. The Barustani people and their chief have heard that you are a great fakir and not a man to provoke. They will let us be, though it is customary to leave a gift of money to acknowledge the right of the Barustani people to exact payment for our passage.'

Jean left ten gold coins in a chest on a prominent rock according to instructions given by Afzul.

Guided by Afzul, the party safely crossed the backbone of the towering Suleiman Mountains through the Jugdullah Pass, some fifty miles from Kabul. As they descended to the plain the hills, which had been bare, changed into scrubland and the temperature rose, though it was now the start of the cool season. Three days later, they had their first sight of the city. Encircled by unburnt-brick walls punctuated by towers, it was dominated by the Bila Hissar, a combination of fortress, palace and prison, which stood on a hill. The country roundabout was fertile and green with meadows and cultivated gardens: was not Kabul the 'City of Orchards'? But at close hand, he found a labyrinth of dirty, evil-smelling streets too narrow for carts, more mosques than he could count and the raucous voices of men of many tribes and nations. He would soon learn the truth of the saying: 'The flour of Kabul is not without lime, nor the women of Kabul without a paramour.' Beneath the modesty of their latticed *boorkhas*, the city's women were said to be skilled in intrigue; and the men, beneath their hospitality, courage and rough good humour, were unequalled in the arts of cunning, cruelty and revenge.

By the time Jean entered the city by the two-storied south gate, his escort had dispersed one by one, each returning to his home. He was left with only Afzul to guide him around the teeming town. With his help, he found a merchant to buy a few of Phara-Padh's baubles and with the money took a house near the remnant of the Char Chutta, the great bazaar once famed for its vaulted roof which had long since been destroyed by fire.

Afzul spread word that his master was a very great man, come to render important services to the City of Orchards, all the while interlarding his stories with anecdotes of other *feringhees* it had been his honour to serve. Once it was known that such a great personage had taken up residence, Jean's house was besieged by men with long beards and flowing robes who offered to procure for him tobacco, wine, women, anything he needed. Perhaps the *huzoor* would prefer the dancing boys of the *Bacha-Bazi*, who were taken off the streets, had their faces painted and were made to dress like women for the delectation of warlords and the merchants of Kabul? He politely declined their offers but did retain the services of a *munshi*, a teacher of languages, with whose help he set about mastering the Afghan tongue.

At first, Jean did not go out and received no visitors but sat for hours on the terrace of his tall, narrow house, where the noise and smells of the bazaar floated up to him. He resumed his efforts, long since neglected, to perfect ways of disguising or concealing his face so that he could walk abroad without attracting attention. At Lakya-Pore, all eyes had grown accustomed to his hideous ugliness and his fellows had thought no more of it than they would of a minor disability such as a limp or a missing finger. On his way down from the mountains it had been an asset, a defence against the hill men who, though they had a casual way with life and death, were afraid of disfigurements as unearthly as his. But here in Kabul, he needed to become invisible again, so that he could operate in shadow, unremarked, away from the light.

Afzul brought unguents to darken his skin and was disappointed that his master had no beard to dye. A turban pulled down over his forehead hid most of his upper face, while a mask of soft leather or a scarf of silk or cashmere covered his mouth. He experimented with false noses made of leather, wood and even silver held in place with gum resin. But only a cumbersome visor could veil his eyes which burned a fiery bronze from deep within their sockets. For the rest, he settled for a long silk shirt, wide trousers of fine cloth and stout laced boots, to cope with streets which were running sewers. Eventually, he was satisfied and walked abroad without attracting undue attention, acquiring a sense of the place and the opportunities it offered, for here he must make his fortune, so that he could leave a free man, or be marooned forever.

The way forward was shown to him by his *munshi*. As a teacher, his work naturally took the man into all manner of houses, and his gossip about the newly arrived *feringhee* aroused sufficient curiosity for Jean to be invited to dine with the assembled *bunnias*, the leading merchants, of Kabul. Afzul picked out suitable attire for him and in due course Jean presented himself at the door of the town house of a high-placed *huzoor*.

It was situated in a narrow street and hidden by a high wall over the top of which the branches of a mulberry tree waved gently in the evening breeze. A door in the wall opened to his knock and a gatekeeper led him through a narrow passage darker than the night and across an open courtyard lit by the stars and made hazardous by tethered horses and heaps of refuse. He was directed up a staircase as narrow as the passage, with nothing to warn the unwary of the threat of low roof-beams to their heads, and was shown into a dimly lit room filled with bearded men who welcomed the newcomer with the prescribed greetings. After returning a formal *Salaam aleikum* to his hosts, he sat with them. Lolling on cushions, they were served fruits and spicy pilau rice and strong, harsh *bang* in glass goblets. A *hookah* was passed from mouth to mouth while a nautch girl performed to jangling, discordant music played with such energy that conversation was well nigh impossible.

Jean knew from his *munshi* that under the old king, a regime of strict morality had made alcohol illegal and banned professional dancing girls. But since the British had put Shah Shujah on the throne, standards had grown lax and the trade in spirits had become the most profitable in the city. Here, he decided, was his route to fortune. Before he left the soirée, he had raised the matter with Edul Kasid, the most powerful of Kabul's merchants who, after further discussions held the very next day, undertook to finance a scheme to the tune of a *lakh* of rupees. Before the week was out, Jean had discovered where the liquor was made and how it was transported and distributed. Within two months, he and his new partner had cornered the market, having dealt forcefully with their competitors.

Half a year went by and his coffers grew full. And then one day he was summoned to a meeting of the *bunnias* who were not pleased by the speed and scale of the success achieved by an upstart *feringhee*, a foreigner and an infidel, in their city.

'*Feringhee* I am, but no *Frank* and certainly no infidel,' said Jean, who had learned that lies were the common currency of Kabul conversation, 'but a man from the hills of Kashmir and as good a Shiah as any of you.'

'Ha!' exclaimed Edul Kasid, whose greed had been awakened by the thought that if his partner failed to satisfy the assembled merchants in this matter, he himself would surely be left the sole master of their venture, 'that is easy to say. But can you prove your knowledge of the faith?'

A black-whiskered mullah was summoned, a scholar learned in all the parts of the Koran. First Jean was tested in doctrine.

Jean, who had been well schooled in the religions of the East by Father Verhoven, professed himself a devout follower of Ali, cousin and son-in-law of the prophet. Then he was asked to name the twelve Khalifahs since Mohammed, which he did, and then the five correct books of Shiah tradition, which he listed, also correctly. The questioning continued until he held up one hand.

'I will answer no more,' he said. 'For the rest, I am as dumb as a corpse and silent as a stone. Never in this land of open doors has such harsh treatment of an honest man been known. I came in peace but am not welcomed! Have I cheated any of you that I should be denied the laws of hospitality? Have I not been open in my dealings that I should be treated as the meanest of your enemies whom you call *kaffir* and sons of owls and pigs? Shame on you!'

Acknowledging that he had answered correctly and unable to deny that he had good reason to be indignant, the *bannias* backed down and Jean was allowed to return to his business.

But he knew he had been granted only a stay of execution. He had outlived his welcome. Some excuse would be found for a charge which would lead to perpetual imprisonment or perhaps death by impalement and his subsequent appearance, hanging by the feet, on a public gallows.

In truth, it was neither a surprise nor a setback. On the contrary, he was weary of the Orient where life was cheap and precarious. He missed the company of people who mostly meant what they said and did what they promised. A Russian tea-merchant, newly arrived from China and now heading north for home, told him of the Great Fair of Nizhnii Novgorod which for two months each summer attracted thousands of buyers and offered opportunities for an enterprising man of business. This chance meeting seemed heaven-sent. Acting through intermediaries, Jean secretly converted his money into portable gems. He had decided to leave.

'Prepare horses, clothing, provisions,' said Jean to Afzul, 'whatever we need for a long journey. We go to Russia!'

'I am the arm that does your bidding, noble Captain,' said Afzul. 'Yet I would tell you that the road you propose to take is full of dangers.'

'What road is not?' said Jean. 'But the dangers of travel hold no fears for the brave. Is not every man's fortune written on his forehead?'

Afzul went away to do as he had been commanded, muttering darkly under his breath. A journey north would lead them through Nuristan, the Land of Unbelievers, where cruel, bloodthirsty hillmen descended like hawks on small parties and preyed on even the best-guarded caravans. To pass safely through such lands, a *feringhee* must be either a holy man or a *huzoor*. Then he brightened: was his master not both? His prodigious ill-looks were the self-evident sign of saintly self-mutilation while his superior white man's manner compelled respect, his gold opened doors and his servants were favoured above all servants.

Afzul smiled. He would soon be a rich man!

But neither was aware that decrees was written on both their foreheads which would surely be fulfilled and bring no joy.

Chapter 10

Though Jean had faced down the hostile *bannias*, he knew he was living on borrowed time, for his enemies would not let matters rest. He put on a bold face which told the world that he feared no man. Next he launched an ostentatious demonstration of his confidence and wealth: he moved out of the crowded, noisy centre of the town and rented an imposing villa in a pleasant suburb. It stood inside walled grounds which had shady walks, white statues and bas-reliefs featuring dragons and lions. Many kinds of exotic shrubs flowered in sequence and kept the air perpetually filled with fragrance.

Afzul forgot his fear of the merchants and took immediate control of the house and gardens. His role as major-domo to an important man delighted him, for the change in his fortunes took him higher and higher in his own estimation.

But even he found a fault in this new paradise.

'Captain,' he said to Jean, 'it is not fit that a *huzoor* as important as yourself should have a garden that has no water. It is the custom of the country that an excellency as luminous as yourself should ornament his existence with water. He should be surrounded by its beneficent power and...'

'Don't be flowery, Afzul. If you think there should be fountains and pools, see that water is brought.'

'But there is none to be had, Captain. Water flows to this part of the town, it is true. But it has all been commandeered by your neighbours. To have water in your garden, you must take some of theirs.'

Jean was at a point in his affairs where he did need an unnecessary dispute over something so trivial as the water supply. He had no wish to make new enemies.

'When the matter is explained to them, surely they will readily agree to ...'

Afzul snorted disdainfully.

'Such men as Rahman Nadir, whose garden borders your Excellency's, take but do not give. They would think themselves dishonoured to help, forgive me, a *feringhee* mount even higher in the public's regard than he has already risen.'

'Afzul, I really don't think…'

'Come with me, Captain. And you shall see how much far above you he is in splendour because he has water!'

Afzul would not take no for an answer and showed the way. They mounted the wide marble stairs and eventually paused at a small window in a concealed niche. It had once looked out onto Rahman Nadir's gardens, but it had been filled by a solid wooden screen which completely blocked the view.

'What is the meaning of this screen, Afzul?'

'It was put here by Rahman Nadir's absolute order. Judging the best site for his harm to be next to the property your honour now occupies, he demanded that his women must be protected from prying eyes. And so it was done, for Rahman Nadir is a great *huzoor* and not to be contradicted.'

'But if Rahman Nadir's garden cannot be seen from this window, why did you bring me here?'

'Because,' said Afzul with a knowing look, 'the proprietor of this house is a man who likes looking at pretty women.'

And so saying, he released a catch and opened a small aperture in the screen.

'See, Captain, how pleasant the fountains are!'

Indeed they were. They splashed as they played and the sky was reflected in pools where lotus flowers bloomed. The harem, however, was deserted.

'Yes, yes, Afzul. You are right. But we must be satisfied with what we have. Have you forgotten that our time here in Kabul will not be long? A quarrel with Rahman Nadir will surely not lengthen our stay.'

'If you think, Captain, that making fountains is making me forget the dangers we run, you are right. I shall speak of this matter no more.'

'Good.'

'May your wisdom never grow less, *huzoor*.'

But there was more calculation than prudence in Afzul's reasoning. After buying all they would need for their long journey, he had been left with a sizeable share of the money Jean had given him. This he added to his own purse. By heeding his master, he reasoned, he stood to gain more than by making pools for the sky to reflect in.

But for all that, his preparations for their departure had been thorough. For his lord, he had procured a large, loosely-made Turcoman horse and for himself, an Afghan pony which had long, ill-shaped eyes and was built, so the horse-trader swore on the heads of all his children, for stamina and speed. Knowing that their journey would take them through bandit country, he also bought arms, in particular, a pair of damascened pistols, which would make a handsome gift for any hill chieftain, and a sword, for when bullets ran out a sword was still a sword. He had arranged for the animals, the weapons and the rest of their supplies, to be kept at a secure location outside the city walls, with instructions that all was to kept in a state of constant preparedness and ready to leave at a moment's notice.

And it was as well that Jean ordered him to take these precautions. For there now occurred an event which scattered his plans like leaves in the wind.

That same evening, Jean walked around the garden of his house which thus far he had been too busy to inspect. He ended under the sealed window and sat a while, enjoying the coolness of the air. As he sat, a woman's voice began to sing to the accompaniment of a guitar. The music came from the women's apartments in the grounds of Rahman Nadir's house. The melody was strangely beguiling and curiosity got the better of him.

He climbed the vine which covered the nigh wall dividing the two gardens and cast a tentative glance over the top. He took every care and was as silent as possible, knowing full well what would happen if he were observed: men who broke purdah faced the severest physical punishments, even death. He saw a garden filled with fountains and rose bushes where half a dozen women reclined on richly embroidered cushions and subtly patterned carpets. They were dressed in brightly coloured pastel over-tunics and wide trousers, with hair elaborately plastered, eyelids heavy with antimony, and cheeks adorned with rouge and tinsel patches of gold or silver. In their midst, one of their company, young, no more than a girl, with a blue veil over her hair, was playing a long-necked guitar and singing a song which affected Jean deeply but left the women untouched, for they continued to chat, giggle and play with their heavy bracelets of brass and gold. One by one, they left the garden as night came on and returned to their apartments. The girl played on until, with a start, she realised that she was alone. She laid down her instrument, stood and walked out of Jean's sight.

He climbed down and in his memory heard the song which had wrapped itself around his loneliness. It left him full of sweet emotions. Memories of Françoise, buried for years, swam into his mind, and he saw once more the blue eyes and red lips of Marie-la-Belle who had asked him to dance when he was dreaming but never when he was awake.

Jean felt a hunger stir in him, for he had forgotten the sweet enchantment of women.

That night he dreamed of things which were held in a gossamer web and fanned by the wings of butterflies.

The next night, he returned to his observation post. When the women went in, the girl continued to play as before. She wore the same simple blue veil thrown over her head. It hid her hair but left part of her face tantalisingly obscured. There was nothing Jean wanted more than to see the part of it that was hidden. Her hands were dyed with henna and her small feet in purple slippers extended beyond the hems of her cream-coloured petticoats which contrasted with her red skirts. Unable to stop himself, Jean sang softly with her. The music stopped, the girl looked round her in puzzlement and then, alarmed, turned and disappeared from view.

But as she turned, the veil slipped and displayed her face. The bloom of her cheek, her eyes like dark almonds, the pure line of her nose, the petalled mouth and the invitation of her throat – here was beauty in all its perfection. As she walked away, she moved with feline grace, with a swaying of the hips which stopped his breath. At last he understood what the love poets he had read meant when they spoke of the eyes of does and the sweetness of honey. He felt longings new to him, a stirring in his very depths. Nothing Father Verhoven had taught him helped explain what he felt.

The next night, he watched again. He expected that the girl, alarmed by the fright she had been given, would leave when the last of her companions withdrew to their quarters. But she played on and did not stop even when Jean gathered up his courage and started to sing to the melody she drew from her strings. As she played, she looked straight up at him. Jean felt he was staring at the sun, yet could not unlock his eyes from hers. Astounded, he saw no revulsion in them only an unwaveringly frank gaze. She did not shriek with horror or shrink from the sight of him.

Her face was even more beautiful than he remembered or had imagined. On her forehead, hung a bunch of small silver ornaments.

He felt he could gaze at her forever, find new wonders in her person and never weary of doing so.

'Why do you watch?' she said in a carrying whisper. 'You know that a man who spies on the women of my lord's harem will surely incur his wrath.'

One part of his mind told him this was true. But another part began to tire of merely watching and made him want to be near her.

'Are you not ashamed to behave like this,' she went on, adding: 'though you sing beautifully.'

Before he could reply or stir, a harsh voice from within called several times: 'Eriknaz! Come here, wretched girl!'

Laying down her guitar, she ran in, leaving Jean to the night and his thoughts.

Eriknaz! A whole world in a name! He had the strange impression that all his life so far had been a preparation for this moment. Perhaps there was truth in the oriental view of fate after all! He was ready to believe that his destiny was to love Eriknaz. If any word was written on his forehead, it was surely her name.

The following night found him at his post again. When the women went in and left Eriknaz alone, he lowered himself into the garden and crouched near her, hidden from prying eyes by a flowering bush. She did not stop playing. Both had to be so careful. She had not even looked up once, though she knew he was there.

'You should not be here,' she said turning to him at last. 'You are not my father, nor my uncle nor my brother nor my husband. You cannot speak like this to a maiden without shaming her.'

'I could not stay away,' he said simply.

'Go now,' she said. 'If they find you they will kill you. They will also kill me.'

'My name is Jean.'

'I know who you are. You are the *feringhee*.'

'If you know that, you know I am not handsome to look at.'

'I heard it was so. But what are looks? If a man is handsome, is that a cause for rejoicing if his actions are evil and he proves to be ugly beneath the skin, fair without and foul within?'

From inside the apartments, the same voice as the previous night called:

'Eriknaz! Eriknaz! It is late. Come in now.'

'Stay a moment longer,' said Jean, as Eriknaz set aside her guitar, 'and tell me why you wait after the other women have gone in.'

'Your voice,' she said simply. 'It spoke to my heart.'

'Since you know who I am, tell me who you are.'

'My name is Eriknaz Riza. I am to marry Rahman Nadir. I would rather die.'

'Listen,' said Jean, 'if you wish, I shall take you from this place.'

He could have added that he loved her, for he did, and would love her always. He knew this as surely as he knew anything. But he feared to frighten her. Instead, he asked:

'Will you come?'

She thought for a moment then nodded.

'Then watch for my signal.'

'That I cannot.'

'Why? You must if you wish to escape this prison.'

'I said "cannot", not "will not".'

'I do not understand.'

Eriknaz turned her almond eyes to him.

'I cannot see. I am blind!'

'Eriknaz! Eriknaz! Where is that girl?' called the duenna.

'You say nothing,' said Eriknaz. 'Does that mean I no longer please you?'

Jean did not answer he was because he was overcome with relief and gratitude. The irony, pure and kind and wonderful, was perfect.

'But you do please me, Eriknaz. You please me very much. For your sake, I regret that you cannot see the beauty of the world. For mine, I rejoice, for you will never see my ugliness and will not turn away from me. It is well thus. Heaven has arranged our lives to the best advantage.'

'Eriknaz!' came the insistent voice. 'Don't make me come and look for you!'

'Go now,' said Eriknaz. 'It is too dangerous for you to stay.'

'I will come again tomorrow,' said Jean.

He watched her go and then, his heart as light as a child's dreams, he swarmed up the vine and returned to his chamber. Before composing himself for sleep, he considered how he could spirit Eriknaz out of the harem, out of Rahman Nadir's grasp and out of Kabul. The difficulties were great and the dangers fearsome. But, he thought, in all countries doors that are locked with iron keys can always be opened with gold.

During the days that followed, Jean planned his escape. When Afzul learned what he proposed to do he was horrified. But Jean overcome his qualms by filling his mouth with enough gold to keep him loyal and prevent him informing Rahman Nadir that the wife he was shortly to marry was about to be abducted. He also instructed him to offer generous bribes to anyone who was prepared to help them. Each night, after the women retired to their apartments, Jean climbed down the vine and spoke to Eriknaz, telling her of his feelings, hearing her speak of hers.

On the fourth evening, Jean told her how his plans were progressing, Suddenly there was a disturbance inside the women's quarters as if furniture was being overturned. Over the feminine squeals of terror and outrage at the male invasion of their privacy, men shouted and made way for a burly personage in rich robes, no longer young and run to fat, who barked:

'Guards! Seize them!'

Jean stood up and attempted to shield Eriknaz but he was outnumbered and quickly overpowered.

'I am Rahman Nadir,' snarled the man who had given the order. 'And you are the *feringhee*, who does not understand the rules of hospitality and think he can treat the true religion with contempt! On your knees! I shall see to it that you are taught how to behave!'

He was incandescent with rage.

'As for this whore,' he went on, 'she blasphemes and does not know the meaning of respect and honour. She is not worthy of my consideration!'

And taking his sword from his belt, he ran it through Eriknaz's body so hard that its point emerged at her back.

Jean gave a great cry of anguish and struggled with his guards.

'So much for the woman who bewitched you,' Rahman Nadir cried. 'You are not what you have claimed, a devout man and learned in the faith, but a *feringhee*, false-hearted, treacherous and my enemy. For you I have a different punishment. Bring him!'

But before anyone could move, there was the crack of a carbine and Rahman Nadir staggered and collapsed on to the floor.

'Come, Captain!' came Afzul's voice. 'Climb the vine! Quickly!'

Jean hesitated a moment. Afzul loosed off a second shot, One guard fell dead and the rest scattered and ran.

Jean bent over the body of Eriknaz. There was no breath in her. He kissed her mouth, as if he could hold back or even receive the soul that was departing from her. Then he stood and looked around him. A moment later he was scrambling up the vine and disappeared over the wall.

'What now, Captain?' asked Afzul.

'Take us to the place where everything is ready and our horses are waiting. We leave Kabul tonight!'

They rode fast, stopping occasionally to look or listen for pursuers but saw and heard nothing. They had disappeared without trace. After travelling east for some miles along the Kabul River, they turned north into Nuristan through the Panjshir Valley and into the mountains. They climbed steadily through the rich, upland country where mulberry bushes and holly oaks shaded the roads. They passed through villages of flat-roofed houses made of brown mud with narrow windows and wide overhanging eaves. They exchanged greetings with men herding goats or travelling to Kabul to purchase matchlock guns and powder. At Marz Robat, they turned north west along the caravan route which would take them over the Parander Pass and the Hindu Kush. Once through the pass and on the upland plateaux, they would make for Bomiyan and then on to Bokhara.

For the first week, they made good progress northwards. But once they were among the high mountains, game became scarce and their progress slowed. They finally negotiated the Parander Pass, a defile clogged by large boulders through which a rough trail wound a tortuous way. As they began the descent on the other side, the temperature rose and game became more plentiful.

At the end of a long day's riding, they were sitting around a spit roasting a goat which Jean had shot earlier in the day when a tall hook-nosed tribesman walked out of the darkness into the pool of light cast by their fire. He wore a turban and a *poshteen* cloak. A curved, unsheathed dagger was stuck in his belt. He sat down cross-legged on the ground. Without speaking, he reached out, cut a slice of meat from the roasting carcase with his dagger, and bit off a mouthful.

'This meat is good,' he said, chewing. 'But it could not be otherwise because it is mine. All this land, from where the sun rises to where it sets, is mine. All that lives and breathes between those two points is mine. You,' he concluded, 'are mine. I am Abdul Ghias.'

The light of the fire revealed coarse, cruel lips, dark, compelling eyes, a high forehead and a full beard.

'There was no one to ask for permission, *huzoor*,' said Jean politely, 'no one to pay for either meat or passage. We are not rich men and travel as pilgrims, but we know the law of the country and always pay our way.'

'Will you give me rupees as an apology for stealing my goats and riding over my land?' said Abdul Ghias.

'Willingly,' said Jean. 'I told you we are honest pilgrims.'

'What else do you have to pay me with?'

Without waiting for an answer, Abdul Ghias stood up. Jean and Afzul followed suit as a mark of respect. The chief made a sign. Immediately a dozen tribesmen stepped out of the darkness and began rifling through the travellers' possessions which they laid out neatly on the ground at their leader's feet. Abdul Ghias picked up Jean's sword and a screw-barrel pistol. He weighed each in his right hand. He raised the pistol in the air and pulled the trigger. The shot rang round the hills and the echo died slowly. Satisfied that the weapon was good, he stuffed it into his belt. He tried a pass or two with the sword and then, with a vicious horizontal slash of the blade which started behind his right shoulder, he removed Afzul's head with a single cut.

The head rolled in the dust and came to rest at Jean's feet. What was one life in the great reckoning of things? Killing a man meant no more to Abdul Ghias than wringing a chicken's neck. But an insult had been offered and could not be left to lie.

'Have a care, Abdul Ghias,' Jean said quietly, 'you do not know who I am. The man was my servant! What will you give me as a compensation for killing my property?'

'Me, pay? You ask me to pay? I pay nothing, pilgrim! Especially to a pilgrim as ugly as a whore\s backside! This land is mine and mine alone is the right to give or take life.'

Before anyone could move, Jean bent down, picked a burning brand from the fire and thrust it his face. Abdul Ghias staggered and beat out the flames of his beard which had begun to burn. Then he straightened and faced Jean. But before he could make a move, Jean had snatched the curved blade from his belt and rammed it into his abdomen. Abdul Ghias' face was filled with astonishment at the idea that a wandering pilgrim should launch such an attack on a *huzoor* of his greatness.

While his men stood by, stunned into immobility, Jean hissed:

'That first strike was vengeance for Afzul, my servant and friend. But this – '

Holding Abdul Ghias up with his left hand, he turned the blade in the wound, this way, that way, up and down, and *rummaged*, until the astonishment left the hill man's face and was replaced by agony. A woman's scream emerged from his throat but was strangled abruptly. In the silence, Jean said:

'But *this* is for Eriknaz!'

After one last thrust, he released Abdul Ghias who collapsed in a mass of blood and ravaged flesh. Then he turned and glared at the tribesmen who had been struck dumb with the speed, the horror of what they had seen. His face, in which his eyes burned like torches, was a grinning mask in the firelight. As one man, they turned and fled into the night.

Jean stood over the butchered remains of Abdul Ghias who had paid for all the casual savagery and unfeeling brutality he had met with since he has come to the Orient. He had also avenged the death of Afzul and thus made good his debt to him for saving his life by shooting a bullet into the black heart of the man who had so contemptuously killed Eriknaz. His Eriknaz, doe-eyed and sweet as honey, Eriknaz whose death had taken all joy from the world and left it grey and empty.

At that moment, Jean Dartigoyte knew his life had ended even though his carcase lived on — if living without Eriknaz could be anything other than a living death. So why go on? He looked down at the dagger which he still held in his hand.

But if he died, the woman he who he had stirred to love would also die. Worse, she would be forgotten, for the Eriknaz who had known love existed now only in his mind.

No, he would not die. He would live on. Yes, he would take her name. That way her memory would not fade for as long as he breathed. As Erik he would keep her always alive. He would live for both of them. He must survive for her sake: he was doomed to live. Oh! He would treat the world as it had treated them. He would punish it for treating selfless love and goodness as delusions, for destroying the purest impulses that fill the human heart.

He wondered if his reason had snapped, if he was mad.

'May the length of your shadow never grow shorter,' he said to Erik, his new self.

And the hills echoed with his wild laughter.

When it was light, the horses which had run away, returned.

Later, Erik broke camp.

Chapter 11

The postilion of the twice-weekly coach from Moscow sounded his horn in the paved street and the swaying, lumbering carriage clattered into the stable yard of the Hotel Terminus in the main square of Nizhny-Novgorod. Passengers could have travelled, albeit more expensively, by paddle-steamer along the Volga. Instead they had chosen to try the new Moscow-Siberia road which, as Mother Russia faced the second half of the century, was an emblem of progress.

It had been a two-day purgatory.

'I've said it before,' grumbled Grigory Yegorov, wiping his brow with a handkerchief that had been damp for hours, 'but why in God's name don't they get on with building this damned railway they keep talking about? Take the coach in winter and you freeze, in summer you bake. I can't see men of business in England or France putting up with this sort of thing, don't you agree, sir?'

This remark was addressed to a man dressed in black from head to foot who had spoken only a few words during the whole voyage. He wore gloves and a large Russian fur hat pulled well down. Around his neck was a knot s of cashmere scarves.

'I would, sir,' he replied in passable Russian, then fell silent.

'I see you are a stranger, sir,' said the man, undaunted. 'You should know that my name is Grigory Yegorov. 'I have a certain standing in this town. If I can oblige you in any way, please do not hesitate to apply to me. Here is my card. I would be honoured if you would dine with me. And now I bid you good day.'

The staff of the Terminus spilled out into the warm afternoon sunshine watched by the fat wife of the landlord from the welcoming position she had taken up in the doorway. The horses snorted, dogs yelped, and beggars appeared from nowhere hoping to make a kopek or two by carrying a bag or giving directions to weary passengers who were new to the town. The district constable watched from a doorway across the road. Above him windows went up and the heads of giggling *dashas* (and sometimes their mistresses) appeared, anxious not to miss a moment of the excitement which had disturbed their afternoon rest. For in addition to the passengers, whose clothes, manners and faces were always an object of interest, there would be mails and newspapers.

Grigory Yegorov shook the dust from his coat, wiped his damp face again and nodded to Semyon Korsakov, his manager, who immediately began to give him account of what had been happening at the yards during his absence. But Yegorov held up his hand for silence observing: 'First things first'. He barked instructions for his luggage to be taken to his home and then, with his manager in tow, he strode into the inn where he ordered a bottle of wine and the good dinner he could no longer wait for.

While he ate, Korsakov spoke of orders received, orders met and orders expedited. When his plate was empty and his mouth was again available for speech, Yegorov barked:

'And the Hyena? Have they caught him yet?'

'No, sir,' replied Korsakov. 'Last Monday night, he robbed the house of Countess Askaya. They say he got away with a fortune in jewellery. They say there were twenty of them, all armed to the teeth. They say the poor Countess is still in bed recovering...'

'It's outrageous. I don't know what we pay Steklov and his squad of lead-footed policemen for. What's on this week at the Glavnyi Dom?'

'I thought you'd want to know, sir,' said Korsakov, 'so I brought you the playbill. It's a new piece called *The Lady of the Camelias'*.

'Ah, I've heard of it. French. A very touching story about a pretty young woman who is no better than she should be. No need to mention it to my wife. I shall go alone. Get me a ticket...'

Meanwhile, the passenger in the long black coat and fur hat who kept his face buried in patterned scarves, was shown up to the room where the fire which, despite the heat of the day, he had ordered to be lit was giving out welcome warmth. He gave a few small coins to the *dvornick* who carried his bags. The man bowed and closed the door behind him as he went out.

As soon as he was alone, he removed the coat, hat and scarf and poured water into a basin from the ewer and splashed it over his face. The water felt icy and it told him how far he was from home. He was used to the hot suns of Persia and even in summer Russia was too cold to keep his blood warm. He stared at himself in the cloudy mirror. He saw fatigue in his dark eyes. His cheeks were sunken and his nose had a pinched look. He reached for his Russian hat and scarves. He would need them more than ever now that evening was coming on.

The same *dvornick* volunteered eagerly to find him a *droshky* which took him over the Oka River to the notorious suburb of Kunavino. The driver had been reluctant to take him to the address he gave but was persuaded by the promise of a large tip. Once he had his money, he drove off briskly through the now twilit streets leaving his passenger staring up at a sign which said: *Misha's*. He went in and sat down at a corner table. In the middle of the white cloth which covered it was the inevitable slop-basin which indicated that tea was the most general fare of the place. Immediately, a waiter with a long beard wearing a dirty apron over a swelling paunch unceremoniously set down a samovar in front of him and poured black tea into a cup with no handle. The stranger warmed his hands on the cup before drinking the contents. Then he gestured to the same waiter who, in his own time, sauntered across to his table.

'You wish to order food?' he asked in a bored voice. 'Our food is very good. Today is a savoury stew of meat, vegetables, mushrooms and potatoes. Very popular, sir. Shall I bring a plate of this stew?'

The stranger looked up coldly and said: 'I would speak with Hájí Tabarsi. Go tell him I am here.'

The waiter straightened, pulled his apron up over his belly and hurried away. He was soon back and, all respect and deference now, he asked the stranger if he would be so good as to follow him.

The stranger walked to the back of the room, through the kitchens and up a flight of stairs. The waiter halted at a door and knocked.

'Come in, daroga. *Selam aleikum*, peace be unto you. You are most welcome. I have been expecting you daily ever since I received the letter.'

Hájí Tabarsi's welcome was as fulsome as his girth. He was fat, middle-aged, yellow-faced and grandly moustachioed. He wore laced boots, dark cotton trousers and a blue blouse belted at the waist in the Russian style. But that was the only concession to his country of adoption. The decor of his apartments was entirely Persian, with divans standing on elaborately figured rugs, ornate brass lamps hanging on the walls and pastel cloths bellying down from the ceiling. The room could have been a tent in an Oriental desert.

'May I offer you refreshment?'

Ignoring the invitation, the stranger said impatiently: 'Have you found the man?'

'I have, daroga. I can offer you an excellent honey cake. You would honour me if...'

'I want nothing. But still, perhaps a stove could be lit. I feel the effects of this damnable climate.'

Hájí Tabarsi clapped his hands and gave instructions. While the stranger warmed himself, he began to summarise what he knew.

'His rise has been remarkable. He arrived out of nowhere less than a year ago. At first, he sat on street corners selling nail-clippings and combings from the hands and beard, so he claimed, of a holy man in the mountains, which were a sovereign remedy against ailments of all kinds. He was very persuasive and had soon exchanged his rags for serviceable clothes and his street corner for a cheap room, then an apartment and finally a house. It is said he was helped by a woman on whom he cast a spell. I do not believe this myself but many do. It is one of the thousand stories that are told about him. That he never shows his face is true, but that he never eats or sleeps, moves objects by an effort of will and knows people's thoughts before they do, is merely fanciful and superstition.'

'So far he seems a common mountebank and nothing like the man whose reputation has so intrigued our little Sultana. She will not be pleased to learn that she has been misled.'

'Wait, daroga, there is more. With the help perhaps of his anonymous and, to my mind, non-existent patroness, he next set himself up as a giver of consultations, calling himself Count Kuzow. Among his admirers are high burghers of Nizhny-Novgorod and titled personages of both sexes. His séances attract the curious from as far as Orenburg and even Moscow. He has become a phenomenon.'

'And what do the curious expect to see?'

'Marvels! And they are never disappointed.'

'I must see these marvels for myself.'

'You shall, daroga. For I, Hájí Tabarsi, special envoy of his Excellence the Governor of Mazanderan, have arranged it, and at this time!'

'What is so remarkable about this time?'

'Why, the Fair! The famous Fair! Many tens of thousands of persons of every degree come to Nizhny-Novgorod in the summer months.

Merchants sell their goods which others buy. Even noble persons come to acquire not just luxuries but winter provisions for their estates, for in this place a man with money can buy anything he needs or wants, from church bells to ostrich feathers! Imagine, then, the number of those great and moneyed personages who have clamoured for the chance to see Count Kuzow performing marvels! And yet I, Hájí Tabarsi, have forestalled them!'

'When shall I see these marvels?' said the daroga matter-of-factly.

With the wind taken out of his sails at having so miserably failed to impress, Hájí said that the daroga would have to wait one week. It was the best that could have been done.

The daroga returned to his rooms in the Hotel Terminus. He ordered another fire to be lit.

In the next few days, he got the measure of Nizhny-Novgorod. Hájí was right. The small town was a mass of humanity. The streets bulged with white-faced, flat-nosed furriers from Archangel, bronzed, long-eared Chinese tea-merchants, Bokhariot merchants in snowy turbans, Tartar pedlars, Cossacks with leather goods from the Ukraine, French drapers, Manchester cotton masters, Swiss watch-makers and dark-haired men with loose robes bringing perfumes — a whiff of home — from Persia. The daroga visited the kremlin and savoured the view, wondered at the clusters of pepper-pots on roofs and stared at the red and white cathedral capped with five blue cupolas. He drank tea in *traktiry* and ate caviar and pease-pudding. And everywhere he went, there were but two topics of conversation: business and the Hyena.

'Why hyena?' the daroga asked a diner with whom he shared a table.

'Because it is well known that the dried foot of a hyena is a sovereign protection against all enemies …'

'Including the police?'

'Especially the police,' said the man. 'And they have been so assiduous in their search for him that a hyena charm is the only explanation for their failure to apprehend the villain.'

The daroga marvelled that such a modern-minded, hard-headed people, and Christians to boot, could believe such nonsense. But the encounter made it easier for him to understand how someone like Count Kuzow could impose himself on the multitude. But that did not stop the man being a charlatan.

Protocol and professional courtesy required the daroga, head of police in the northern Persian province of Mazanderan, to call on his equivalent in Nizhny-Novgorod. Captain Kiril Steklov lived in the Upper City and received him politely but without warmth. The Captain was tall, gaunt and dressed in black trousers and a frock-coat buttoned to the throat where a white cambric cravat frothed in a generous bow with hanging ends. After the usual pleasantries, he asked:

'And to what, sir, do we owe the honour of your visit?'

'I travel for reasons of health,' said the daroga, with his most ingratiating smile. 'But I cannot escape the observing old habits, a professional hazard, I fear. Like you, I am charged with bringing to justice the perpetrators of whatever crimes I cannot prevent. I am always interested in other approaches to our work. To this extent, I confess I am a thief myself. When I see a good idea which will improve some aspect of my own administration of justice, I steal it without compunction.'

Reassured and delighted by the implied flattery, the Captain said that for ten months of the year, the town was law-abiding enough. But there were two problems which made his life difficult. First, was the dramatic rise in criminal activity during the Fair, when the population increased tenfold.

'The other challenge is subversive activity. Politics! Hah! You would not believe the enthusiasm for revolutionary causes which has reached our town. My men are constantly arresting orators and seizing dangerous pamphlets clamouring for reforms of all kinds.'

'You have my sympathies, Captain. We in Persia are fortunate. We deal with common criminals only. We do not have the problem of subversive ideas. Our people cannot read and do not think. It makes life so much easier.'

'I envy you,' said Captain Steklov and offered to show him the inside of the prison nearby, a large, new, grey building with four towers which looked down sternly on Ostrozhnaya Square. The jail was a hell-hole, but the daroga expressed admiration for the lenient treatment of prisoners. But in truth he was appalled by such laxity. If there were such prisons in Persia, the honest poor would be committing crimes so that they too might be sent to them and be so well looked after.

That evening, at *Misha's*, the daroga took out the card he had been given by the traveller in the coach. Hájí Tabarsi said that Grigory

Yegorov was the manager of the Sormova shipbuilding works, the largest employer in the town.

'I shall call on him. I might learn things that you cannot tell me.'

The daroga left his card after the European fashion. He was rewarded with an invitation to dine three days hence, the day after he was to form part of the audience for the display of marvels promised by Count Kuzow.

The Count never performed his marvels until after the sun had set. It was dusk when, two days later, the daroga joined some forty well-dressed men and bejewelled women who had gathered in a square in the centre of the town and handed the tickets they had paid for to a giant Nubian who seemed to be dumb, for he never spoke. The daroga felt conspicuous in his long, black coat and ottoman fez. Speaking to no one, he halved the entrance fee Hájí swore on the head of his children that he had paid for the ticket, and multiplied by the number of takers. It came to a small fortune. Kuzow might not be a Count but he was certainly a clever operator.

The crowd spoke in subdued whispers. Most looked nervous and some were openly apprehensive.

When the Nubian had collected the full complement of tickets, he gestured to his flock to follow him. He led off through a maze of narrow, busy, muddy streets between shops selling cucumbers, black bread, ropes, harness and goods and comestibles of all kinds. Soon they left the crowds behind them. Without warning, they were brought to a halt at a brass-studded door built into the steep slope of the hillside. The Nubian produced a key, opened the door and counted them in to make sure no interlopers had joined the group. After locking it behind him, he led them up a short flight of steps. When they reached the top, the Nubian halted again and surprised them by ordering them to be silent.

'No talking please,' he said in a deeply resonant voice. 'There must be quietness. If you speak you will fall down dead, that's for sure. This is a place of evils. Much cruelty has been done here.'

The effect of his words in such a place was instant and all fell silent. Then he led off again. A short passageway took them to a vaulted hall with a floor of broken tiles. Around the walls were bas-reliefs depicting grimacing deities slaughtering animals for sacrifice on altars where oil-lamps were tended by partly-clothed female figures. They had time to observe these details in the gloom while they waited to pass one by one through a low door which led down a flight of steps to a low-ceilinged room. From the walls, painted bears snarled at them and tigers bared their teeth. They descended again to a lower, circular chamber, passing a succession of divinities with ferocious faces. There was just enough light to enable the newcomers take in their surroundings. The atmosphere was heavy and they could well believe that the place was steeped in the blood of centuries. All round the circumference ran a stone bench on which they were told to sit. The walls were undecorated. In the centre of the room was a low altar. On it sat a cross-legged yogi, unmoving and naked save for a simple loin cloth and a crude painted mask of the kind the daroga had seen among primitive tribes. The man was disturbingly thin, emaciated even.

The spectators felt a chill for which the temperature of the cellar was not solely accountable. The Nubian lit candles arranged on the floor in the form of a star. Each burned with a different colour. Around each he drew a ring in its own colour. Then into tall incense burners, where fires of olive stones smoked, he threw various powders. The fumes glowed orange, blue, green in the light of the candles and an acrid, unpleasant smell filled the room. Too late, the daroga clamped a handkerchief over his nose and mouth, for he detected belladonna, Indian hemp and white poppy which were known to cloud the mind and confuse the senses. He felt nauseous and found it hard to breathe. The feeling passed quickly but was replaced by a chill which made him shiver. This too faded and was succeeded by a strange sense of wellbeing. He felt serene, wide awake, tireless.

The Nubian stepped forward and tossed liquid from a small goblet into the middle of the star where it left a glistening stain. The yogi stirred, produced a long wooden reed-pipe from nowhere, and began to play, very softly, caressing the instrument with his bony fingers. The music was tuneless, monotonous, repeating the same notes and phrases over an insistent, mechanical rhythm which the Nubian picked up on a drum. Imperceptibly, the rhythm accelerated and as the music speeded up, the shapeless patch of damp quivered, as a breath of wind ruffles the surface of standing water. It shrank, expanded and writhed, undeniably, disgustingly alive. The daroga could not take his eyes off it. The music grew louder, faster, more insistent, as though the notes were commands which could not be disobeyed. A mound appeared in the centre of the damp patch whose jagged edges flexed and then coiled and uncurled like springy wood shavings. The hair rose on the back of the daroga's neck. This was impossible! Yet it was happening!

The music grew faster and more irresistible The mound swelled, its surface convulsed by the frantic efforts of whatever creature was separated from the air outside by the thinly stretched membrane. Enraged, driven frantic by the insistent beat of pipe and drum, the thing pushed this way and that, stretching, growing in size, assuming a shape, an unrecognisable form. The music rose to a frenzied climax and then suddenly stopped. At the same instant, the skin burst and a double-headed creature emerged. After a titanic struggle it freed itself from the clinging membrane and stood tremblingly on four legs. It shook itself like a dog: the daroga flinched as he felt drops of its unspeakable birth-spittle fleck his cheeks. It was small. But it grew alarmingly fast. Now it was as tall as a man and covered with long matted hair which it proceeded to lick. From time to time it stopped and glared at the daroga, singling him out, he knew, for special attention. It was like the hound that guards the entrance to hell in every fable and legend. Its four eyes were sunken, small and red and its twin snouts no more than glistening, black holes. The twin slack-jowled mouths barely covered long, sharp fangs. It exuded ferocity and cunning. It faced the daroga who flinched as it took a step in his direction. But it was stopped by an invisible barrier which prevented it from leaving the charmed star inside which it had been born. It whined and turned to the yogi, as if pleading to be set free.

The daroga raised his eyes too. After the astounding materialisation he had seen, he was hardly surprised to see the yogi floating three feet above the altar.

As he watched, the enchanter took up his flute again and began to play. The music now turned lugubrious, funereal. When the daroga lowered his eyes from the player to the creature, it had vanished. In its place was the damp patch inside the star of candles which had almost burned down. As he watched, they guttered and went out one by one. He looked up again. The yogi had vanished too and the room was as dim and as empty as when he first saw it.

'There is no more. Spectacle finish,' growled the Nubian in the same dark, bass voice. 'It is time to go. Follow me. And please not to talk.'

He led the way back through the low-ceilinged room and the vaulted hall and let them out through the brass-studded door which he closed and locked after showing the last person out. The entire party breathed the cool night air deeply. It was late. The daroga's watch told him how very late it was. He could not believe that they had been inside for five hours!

He wondered what he had seen. So did everyone else. He heard them arguing. All were convinced that they were right and everyone else was wrong.

'It was a fire-breathing dragon — No, a hissing lizard — a giant reptile with leathery wings — a bear with massive paws — legless — four legs — no, five —It roared — barked — growled — hissed …'

'Well?' asked a voice at his elbow. 'Did you see marvels?'

The daroga turned and found Hájí Tabarsi who had brought a *droshky* to take him wherever he wanted.

'Questions later. But now there is something I want you to do. Hide yourself, keep watch, then follow the Nubian when he comes out. I must know where the Count lives. When you have the address,' added the daroga in a whisper, 'come to me at *Misha's*. Do not fail me.'

Hájí disappeared into a shadowy doorway to wait.

The daroga climbed wearily into the *droshky*. When he reached the *traktir*, he ordered a stove to be lit and tea to be brought. It had been a tiring night.

Hájí arrived an hour later.

'There were two men, the giant Nubian and another.'

'What did this other look like?'

'I could not see. He was too well wrapped against the night.'

'What did they say?'

'They did not speak.'

'Where did they go?'

'To a rich man's house, guarded by a high wall, near Sennaya Square. They did not come out again.'

'Good. I shall call on the Count soon.'

Hájí threw up his hands in horror.

'But he is a wizard, daroga!' he said, appalled. 'You will go there at the risk of your sanity, your life!'

'I think not. Tonight I saw a marvel. But I believe it was more spectacle than miracle. Count Kuzow is clearly a man who has lived long in the Orient, for he is skilled in the arts of the fakir. With narcotic incense and hypnotic music, he drugged his observers who saw what he wanted them to see and what they saw was the shapes of their own thoughts which vary from person to person. Even I was not immune. The man is very clever. I am only too pleased that he uses his skills to make money. If he stood up in any public square and preached revolution, he would quickly have ten thousand followers and be very dangerous.'

'But why does this young Sultana wish to have him at her court? She has plenty of magicians to amuse her.'

'But none as skilled as this man. But who are we to question the wishes of the principal wife of our master?'

The next night, the daroga, dressed in European clothes, presented himself at the home of Grigory Yegorov, shipbuilder and man of substance. It was an imposing mansion standing on a vantage point above the Volga. A flight of stone steps led up to its classical portico. Guests were received in a spacious vestibule. The first person the daroga saw was Steklov who, at his request, put names to the more prominent personages and their wives. Although the daroga had lived for periods outside Persia, he had never grown accustomed to mixing with women in social gatherings. Their bare shoulders, uncovered hair, the way they looked directly into his eyes all offended him. But it was not only their immodest physical presence which was wrong but their forwardness in other ways, above all in holding and expressing opinions. But he was in another land, and knew how to comply with the customs of the country.

At dinner the topics of conversation bored him. He sat between the owner of a dye-works and the proprietor of a brick factory. One favoured modern methods of production and the use of steam engines, while the other favoured the old working practices. Their discussion, which grew heated at one point, did not interest the daroga. Wealth did not come from making things but from selling them. Its only source was land and in the vassalage of the villages and tribes which were allowed, for a price, to exist on it. His mind wandered. His thoughts were interrupted by his host who barked, from the head of the table:

'And how do you, sir, in your country, treat criminals like the Hyena?'

'We catch them and put them to death, sir.'

'So do we, sir. The problem is that we cannot catch him. Isn't that so, Steklov? He's too clever for you.'

'It is true that thus far he has eluded us,' said the police chief.

'Would he elude you, sir?' Yegorov asked the daroga.

'For a while, perhaps. But when we offered a reward —'

'There is already a hefty price on his head,' said Steklov quickly.

'— and made it known that terrible punishments awaited friends and family who hid him or the village or tribe which aided him in any way, he would soon be surrendered. Besides, God, who is great, does not allow the guilty to go unpunished.'

A murmur of approval for such outright trust in civic duty and religion rose from the table.

'Perhaps you have not heard his latest outrage,' Yegorov went on, still addressing the daroga. 'He personally led an assault on the house of a very dear friend of ours, Countess Askaya, who cannot be here tonight because she has yet to throw off the shock to her system.'

'I did hear something of the affair,' said the daroga. But Yegorov ignored him and he went on:

'Her house was not robbed so much as attacked. She was entertaining at the time. I was not back from Moscow, otherwise I would have been there and, by God, I would have given this Hyena something to think about. Armed men suddenly appeared in her dining–room, took valuables from her guests and also from her vaults which her servants were obliged to open. Her late husband, a military man, must be turning in his grave.'

'I heard somewhere,' said the portly brick-maker, 'that this Hyena fellow commands a virtual army of cut-throats …'

'They say,' said a lady wearing three rows of pearls, 'that he has an impregnable fortress somewhere …'

'I was told,' said a guest with a military manner and moustache, 'that he is a strong disciplinarian. To punish one of his gang of thugs, he tied him to the mouth of a cannon and trained a magnifying glass on the other end. When the sun reached a certain height, its rays ignited the fuse and blew the man to pieces. He may be a rogue but I take off my hat to any man who can keep his foot soldiers in line.'

But not all found much to admire in such actions. The men fell silent and the ladies shuddered and put their hands over their mouths in horror as they thought of how the poor robber must have felt as he watched the sun rise relentlessly in the sky... Then Yegorov's wife, taking her duties as hostess seriously, broke the silence. Speaking in a nervous, brittle manner, she said:

'I hear a new opera is to be performed at the Glavnyi Dom. Italian, I believe. I do so prefer the Italian opera ...'

And the company began talking of their musical tastes.

But within moments, the room was plunged once more into shocked silence. A servant with a soiled apron, a face as white as lilies and hands that kept clutching at the air, burst into the room and cried:

'She's gone! They took her!'

The woman stopped, covered her face with her apron and sobbed.

'Who's gone?' barked Yegorov.

'Masha, your honour! They took my little Masha! They gave me this letter and said I was to bring it to you, sir.'

Yegorov took the letter and read it quickly.

'It's signed by the Hyena. He's kidnapped my darling Marya Vasilissa and he wants a king's ransom for her return!'

Madame Lizaveta Yegarovna fainted. Ladies gathered round and waved their fans over her. Steklov made a sign to an underling who had been stationed in an alcove and told him to order the constables on guard outside to be on the alert. Then he approached the servant, whose name was Fekla, patiently started asking questions and, with some difficulty, established that three armed, masked men had entered the kitchen. One stayed to ensure that the servants made no trouble. The other two made her take them to Marya Vasilissa's room. They tied the terrified girl's hands and put a gag over her mouth. Then they went back down below stairs and, after giving Fekla the note to take to her master, disappeared with her young mistress into the night.

'Search the grounds!' screamed Yegarov to the servants who had followed Fekla into the hall. 'I want those men found!'

Steklov said: 'I have the matter in hand. My men have been alerted. But I fear they will find nothing. The kidnappers will be long gone. Our only hope is that there are witnesses who can tell us which way they went.'

Several passers-by had seen three men helping a fourth person into a private carriage. The vehicle had been traced as far as the Oka river. The trail had gone dead once it entered the squalid web of Kuzowina's backstreets.

'Why does not our host just pay the ransom?' asked the daroga on the steps of Yegarov's house. 'He is very rich and it is the quickest way of getting his daughter back.'

Steklov looked at him coldly.

'It is not our practice in Nizhny-Novgorod to accede to the demands of criminals.'

The daroga shrugged and, since he had no role in the affair, ordered his carriage and returned to his rooms where he ordered a fire to be lit. Then he sent for Hájí Tabarsi and told him to bring him a reliable locksmith and a dark lantern. Hájí protested that it was late. But a sharp word sent him scuttling about his errands. Within the hour, he and a short, stocky man who smelled of onions and carried a bag which clinked climbed into the *droshky* where the daroga was waiting for them. They drove in silence across the bridge over the Oka, proceeded through the now deserted streets and stopped at the venerable brass-studded door to the mysterious halls where the Count had performed his miracles. Hájí lit the dark lantern, opened the shutter and directed the beam on to the lock. It took the locksmith five minutes to open the door. Telling Hájí to pay the man off and keep watch outside, the daroga took the lantern and entered the magician's den alone.

He reached the vaulted chamber with the floor of broken tiles. It was as silent as the tomb, but the silence was colourless, neutral, an absence of sound not an atmosphere in which suitably prepared minds would believe they could feel the blood of the centuries flow from tortured bodies. He examined the bas-reliefs on the walls. The grinning figures were not embossed in the stone but merely painted friezes, recently completed and skilfully worked in trompe-l'oeil; in a dim light they easily passed for the work of ancient masters. As he went down to the steps into the lower chambers, he peered closely at the bears, tigers and ferocious divinities which had sent shivers up the spines of the Count's paying customers. He found that that the seeming bloom of age on them could be removed with a thumbnail which revealed fresh plaster underneath. But the last, circular chamber was as bare as before, with the altar still standing at its centre. The daroga now saw that it was not a holy relic at all but a cold slab of the kind used by the butchers of Nizhny-Novgorod to cut up the carcases of animals.

Thus were confirmed his suspicions that the door with the brass studs had not concealed some ancient place of torture. It had been cunningly turned into a theatrical set on which a mystification had been staged.

He sat on the slab for a moment to collect his thoughts. He set the lantern down beside him. The sound of metal on stone seemed loud in the utter silence. As it died away, he seemed to hear faint cries. Yes! A voice was calling, far away. It came from the centre of the room. Perhaps he had been wrong! Perhaps this place had once been a chamber of horrors! Perhaps ancient screams of pain still reverberated in the small hours while the world slept!

There was the voice again! It emanated from somewhere in the centre of the room, no, from beneath his feet, from inside the cold slab! He picked up the lantern and began examining every inch of its four stone sides. The first two told him nothing, but as he ran his hand under the lip of the third, his sleeve caught on a projection. It was a metal lever. He pulled on the lever and a section of the side of the cold slab slid open. It made a low grating noise which was audible in the silence but would be easily covered by the sound of, say, a pipe and drum.

He had found the secret of the yogi's mysterious disappearance!

He showed his light into the hole and saw steps descending. He eased himself through, climbed down not knowing what to expect and found himself in a small, square chamber. In one corner was a truckle bed on which a body was lying. The daroga walked softly across to it, looked down at a pair of terrified eyes and said:

'There you are, Marya Vasilissa! Your parents will be delighted to have you back.'

He sat her up and waited until her teeth stopped chattering.

Then he led her up through the altar, closing the moving panel behind them. The metal of the lever was new and the panel itself had been expertly cut and mounted on runners. The slider mechanism operated with amazing smoothness. If any marvel had been enacted in this place, it was the construction of the yogi's false altar.

Keeping a few steps ahead of her, with his lantern pointed at her feet so that she would not be frightened by the figures decorating the walls, he brought her up to the vaulted hall and from there out into the cool night. He shivered. Damn this Russian climate!

Hájí had kept the *droshky* and they loaded the barely conscious girl into it.

As they got in, Hájí told the driver to take them to the house of Grigory Yegorov, but the daroga countermanded the order.

'Take us to the Upper City, to the residence of Captain Kiril Steklov.'

'Forgive me, daroga, but are you mad? Steklov will take charge of the girl and will receive all the credit!'

'I trust he will. Hájí,' said the daroga who told the coachman to drive on.

When they arrived they propped up Marya Vasilissa on a couch in an antechamber and told the servant to fetch Steklov. The police chief froze when he registered her presence. He ordered tea to be brought for the girl and then with a brusque gesture, he motioned the daroga to step into his study.

'What is the meaning of this?' he said in a tightly controlled voice. 'How did you find the girl so quickly when my men have failed to find any trace of her?'

With infinite courtesy, the daroga said that a chance encounter (he would not be drawn on the identity of his informant or the circumstances in which they met) had led to the girl's recovery. As a stranger in Nizhny-Novgorod and not knowing what to do, he thought it best to deliver her to the proper authorities rather than return her directly to Grigory Yegorov.

'Your tale of rescue sounds very fanciful. Indeed, your whole story makes me very suspicious.'

The daroga laughed: 'No, Captain, I am not the Hyena. How could I be? I never set foot in Nizhny-Novgorod until last week. I am passing through. I had a stroke of luck and, since I am in no position to profit from it, I thought that perhaps you and your service might prefer to have the benefit of Grigory Yegorov's gratitude. Yours shall be the triumph.'

Placated, the Captain thanked the daroga for his generous gesture and hurried off to Yegorov's mansion where he was ecstatically received. The master shipbuilder ate the disparaging words he had pronounced about Steklov's policing methods and was suitably grateful.

Next morning, the daroga took a cab to the address near Sennaya Square which Hájí had given him.

He was obliged to ring the bell several times before the door opened. The daroga asked to see Count Kuzow. The giant Nubian told him no one of that name lived in the house.

'Humour me,' said the daroga, 'by giving your master this. I believe he will see me.'

The Nubian's eyes widened when the reed-pipe which had been used in the materialisation was placed in his hand.

'Wait here,' he said and closed the door.

Within minutes, he opened it again, stepped back and allowed the daroga to enter the house. He escorted him to a high-ceilinged drawing-room furnished in the European style. A man, gaunt and of above-average height was standing with his back to a blazing fire. He had long hair which might have been a wig and the part of his face not hidden by a full beard, which might also have been false, was catered for by a pair of smoked eye-glasses.

'Ah, come in, sir. I hope the heat does not inconvenience you. This damp Russian summer is a trial to me.'

'To me also, Count. I shall bask in the warmth of this handsome room. But forgive my unexpected appearance here. Let me introduce myself, I have the honour to be daroga of police of Mazanderan, the northernmost province of Persia. Your fame has come to the ears of the principal wife of my master, his Excellency the Sultan-Governor. I have been sent on a mission to invite you to spend a season at the Court of Mazanderan where the Sultana hopes you will entertain her friends and her guests with the marvels for which you are justly celebrated.'

'Before you tell me more about your mission,' said Count Kuzow, 'be so good as to explain how you found me. I have gone to considerable trouble and expense to protect my privacy.'

'I was fortunate enough to attend your most recent performance. It was a very memorable experience. Less impressive, however, was the ill-conceived kidnapping of Marya Vasilissa from that boor Yegorov's house.'

'Ill-conceived? What do you mean?' drawled the Count, unimpressed.

'And so badly-executed that the girl has been restored to her father.'

The Count stiffened.

'You could send your man out to confirm what I say, but there is no need. I have brought you your pipe, the one you use when duping the paying public. It should tell you that I know everything.'

'Since you are so well-informed, daroga, why don't you tell me what you think you know?' said the Count in a thin, controlled voice. 'I shall correct you if you are wrong.'

The daroga gave a detailed account of what had happened from the time he left the fake chamber of horrors until he handed the girl to Steklov.

'I think I shall kill you, daroga. You know far too much about me,' said the Count. 'I have many ways of killing a man.'

'You could not hope for a better opportunity. No one knows I am here. I would not be missed. But before you send me to paradise, the destiny for which all true believers yearn, perhaps you would like to consider the purpose of my mission? You shiver here in Russia with winter in the offing. You waste your talents deceiving Christian clods for money. My dear Count, Mazanderan is a place in the sun and the satisfaction of knowing you are the ornament of the Sultana's court would have definite advantages.'

'What is your Sultana like?'

'Young and full of tricks.'

'And my reward?

'If the honour of serving her Highness is not recompense enough, the material benefits would be very considerable.'

The Count did not speak for a while. Suddenly his body relaxed and his manner suddenly lost its menace.

'Daroga, you are a fortunate man. You intrigue me. Moreover, you have come at the right time. A week ago, you would not have left this house alive. But you have reminded me just how bored I am here. I have done all I want to in Russia. Repeating a fakir's tawdry tricks has become a chore and the Hyena has ceased to interest me. The Fair will soon be over and Nizhny-Novgorod will go back to sleep. Another freezing winter of tedium in this place is not an agreeable prospect. I am tempted by the Sultana's invitation.'

'You will come?'

'Before I answer, tell me one thing. Why did you take the girl to Steklov rather than back to her father? Doesn't it matter to you that he, not you, will reap what you have sown?'

'No, for the reward I sought was his good will. I believe I now have it.'

'Why should you want his good will?'

'I thought that you might need a passport. To reach Mazanderan we shall pass through several countries which are disagreeably suspicious of strangers. I'm confident that if I asked Steklov, he would oblige by providing suitable travel documents in whatever name you choose. May I enquire what that name might be?

'Erik,' said the false Count. 'Have Steklov write 'Erik' in my new passport. And while he's about it, ask him to provide papers for the Nubian.'

'Then you will come?'

'Daroga, you amuse me. How can I refuse your offer?'

Chapter 12

Leilah, newest wife of Osman Oullah, Sultan-Governor of the province of Mazanderan, leaned back on the large down cushions covered with cloth of gold, wiggled her pink toes in her slippers and sighed. She was seventeen and bored. Her lord and master was already losing interest in her. It was said that he had a new favourite, a Georgian slave who had green eyes and called herself Nûr Jehan, light of the world. Such airs! Leilah hated her whether the rumours were true or not, though they probably were. She felt miserable and neglected. Osman Oullah had stopped devising new entertainments for her. Instead of being at her side at this moment, he was elsewhere. He had told her he would be busy all day discussing with his Vizir new plans for diverting public tax monies into his personal coffers. But Leilah did not believe him. He was probably with *her*.

She sighed again. Would no one pay proper attention to her feelings and wishes? She called for her old nurse and commanded her to tell her stories of old, heroic times. But today even the sad tale of her namesake Leilah, the most beautiful and perfect of her sex, who was adored by Majnoun, the ideal lover, seemed flat and dull. Instead, she told the nurse to bring her street clothes, for of late she had taken to staving off boredom by leaving the palace secretly and going to the medina dressed as a seller of spices. She went well protected by the harem eunuchs who told passers-by who she was and left them no choice but to buy spices they did not want. She charged fanciful prices. For a pinch of saffron, she asked a gold *tomaun* from this man; from the next, one copper *ghauz*. Only she took pleasure from such outings.

Then Leilah changed her mind. She stamped her foot and shouted at her women, calling them fools and saying that she would not go out after all. It did not amuse her to rub shoulders with flea-ridden, evil-smelling common people. She broke off when she saw Taki, principal eunuch of the harem, enter the place of women, the *anderún*. He salaamed.

'What is it?' she snapped crossly.

'The magician is here, lady.'

At first Leilah did not understand, but then remembered. The Master Magician of Nizhny-Novgorod! So the man had been sent for after all! She had begun to think the Sultan had forgotten his promise. But he hadn't and she felt reassured. Perhaps he hadn't tired of her after all.

'Where is the man?'

'In the marble hall, lady.'

Without another word, the young Sultana of Mazanderan skipped lightly through the harem door and up to the latticed gallery running round the central atrium of the palace which was open to the sky. From there, ladies of the court could see unobserved all those who came and went. She looked down and saw a man of above average height in conversation with another she knew to be the daroga, the magistrate in charge of the Sultan's police. The Magician was not dressed like a wizard but as a wealthy merchant or perhaps a tax-gatherer, in a shot silk coat trimmed in front with gold lace and gold buttons. A dagger with a jewelled handle was stuck into the cashmere shawl he wore round his waist. But his face was hidden by a large turban cloth held by a glinting diamond pin.

The Sultana turned to the duenna who had followed her mistress up to the gallery.

'I will speak to the man,' she said. 'See to it.'

She waited while the duenna gave the order to Taki and then watched Taki approach the Magician who parted from the daroga and was led to the little parlour where women of the harem, faces hidden and closely chaperoned, could speak with men. Leilah, suitably veiled, kept him waiting before making an entrance...

'Magician,' she said through the carved wooden grill which separated them. 'I cannot see your face. I command you to remove your turban-cloth.'

'My face, lady, is not pleasant to look at.'

'Nevertheless, I will see it,' said Leilah imperiously, as befitted the Sultana of Mazanderan.

The Magician unwound the cloth and put it to one side.

The duenna uttered a cry of horror, for she believed she was looking at a *ghôl*, even though she knew full well that *ghôls*, which ate corpses, never appeared in the light of day. But Leilah clapped her hands and laughed delightedly. Never was there a face so hideous! Truly, a man who looked more like a master of dark arts could not exist! She stared at this wizard from the north.

'You sent for me, lady,' said Erik. 'I am here. I have come a great distance to serve you. What is your will?'

Leilah said nothing but continued to inspect that face: burning eyes buried deep in their sockets, the lank strands of white hair, the half-bared, grinning teeth...

'It is not polite to stare,' said a man's voice at her back. The Sultana whirled round in alarm but saw only her duenna, still terrified, cowering on her stool.

'Not polite at all,' said the same voice, though this time it came from a small chest to her right.

She smiled: 'I caused you to come because I wanted you to perform magic tricks for me. You have made a good start. I have heard that religious men of the east throw their voices. I see you have mastered their art. You shall teach me. What else can you do?'

Erik did not reply but raised his eyes to meet hers. She was about to say that it was insolent to stare then thought the better of it. Without releasing her eyes, Erik wordlessly unsheathed his dagger and with it cut into the flesh of his forearm which began to bleed profusely. He held the arm out straight, so that she could see. She could not look away. The bright crimson blood and the open lips of the wound drew and held her gaze in the tightest of grips. She craned forward to get a better view. As she did so, the blood stopped flowing, checked itself and seemed to return to the gaping wound which began to shrink until it had closed up, leaving no scar. She blinked in disbelief.

'Wizard, you are every whit as accomplished as I was told.'

'I am at your service, lady,' said Erik, with a respectful bow.

'I shall think how you shall serve me. Now leave me. You may expect my summons.'

When Erik had gone, Leilah returned to the women's apartments. She avoided the other chattering concubines and sat pensive and alone at a little table on which was a painted box. She opened the box and from it took collyrium and Chinese rouge. After applying the first to her eyes and the second to her cheeks, she picked out a pair of silver armlets containing talismans, and a ruby on a silver chain which she hitched into her hair so that it hung down on the centre of her forehead. By the time she had finished, she had made up her mind.

'Beware, Nûr Jehan! I'll put out your light!' she whispered to herself and smiled.

Erik had been given an apartment in the palace. From its balcony he watched the comings and goings of the men of the court of Mazanderan. Months on the road with the daroga had enabled him to add Persian to his collection of foreign languages. The snatches of conversations he caught were the standard fare of courts everywhere: who was in, who was out, do this for me and I'll do that for you. But the Sultana did not keep him waiting long. Taki brought her summons.

He was ushered into to the same parlour where Leilah was waiting. He bowed respectfully.

'I can kill parrots with a sling,' said the Sultana without preamble.

Erik knew little about women. Since leaving France five years before, he had known only the company of men — with one exception, but do not think of her! Never think more of her! Thinking of her will make you mad! Françoise had loved him but as a mother loves a boy and ever since he had been separated from her all he had known of women was their unkindness. He now recognised spite and malice in the words and gestures of the Sultana who was, so the daroga had told him, Osman Oullah's current favourite. He also sensed danger. It would not be to his advantage to ruffle her feathers.

'Yes, lady' he said, 'a sling is a good weapon for killing a parrot. But killing a bird is nothing next to killing a man. To kill a man, a bamboo pellet bow is better. It shoots pellets of clay baked hard in the sun. If you wish, I will make you one and teach you how to use it.'

If the Sultana thought this forward and impertinent, she did not show it.

'Yes you shall,' she said quite seriously. 'But not today. What I want now is a... a sleeping draught, such as wizards in legends make use of to lull their enemies. I command you to make me such a draught.'

Erik wondered what enemies the Sultana had that she needed poison, for clearly that was what she wanted.

'Shall it be in the form of a powder or a potion?'
'Potion.'
'And is it to be mild, to bring rest to a weary body, or strong enough to induce sleep of the wakeless sort?'

'Let it bring the wakeless sort. So much more lasting.'

The next morning, the Sultana received a small flask with a silver stopper. She removed the stopper. The fluid inside was colourless and without odour.

Later that day, there was uproar in the women's quarters. There was a sound of running feet, screams and lamentations. The court physician was summoned. Then peace returned.

'Ah,' said Leilah when she was told the news, 'the Light of the World is extinguished. Yet,' she added, 'the world shines no less brightly. In fact just the opposite'

Erik heard of the disturbance. When he questioned the daroga, he was told that one of His Excellency's concubines was dead, poisoned by her own hand.

'A tragedy,' sighed the daroga, 'but a death not entirely natural, I suspect. Nûr Jehan was the new ornament of the Sultan's court and her regrettable demise serves the Sultana well, for she is now confirmed in her position.'

Erik decided he must make himself indispensable to the Sultan's favourite. If he did not, he would find himself next on her list.

'I shall call you *feringhi*, since you are a foreigner,' said Leilah when next they met. 'I want you to teach me to shoot clay pellets with the bamboo bow.'

This was not easy to arrange for only the Shah himself was permitted by law to enter the harem and be in the company of the women of the *anderún*. But Leilah, with a mixture of rewards, threats and presents of money – for nothing was achieved in Persia without the giving of presents – smoothed away all difficulties. She appropriated for her own use an unfrequented, circular courtyard with a fountain playing at its centre. The customary latticed gallery for women ran round the circumference. Behind it, old Fatmeh, the duenna, was posted. She kept her mistress and the *feringhi* in view at all times, though her prime duty was to give warning if any member of the Sultan's entourage approached. Thus, under the strictest supervision, Leilah was able to receive instruction directly from her *feringhi*.

Of course, she was quite aware that her Magician had no supernatural powers, that there was no magic in his mysteries. He was a mere trickster, a master of illusions, manipulation and mesmerism. She thought none the less of him for that. On the contrary, she admired his skills and was eager to learn all his secrets which would help her to bend the world to her will. When she was proficient with the pellet bow, he advised her that, for close-quarter work, the Punjab noose was quicker, more deadly, more silent. He offered to demonstrate.

For an hour, the circular courtyard was turned into an arena. From the gallery, Leilah watched as a palace guard was brought, a man so huge that he might have been cousin to Gargantua, He was told that if he overcame the *feringhi* in single combat he would be richly rewarded. If he did not, he would die. Erik, unarmed except for a noose, circled his man who jabbed at him with a lance. Seeing an opening, Erik pounced without warning. Ducking under the guard's flailing arms, he got behind him and slipped the noose around his neck and tightened it. The guard choked, his face turned purple and within moments his whole body had gone as slack as an empty wineskin. Erik released his grip. The man collapsed gasping in the dust like a floundering fish.

Leilah clapped her hands delightedly. She ran down into the courtyard and demanded to hold the noose. She ran the silken cord through her fingers and pulled on it, testing its strength. She was so engrossed in it that the guard succeeded in crawling away unnoticed and forgotten. She demanded to be taught how to use the Punjab noose.

Knowing she would ask this of him, Erik called for the manikin of straw he had brought with him and demonstrated the fine art of garrotting a man. 'Approach silently... do not lose the element of surprise... ensure that there is nothing on or near the neck to obstruct the cord... slip it quickly over the head and tighten it... thus.'

The Sultana was a quick learner. She insisted both on keeping the noose and on having further demonstrations. She commanded the daroga to bring convicted criminals to the improvised arena where, like Christians in the Coliseum of Rome, they were given tridents, nets and battle axes and ordered to do gladiatorial battle with Erik, Master of the Punjab noose. Erik was always victorious. Eventually, the Sutana found his invincibility tedious. But she kept the sport alive by testing her own skill on several of her women, of whom two died.

She persuaded Erik to perform fakir's tricks for Sultan Osman who was delighted. He made Erik a present of twenty gold *tomauns*.

Alone in his apartment, Erik took stock of his situation. Though he was now free to come and go at will in the palace, he was in effect a prisoner. As long as he kept the Sultana amused, he was safe. But the moment he started to bore her, he knew that his days were numbered. He must make himself necessary to her, become her ally, her right hand. Then, when he had lined his pockets, he would shake the dust of Mazanderan from his feet.

Soon after he had taken this decision, the court began to hum with rumours that Sultan Osman was to be replaced. The daroga explained that he owed his appointment as Sultan-Governor of Mazanderan to Shah Nasr el din, King of Persia, who had conferred it upon him in his palace of Golestan, the famous Rosy Garden of Tehran. Osman Oullah's predecessor had been dismissed for corruption. On taking his place, Osman had promised his sovereign that he would collect taxes faithfully and protect the interests of the province and its population. He duly collected taxes but kept what he could for himself, deceiving officials in Tehran by saying that harvests were bad, trade was slack and the cost of public works higher than anticipated.

He had now been in Sari, his capital, for four years and had amassed a considerable fortune. Accusations of corruption were now being made against him. Soon he would be recalled to the court of Tehran to explain himself. He would be asked if he preferred to return the funds he had embezzled or repay a stated sum, probably half or two-thirds of what he had stolen. He would hand over the agreed sum, and then, with what remained, give presents to the Shah, the Shah's ministers, the ladies of the Shah's harem and influential officials of the Shah's court who would intercede for him. Then he would be given another province to govern and the process would be repeated.

'So you see,' concluded the daroga, 'no one loses. The people are happy to see that not even a Sultan can escape justice, the Shah and his government get rich without having the worry of governing the realm and the Sultan-Governor moves on to pastures new. It is a system which pleases everyone.'

'Not quite,' said Erik. 'The Sultana is not at all pleased. She has her family here and has told me she will not be parted from them or from her province, though it is a marshy, pestiferous place.'

'The Sultan my master will persuade her to change her mind with presents. She likes pretty things. It is how things are done in Mazanderan.'

'Perhaps, but her mind is made up. She will not be moved. She has a high opinion of me and has given me instructions to find a way of persuading the Shah in Tehran to change his mind and leave Osman Oullah here, in Sari. If I fail, I die. She did not say it in so many words, but that is what she meant.'

The daroga looked at him.

'Then I wish you good fortune,' he said.

Shortly after this conversation took place, a man came out of the west, Mirza Ahmak by name. He travelled from place to place rousing the people with talk of justice and universal peace. He preached to great crowds saying that the Sultan bled his subjects dry for love of money. His words sowed the seeds of a cause which seemed destined to write the next chapter of the history of Mazanderan in letters of blood.

Osman Oullah was very afraid. He sent soldiers to stop the mouth of this Mirza Ahmak. They failed. He urged the clergy to stiffen the resolve of the faithful against him, but though they butchered Mirza's disciples and threatened those who heeded their preaching, the tide could not be stopped. The Sultan wrote brave replies to alarmed missives from Tehran where Shah Nasr el din had not yet recovered from the late rebellion of the Babi faction. The Shah replied warning him that an armed insurrection was in the offing which would spread rebellion throughout Mazanderan. From there it would travel with the speed of flames in tinder and ignite the whole of Persia. The Shah made it clear that it was Osman Oullah's responsibility to end the disorder in his province.

In an intimate moment, Osman confided his worries to Leilah who saw at once that the wretched Mirza was a gift from heaven. If the rebel could be stopped, and if the man who stopped him proved to be her poor, dear husband, the Shah would be so grateful that there would be no more talk of leaving Mazanderan. Of course, the Sultan was a booby and not fit for the task. But the Wizard was a man of infinite resource, and discreet. He was a man who could be trusted to put a speedy end to the revolt.

She commanded him to come to her. She told him what she wanted.

The palace of Osman Oullah now held no secrets for Erik. With the Nubian, he had explored every corner, every corridor, every cellar. The skills which had enabled them to build the secret altar with sliding panels in the circular chamber at Nizhny-Novgorod now allowed him to walk through walls and drop from one level to another through undetectable trap-doors. He had perfected a way of raising a whole section of a wall by means of a counterweight which was operated by a lever. Once the balance was achieved and the wall was in position on its pivot, a child could push it open with one finger and step into the next room. Working with the Nubian at night, he had installed a sufficient number of these secret traps for him to be free to leave the palace unseen whenever he chose and return just as freely by the way he had left. He was no longer a prisoner in Osman Oullah's palace.

In this way had he made sure of having an escape route. He could now go out into the city by day or night and wander through the *medina* or listen to the gossip in the mosques. He smoked a pipe in places of refreshment and learned that the Sultan was as much hated as he was feared. There was excited talk of the Man from the West. Erik travelled beyond the city limits to attend forbidden gatherings where the bold and curious elements of the population heard Mirza Ahmak sow the seeds of revolt. The man was personally ambitious and a persuasive orator. But Erik saw at once that sowing seeds was all he could do, for he lacked the means to rouse the rabble to rise up against its masters. His aides were poorly equipped and his bodyguard did not look like warriors. His meetings were secretive and had a hole-in-corner feel, as though Mirza was expecting them to be disrupted at any moment by the Sultan's troops. He did have the manner of a man about to bring down a regime.

After one such meeting, Erik, wrapped in a lambskin *poshteen* against the cold, mingled with the crowd outside Mirza's tent and petitioned for an audience. He was told to wait. Other, more important, men came and went and he was not called even when he was left alone in the antechamber. He was told to go home, for Mirza Ahmak would receive no one else that night. Erik said he would wait. When the dawn came, he was still waiting. No one thought to bring him refreshment all through the day. But as the sun was beginning to set, Mirza Ahmak came in person to find out for himself what important reason was greater than the physical fatigue and the impatience of this singular visitor.

'You wish to speak with me?'

'Yes, Excellency,' said Erik

'I see your eyes but not your face. I do not speak with anyone whose expression I cannot read. Only men who wish me harm come to me masked.'

Mirza Ahmak gestured to a guard. But before the man could move, Erik unwound the scarf that hid his face.

'Are you any further forward?' he said. 'Can you read such a face as this?'

Mirza Ahmak paused a moment, then said: 'If you wish to dispute with me,' he said, 'you waste your time. My aim is justice for all men and peace for all nations …'

'I expect you are sincere in wanting these things, lord, but your beliefs are not my concern. I am here to speak of money.'

'Money?' said Mirza Ahmak cautiously, for other men, skilled in debate, had been sent to trap him into making hasty statements with which to discredit him.

'Money. For horses, supplies, to pay men. Men will not fight your cause if they are not fed or paid or given weapons. You will win your cause by fighting, not with words. But you know this. Those who sent me are prepared to finance your … work. They are not all as hot in the cause as you, but all have their reasons for wanting to see the back of Osman Oullah.'

'Who are these men and what are their reasons?'

'I am but their messenger, lord. They will tell you all you wish to know. Come with me. I will take you to them.'

Mirza Ahmak threw back his head and laughed.

'I, come with you? No, no. You cannot think that I will allow myself to be trapped so easily! I have many enemies and they all wish me dead. Do you think I will put my head in a noose? Leave me before have you seized.'

Erik did not move. Instead he reached inside his robe. Mirza Ahmak took a step back but stopped when he saw what his strange visitor was holding out to him.

'The men I serve ask you to accept this token of their good faith. Will you come? You may bring men to guard you, though not many. The meeting must remain secret. A large force would attract attention.'

Mirza Ahmak studied the ruby which Erik had placed on his palm. It was clearly a stone of great worth. Surely there could be no danger in speaking to men who were so lavish with their gifts?

Chapter 13

When Osman Oullah was told that the severed head of his enemy Mirza Ahmak had been left at his door, according to the custom of honouring the victories of great lords, he felt great relief. After examining it, he despatched a messenger to inform the Shah that the realm had been delivered from the threat of fanaticism and that he, Osman Oullah, Sultan of Mazanderan, had done this thing. Word came back from the Golestan, the Shah's 'Rosy Garden' Palace at Teheran, congratulating his faithful servant on his signal achievement of saving Persia from its enemies. A present of elephants followed. Osman Oullah expressed his own pleasure by making lavish gifts to his Grand Vizir, the Great Muphti, his General-in-Chief, his Lord High Treasurer, his lord Chamberlain and his Master of Horse, all of whom claimed to have had some hand in the defeat of the Shah's great enemy. Wherever he went, his name rang with praises:

'May the Sultan's s wealth increase!'

'May his kindness never be less!'

'May he live forever!'

Osman Oullah also made gifts to Leilah, queen of his heart, and she in turn gave presents to Fatmeh, Taki the eunuch and her favourites. To Erik she offered a richly-bound book of her very best poems written in her own hand and charming spelling.

Erik smiled but did not feel slighted. He had ensured that Osmon Oullah and his entourage would not move elsewhere, and with this he was content. But he knew the time was coming when he should think of leaving. He had been in Persia now for a year and a half. He had established himself as court jester to a capricious Sultana who delighted in inflicting pain on others. The fact that his own life hung on the whims of a spoilt, spiteful girl offended him. It would be a simple matter to relieve the earth of her presence, but she was still useful to him. She continued to give him presents when he amused her and, at her bidding, the Sultan had already filled his mouth with gold on three separate occasions. Perhaps he should now turn his attention to pleasing the Sultan-Governor himself.

He kept the fruits of his labours securely in an earthenware amphora hidden behind a false wall which he had built in his quarters. It was now three-quarters full. When it was full, he would shake the dust of Mazanderan from his feet.

He needed a triumph, something spectacular.

He recalled Father Verhoven once telling him of an oriental court where skilled craftsmen had built a palace with walls honeycombed in such a way that voices in one room could be heard in distant apartments. It had been done using hollowed walls, vents, ducts and all forms of air-passageways. Having no army of artisans to call on, he could not replicate that marvel of the builder's art. But he could reproduce some of its effects. With the help of the Nubian, he fixed metal canopies over fireplaces and obtained permission to make apertures in walls and ceilings which, he claimed, would increase the circulation of air and keep the palace cool in the hottest summers. The canopies and apertures acted as funnels. They captured sounds which rose and were magnified and redirected by means of ducts and conduits which formed an interconnected system of flues and airways. Propelled upwards by the warmth of the air the sounds would emerge through the ornate outside vents which kept the Palace cool. Then on one windless evening, as the Sultan strolled in his garden and the Sultana sat with her women in her quarters, Erik brought court musicians armed with trumpets, rams' horns, cymbals, tambourines and drums to the atrium and commanded them to play.

In his garden, the Sultan looked up in puzzlement. In his *anderûn*, his women lay down their needles and looked tremblingly at the Sultana. Their fears evaporated when they saw her laugh with delight.

'It is my Wizard!,' she exclaimed. 'Only my Wizard could make the rooftops sing! Bring my Musician to my parlour. I will speak with him.'

But when Taki was sent to fetch him, Erik was not in his quarters. For the Sultan had also thought of the jester, the *lûti bashi*, whom Leilah had caused to be brought from distant Russia. Osman Oullah had no ear for music but he had a keen eye for his own interest. If this *feringhi* was capable of making trumpets played in an atrium audible to persons in other parts of his palace, then surely he could make buildings where what was secretly said by courtiers in one room could be heard by a listener in another. Plots and intrigues would be nipped in the bud and he, Osman Oullah, would no longer have to fear what his enemies were doing behind his back.

He put the matter to Erik who said it could be done and recommended the construction of new quarters where his Excellency's court would be installed.

'You will start at once,' said the Sultan eagerly. 'And you must not think of the cost. You may have whatever you need,' he said, before adding, 'within reason.'

The Sultana was no less pleased. Her Wizard from Russia had for some time long lost his novelty value. She had wearied of the Punjab noose, the gladiatorial combats had ceased to excite her and she quickly forgot his role in ridding Mazanderan of the rebellious Mirza Ahmak. But singing roofs! Trumpets in the sky! Pure surprise and delight! She rewarded him with a ruby. When Erik had time to examine it, he saw that it was worth rather less than the one he had given to Mirza and had never retrieved. He would have to do better if he was to fill his amphora.

The Sultan's service included a large number of slaves, for while he was forbidden by religion to enslave co-religionists, he was as free as any other Sultan, Sheikh or Bey to deprive Christians and other infidels of their liberty and put them to work. Among them were some who were skilled in brick-making, masonry and allied building crafts. Erik appointed overseers and gave the Nubian overall responsibility for ensuring that his plans were followed to the letter and that the work progressed briskly. A suitable site was chosen in a garden close by the Sultan's palace. Workers were commanded never to speak to anyone about the building under construction on pain of death. To ensure that security was observed, they were isolated in a well-guarded compound. A high wall was built around the site to defy prying eyes. If his listening palace was to serve its purpose of allowing the Sultan to eavesdrop on his courtiers, then its secrets had to be guarded closely.

Erik understood Osman Oullah's fears. The times were dangerous. Of late there had been insurrections in a number of provinces, notably at Yezd, Zanjan and Niriz. The rising in Mazanderan was finally suppressed only after the general commanding the Sultan's army was replaced by Zadeh Kassem, a more competent, but also more ambitious, leader. The loss of many lives had left lingering resentments among the population. To keep the peace and root out any remaining malcontents, Osman Oullah counted on the daroga, his chief police magistrate. The Persian was thorough but his persistence made enemies. There were attempts on his life, which he was able to foil. But more serious was the whispering campaign which was designed to blacken his name at court and arouse the hostility of the Sultan.

It was said that he had spoken disrespectfully of religion, the Sultan and the Shah himself, but he was always able to show that the allegations were falsehoods put about by the Sultan's enemies. But when a chest of gold *taumans* missing from Osman Oullah's apartments was found in the Persian's quarters, he was unable to explain their presence there. He was brought to the court where he was required to say before judges how a chest of treasure belonging to the prince-governor of Mazanderan had found its way into his possession. Since he could not provide a satisfactory answer there and then, he was thrown into a dungeon and told to produce one that satisfied the court. If not, he would be put to death.

He conveyed a message to Erik who came to him in his cell.

'This smells of Zadeh Kassem,' he said.

'Of course,' said the Persian. 'But I cannot prove it.'

'Where is the general now?'

'He is here, in Sari,' said the Persian.

The next day, Osman Oullah, who took a lively interest in the progress of his 'Palace of Ears', was due to make one of his periodic inspections of the site. As usual, given the need for discretion, he came without his usual large retinue, attended only by only two guards who had been long in his service and on whose silence he counted absolutely. The ground-floor lay-out was complete and the walls of most of the chambers and the main atrium were already head high. Several rooms even had ceilings and were finished, apart from the tiling of the floors and the final decoration of the walls. Erik, who had greeted His Highness, had begged permission to be excused as guide of the tour, for a matter requiring his urgent attention had arisen. He added that it would not take long and that he would return in a few minutes only. The Sultan readily agreed, for in his impatience he had no wish to delay the work. He was left in the care of the chief overseer, a nervous Copt who prayed inwardly to his God that he would be able to answer the great lord's questions to his satisfaction.

The Sultan entered one of the completed rooms. It was bare and smelled of damp plaster. The Copt led him to a niche in one corner of the room where, he said, the mighty Lord would see the room to its best advantage. As he stood there, Osman Oullah heard voices though there was no one in the room but himself and his guide.

'Why did you ask me here?' said a deep voice.

'Because I knew you would come, *agha*. Everyone wants to see the Sultan-Governor's gorgeous new palace but no one has been invited. You are the first. I knew you would not stay away.'

'There is as yet little enough to see. So I ask again: why did you really ask me here?'

Osman Oullah stood fascinated. He was hearing the conversation as clearly as if it were taking place in the very room where he was standing. He recognised his master-builder's measured tone. The other voice too was familiar, but for the moment he could not put a name or a face to it.

'Because I want to know why, *agha*, you ordered the chest of gold *tomauns* to be removed from the Sultan-Governor's apartments and placed in the daroga's quarters.'

'Which of my servants told you this? Be warned, insolent *feringhee*, I will not buy your silence. But say one word of this matter and you will die. Still, who listens when an infidel speaks, even if he speaks the truth?'

The Sultan's face began to turn red with fury. Zadeh Kassem! How dare he!

'... The daroga is my enemy. He has crossed me in many things. Through his interference, I fell from favour and lost my command of the army of the north. I will rid the earth of that insolent policeman.'

'But the daroga is innocent of stealing his Excellency's gold pieces! You must find a way of bringing about his release.'

'Never!' snarled Zadeh Kassem. 'I intend to see him hang!'

'In that case, *agha*, here is no more to say. Please follow this man. He will take you back to the gate.'

When Erik rejoined the Sultan only moments later, he found him in a rage. He issued orders for the immediate arrest of Zadeh Kassem and the release of the prisoner. Next day, the daroga, fully vindicated, stood by the side of his Excellency the Sultan-Governor and Erik while the former general had his right hand cut off by the public executioner before being hanged on a gibbet and riddled with bullets. His body was then thrown outside the city walls to be devoured by dogs and jackals. After the sentence had been carried out, Osman Oullah instructed Erik to speed up the work of construction. He could not wait for it to be finished. He thanked God for the miraculous chance which had led him to the niche where he had heard the vile Zadeh Kassem condemn himself out of his own mouth. His palace was not yet complete and he had already foiled one plot. What other intrigues would he not uncover when all was ready?

After he was reinstated, the daroga said to Erik: 'It would be ill-mannered of me to ask how you managed to unmask Zadeh Kassem. I will say only that you are truly a magician. You swim in muddy waters but, like the swan, your feathers never get dirty. You have my undying gratitude.'

'We are allies you and I, daroga. Perhaps one day, you will do as much for me.'

'His Excellency is evidently much pleased with you — and himself.'

'May his gullibility never grow less.'

Erik pressed on, though once he had completed the plans of the new building, he was able to hand much of the work of executing his orders to overseers and inspectors, leaving him with time on his hands. Leilah kept pestering him to reveal the secrets of the mysterious new palace. He wondered how long he could go on saying no before she became angry and made serious trouble for him. She could poison the mind of the Sultan against even his most loyal servants. So he trod warily. He looked for a way of distracting her. Eventually found one.

One day, a section of scaffolding collapsed killing and injuring a number of skilled men. Without them, there would be delays. The Sultan readily authorised Erik to travel to Rasht, a journey of several days, along the marshy southern shores of the Caspian Sea, with a view to finding replacements. As darkness fell on the third night, the leader of the caravan declared it was too late for them to reach any town or village and that they would have to camp where they were. In the night it rained heavily so that by daybreak their road was waterlogged and impassable. Disliking enforced inactivity, Erik took one man with him and rode out to explore the area.

He had not gone far before he came across a group of semi-ruined buildings, an old monastery which housed seven monks. He did not understand their language but their neatly-kept chapel showed that they were Christians. There was a small library and, having been starved of books since arriving in Persia, Erik lingered. The leather-bound volumes were dusty and had the smell of the ages on them. But one took his eye. It was a work of science, written in Latin by Athanasius Kircher and published in Amsterdam in 1646. It was entitled *Ars Magna Lucis et Umbrae*, and was a treatise on optics. It described various experiments with lenses and prisms but Erik's attention was caught by the description of what Kircher called a 'polydiptic theatre'. It consisted of a box lined with 60 small mirrors, with peep-holes at intervals and a hinged lid through which objects could be inserted. The observer with one eye to a peep-hole would see a leaf placed inside reflected many times by the mirrors so that he would think he saw a forest. In the same way, a lead soldier became an army and a single pebble a beach. The 'polydiptic theatre' would be simple to replicate. With this box of delights, Erik would keep the Sultana happy and stop her pestering him.

And so it proved. On returning to the Sultan's palace at Sari with his new recruits, he made her a 'polydiptic theatre' which was a great success. Leilah could not be parted from her new toy. When she wearied of seeing the single soldier who was an army and the leaf that was a forest, she searched for other suitable objects which she could turn into multitudes: feathers, toe-nail clippings or small gems which became a treasure. When she tired of this, she used insects that crawled and insects that flew. The ants and beetles, which turned into whole colonies of creatures all making the identical movements, were amusing for a time. But they showed no sign of distress and Leilah liked nothing better than watching living things suffer. They seemed unaffected by the experience of confronting a thousand selves. Flies and wasps were much more entertaining. They immediately fell into a panic. Surrounded by enemies, they flew at their reflections in a rage which made Leilah screech with laughter. Their exertions exhausted them and they dropped to the floor where they lay inert in a carpet of reflected selves. The beetles continued to be unconcerned and walked around them patiently.

'Wizard,' she commanded, 'make me a larger box of mirrors. It must be large enough to put a rat in. I want to see what a rat will do!'

Erik obeyed and the rat, like the flying insects, tried to attack its myriad reflections. Sometimes it stopped, confused by which image to attack first. Then it leaped, crashing into the glass and falling back stunned before bracing itself to spring again. Soon its pointed face was a bloody mess. The bloodier it got, the louder Leilah screeched with delight.

Erik anticipated her next request by designing a much larger chamber of mirrors. It was ten feet in height and twenty in diameter. Hexagonal and lined with mirrors from floor to roof. As a refinement, each angle was fitted with a tall three-sided, revolving drum which could be turned from the outside. Each face of the drum was painted with a different motif so that the theme of the reflection could be changed at will by the observer who could see what was going on inside through a spy-hole in the top.

Leilah insisted on being the first to try it. Erik let her in and closed the door. She put one hand to her mouth, she danced, she poked out her pink tongue, revelling in the spectacle of seeing her face, her body, her movements repeated a thousand times. But wonder turned to alarm when Erik turned the drums and she found herself in a jungle, a desert, face to face with an army of crocodiles or snarling tigers. She did not repeat the experiment but immediately saw the potential of her reflecting machine as a form of torture. She commanded slaves and convicted criminals to be brought. Through the spy-hole, she watched them over a period of hours, then days, slowly grow disoriented before being driven mad by thirst in a desert or losing their reason a trackless jungle where they felt hunted by wolves and lions. It amused her vastly. She never wearied of it. She stopped plaguing Erik. But she rewarded him generously. She also told Osman Oullah of the pleasure she took in her new toy and he, also glad to be less often the object of her incessant attentions, exceeded her in generosity.

When his new whispering palace was ready, the Sultan-Governor summoned Erik and put to him a delicate question: what should his new palace be called? He himself thought that, like the Shah's Golestan Palace in Teheran, his own gardens were full of the finest roses and now had a hall ot mirrors the equal of the Shah's *Talar Aineh*, so that 'The Rosy House of Sari' would be suitable. Erik replied that since the palace was to be a place where his Excellency would reign over a court where time would pass free of care and every moment would be filled with delight, he suggested that 'Rosy Hours' would be appropriate. The Sultan said the name was original, distinctive and so the matter was settled.

That same night, the daroga came quietly to Erik's quarters to inform him that his Excellency had just given him the order, in his capacity of chief magistrate of Mazanderan, to execute every last slave who had helped to build his new palace. If even one was allowed to live, the secret purpose of its construction would leak out and its value to the Sultan lost.

'True,' said Erik coolly.

'But does not the thought of the slaughter of three or four hundred men …'

'Nearer four than three.'

'… offend you?'

'Offend me? I am not even surprised. I have very low expectations of your countrymen, daroga. Mazanderan is medieval. Medieval things are done here. Europe was just as barbaric five centuries ago. But Europe has used the intervening time learning how to be civilised. Your people have not.'

The Persian stared at him.

'If I were to worry about such things,' Erik went on, 'I would be more offended by the fate of Abani.'

'Abani?'

'My Nubian. He once saved my life and has been very useful to me. Some fool of a guard stuck a spear into him this morning. God knows why. Perhaps one of my enemies paid him to do it. Perhaps it was a mistake or just stupidity. But the reason is unimportant. Only the fact that it happened matters. But he is dead, I live and tomorrow another sun will rise. Albano is already avenged, the offence is cancelled and the affair forgotten'

The Persian looked at him blankly.

'I had the man brought to me. I boiled the hand that threw the spear in hot oil. He too is now dead.'

The Persian shuddered.

'What is the matter, daroga? For a policeman you have a squeamish stomach. I have cured myself of such weakness. I once lost someone who was my very soul. For a time I was mad. But my madness served no purpose and it nearly killed me, for it robbed me of the will to live. When

I recovered my wits I swore I would care for nothing but myself and follow nature for whom nothing matters except survival. To think only of self is to be strong.'

'So you will not intercede for the slaves who built your palace?'

'Not my palace, the Sultan's. No, I will not. It would serve no purpose, for their fate is written. It is not my business, nor is it yours.'

The Persian left without saying another word, not even to observe that if the four hundred who built the palace of whispers were doomed to die, why should the one man who knew every secret of its construction expect to live?

Soon after this difference of opinion cooled whatever warmth had existed between Erik and the daroga, the Sultan of Mazanderan sent messengers to the great of the land bidding them to Sari to attend the inauguration of his new Palace of the Rosy Hours. The Shah was detained in his capital by affairs of state, but he sent word that his Great Vizir, no less, would represent him and repeated that he had not forgotten the service he the Sultan of Mazanderan had rendered in the matter of Mirza Ahmak. When news of this royal endorsement became known, acceptances were received from the governors of the neighbouring provinces of Teheran and Semna to the south, Gilan in the west and Golestan in the east. They arrived gorgeously arrayed and in grand style, and were greeted by rooftop fanfares which Erik had included in the construction of the Sultan's new palace. The sound of rams' horns emerging from golden domes and cupolas produced the most gratifying effect. After welcoming his guests, Osman Oullah stationed himself at strategic points where, thanks to Erik's architectural ingenuity, he could see without being seen and hear conversations at a distance. In this way he learned that his guests sincerely envied him, his palace and the master-builder who conceived and erected the Rosy Hours of Sari.

'I hear,' said the governor of Semna, 'that the Sultan summoned him from Russia.'

'He is a Christian?' asked the governor of Gilan.

'No, but it was perhaps unwise to rely so much upon a *feringhi*,' said the governor of Golestan. 'Can the works of an infidel ever be consistent with the teachings of the true faith?'

In this way did Osman Oullah learn that success is invariably followed by envy and that the envy breeds trouble. He hoped that such talk would never reach the ears of the Shah.

The judgement of his peers gave him cause for thought, for it confirmed the misgivings he had always felt about his Wizard. His Grand Muphti had voiced similar concerns on several occasions and Osman Oullah had a vague sense that there was something diabolical about everything the wizard did. But he had another reason for his growing hostility to his court Magician. If the man had built a whispering palace for him, might he not be lured away and build another for a different paymaster? It was a possibility not to be tolerated.

He summoned the daroga and instructed him to add the Wizard's name to the list of those who had to be executed.

The daroga called on Erik and informed him of their Master's intentions.

'You must get out of Mazanderan at once,' he said.

Erik thought of his amphora. It was not yet full.

'I'm sure I could devise some new toy for Leilah. She would intercede for me. She is good at pestering.'

'Too late for that,' said the daroga. 'There is no time. The Sultan's mind is made up. He has decided that only your death will guarantee that he will remain the sole and exclusive lord of such a palace of marvels as you have built for him.'

'More can be done with his gardens,' said Erik. 'When I tell him of the ideas for enchanted grottoes and fountains...'

'You will never see Osman Oullah again. My orders are to arrest you tonight, when the heat has gone out of the day. You will be executed at once. Delay and you will surely die. You must leave within the hour.'

It was an ultimatum, Erik listened carefully to what the Persian proposed. Dressed in the plain robes of a merchant, he would proceed to the west gate of the city, taking only those possessions which would fit into a small knapsack. Once through the gate, he would find a horse waiting. The daroga thought that he should travel west, to Constantinople, for he would not be safe anywhere in Persia. Meanwhile, the daroga would dress the corpse of a suitably sized slave in Erik's clothes and throw it into the Caspian Sea. Erik was dark of skin and could easily pass for a Turcoman. When the body was recovered, all would see with relief that not even a master of marvels like the Wizard of Nizhny-Novgorod was capable of cheating his destiny.

And so it would be done.

Yet Erik suspected that there was more to his precipitous flight than met the eye. Why should the daroga put himself in danger by helping a *feringhi* to escape the wrath of his Sultan? It could hardly be friendship, because the man disliked him. Perhaps it was gratitude or at least a sense of obligation? After all, Erik had once saved his neck. Or was the amphora not a more likely motive? That was it! The daroga, who seemed so upright, was no different from the rest of his thieving, lying brethren. Otherwise, why was not he allowed to take of his possessions only what he could carry?

He would go to see the Sultan. He clapped his hands for a servant to dress him. No one came. He called. There was no answer. Erik knew it was the way. When a member of the Sultan's entourage fell from grace, the news ran through the court faster than the dust of a storm. His friends vanished and his servants left him. At least one thing was certain: the Persian had told him no lies. But that did not mean the man could be allowed to benefit from Erik's downfall. He donned the merchant's robes and filled his pockets and a large knapsack with gold *tomauns* and gems worth half a king's ransom. Then he hurried to the west gate where he found a horse saddled and waiting.

He rode in long stages west then north to Batumi on the Black Sea where he charted a small fishing boat and made for Constantinople.

The journey by land and sea was long and tedious but it provided time for reflection.

Since leaving France for the Orient on the *Espérance*, he had lived several lifetimes and the experience, he knew, had poisoned him. His expectations of life and human nature were now so low that he was at ease nowhere and trusted no one. He accepted his hideous ugliness with resignation: it was his destiny. He could escape it only by shunning men and avoiding women, especially women, for they had the power to unman him and slip through the chinks in his armour.

But while life was easier when spent alone, solitude was unbearable. He could insulate himself against his feelings and the feelings of others, but loneliness was an enemy. The best he could hope for was to be anonymous, a wave among the multitudinous waves on the vast human ocean. Still, there was always money, and he had money, a large satchel full of golden coins and diamonds. He knew that money could not buy happiness or even peace of mind, but it solved the problems that money can solve. It is a refuge, protection, a place of safety. And acquiring it occupied time interestingly. And chasing money would mean that he could not cut himself off, be a hermit in a wilderness. The pursuit of wealth required him to go among men and be involved in their dealings. It would not make him a full member of the human race but at least he could be lonely on his own terms. The acquisition and enjoyment of money would therefore be his new purpose.

He also knew that he was weary of the Orient and of living with men who spoke the truth only when it was expedient or profitable. Yet he found that the Ottoman capital was very different from primitive Kabul and provincial Sari. Here, at the end of the reign of Sultan Abdulmecid, Constantinople was turning away from Persia and the Orient and looking more and more to the west and especially to the modernising influence of France. He heard French spoken all around him and the place had a cosmopolitan feel to it.

Sitting in a café enjoying strong, sweet coffee and a narguilhe, he observed the endless tide of humanity flow through the streets: porters bent under their loads, Persians in astrakhan hats, Little Sisters of the Poor flapping in their habits, the stately progress of a harem coach closed like a hearse, European businessmen in trousers and frock-coats, Syrians, Bulgarians, gesticulating Greeks and hooked-nosed Armenians. Erik moved among them without hesitation for he had grown accustomed to the oriental acceptance of physical deformity, for it was common enough. Besides, he had perfected techniques which disguised his hideousness. When he passed through crowded streets now he scarcely rated a second glance so effective were the fards, the putty nose, the false beard and moustache and green eyeglasses.

But however much more at ease he felt in cosmopolitan Constantinople and however numerous the opportunities for enrichment there, he decided that his time in the Orient was at an end. He was in a position to begin a new life in Europe and in style, for he was not a poor man. Money would come in useful for settling certain pieces of business he had in France, business of the unfinished kind.

Chapter 14

On a warm summer morning at the height of France's Second Empire, a man of above average height and striking appearance walked through the great west door of Rouen cathedral. He wore a sober frock-coat, less fitted at the waist than was still the fashion in the provincial Norman capital, pale grey trousers, highly polished shoes and a tall stove-pipe-hat. He was bearded and carried his silver-topped cane with a flourish. A pair of green eyeglasses sat high on the bridge of his nose which was hidden by a shaped leather patch. He paused for a moment and looked down all the length of the nave at the high altar. He lingered at the ornate marble tomb of Louis de Brézé, absorbed by the face of the recumbent figure. Its features were twisted into a ghastly rictus, as though the sculptor had caught the final convulsive moment of death itself. Then without warning, he turned on his heel and left. As he emerged into the sunlight, he saw a boy of ten or twelve. The boy held out a ragged cap. The man in the green eyeglasses spoke briefly to him and put a golden *louis* into the cap before going about his business. The boy stared at the coins in disbelief, then ran off.

*

At his hotel the traveller had been told that Maître Gobert was to be found near the rue du Change, in the warren of dark streets behind the Cathedral. His office was on the first floor of a tall, narrow building in a street where, the traveller discovered, the sun never shone. He did not remove his green eyeglasses, though it was dark inside. He climbed the stairs and, on reaching the top, found his way barred by a scuffed door on which was written in faded lettering: 'Maître Georges Gobert, Attorney-at-Law'. He knocked and entered without waiting for a reply. A clerk with a drooping moustache and a central parting which bisected the top of his scalp looked up from the document he was copying.

'I wish to see Maître Gobert,' said the stranger.

'I'm afraid—'

'Today,' said the stranger. 'Now.'

Intimidated, the clerk stood up, wiped his ink-stained hands on his jacket and crossed to another door. He knocked timidly and went inside. After a moment, he emerged.

'Maître Gobert will see you, sir.'

Lawyer Gobert was now about sixty years of age but Erik would have known him anywhere. His hair had thinned and was combed forward to cover his baldness; his chin was sunk in a high collar designed to hide a scrawny neck. But spite and malice were too deeply etched in the lines of his face to be concealed. His desk was littered with papers. The air hung heavily with the smell of dust, brandy fumes and failure.

'Please be seated,' he said in a thick voice.

Erik sat down on a straight-backed chair and rested both hands on his perpendicular cane.

'I am trying to locate a missing person,' he said. 'A document has come into my possession mentioning your name in connection with this person.'

'What document?' asked Gobert suspiciously.

'Please do not concern yourself with the document. The name of the person I am looking for is Gustave Dondedieu.'

If Gobert was surprised he did not show it.

'You may have known him as Gustave Flon,' the visitor continued, 'though that was not his real name.'

Gobert maintained his impassive silence.

'He was also known as Jean Dartigoyte. He must now be in his twenties by now.'

'I cannot recollect anyone with so many names. The document you spoke of is mistaken. I know of no such person. You have been misled.'

'I am sorry to hear it,' said Erik, with a shrug, 'for there is a sum of money due to the young man.'

'Money?' said Gobert.

'A legacy.'

'Ah,' said Gobert sitting up as though he were a becalmed yacht and the mention of money a puff of wind in his sail. 'My memory is not what it was. Perhaps if I looked through my papers I might find that I or my predecessor had some dealings concerning this Flon or Dondedieu or Dartigoyte. Come back tomorrow, Monsieur…?'

'Verhoven.'

'... Monsieur Verhoven, I might have news for you.'

Erik stood, expressed his thanks and left. Once in the street, he entered a café across the street from Gobert's door. He had not been there five minutes when he saw Gobert, wearing hat and coat, emerge from the tall, narrow building and scurry up the street. Erik followed at a distance.

The lawyer headed towards the river through the maze of dark streets. Five minutes later, he took a key from his pocket and let himself into a house with a small garden in the impasse Bossuet. Both house and garden had seen better days. It was a far cry from the handsome villa standing in well-tended grounds which Erik remembered from the time of his belated baptism. Gobert had clearly fallen on hard times. The hotel porter had repeated what he claimed was common knowledge: that his downfall was his own doing, the result of some scandal caused by his incompetence which had been hushed up. Thirty minutes later, the lawyer reappeared at the door and returned to his office.

Erik spent the rest of the day at his bank. He returned to Gobert's office next morning. It was tidier: and had been cleaned. The lawyer looked neater, more kempt and he was much more helpful. Erik attributed these changes to the influence of his Aunt Marie-Thérèse to whom Gobert had run home to consult. Erik smiled at the thought that she had fallen on hard times.

'I must indeed be getting old, Monsieur Verhoven,' his uncle Gobert began with mock ruefulness. 'Or perhaps I had lunched too well, if you follow me,' he added with a laugh which was intended to indicate manly intimacy.

'You have information for me?'

'I do indeed. It has come back to me. A sad case,' Gobert sighed. 'The individual you seek was born in about 1840 – there is no official record of his birth. It was a difficult delivery and the infant was put out to wet-nurse. The mother survived but lived thereafter as an invalid, eventually dying of the consequences some ten years ago.'

His mother, dead! Laurence-Adelaide!

'And the father?' Erik said coolly, for form's sake, for he knew the man was dead.

'A tragic loss. He was a builder, Prosper Dondedieu, well respected in the town. He died in an unfortunate accident.'

'And the boy?'

'He was retrieved from the ignorant peasant woman who had charge of him. I myself personally brought him from the depths of the country to the family home here in Rouen. The boy was illiterate and wilful. It was decided to board him at a school here but he absconded on the very first day. And that was the last the family saw of him.'

'Did either parent or some other relative, an uncle or an aunt, make any provision for him?'

'He had an aunt, sister to his father, but in view of the boy's disappearance there was nothing she could do. She is still extant. I acted for the family and can assure you no property was left to the orphan who was not named in any will.'

'And what of the Flon connection?'

'Nothing.'

'Or from the Dartigoyte family? Perhaps money was left for the boy from that quarter?'

'I have no knowledge of anyone of that name.'

If Erik had been ignorant of the truth, he would not have known the lawyer was lying, so persuasive was his manner.

'And have you recalled anything which might reveal the boy's present whereabouts?'

'You will appreciate, sir that the fact that he has so many names makes him hard to trace. But one thing at least is clear,' said Maître Gobert with a gleam in his eye. 'Any money intended for Gustave Dondedieu that fails to find its rightful home must revert to his aunt, his only surviving relative.'

'In due course,' agreed Erik.

'Naturally, after due process,' said Gobert. 'And in the meantime I shall institute enquiries of my own. If feel I owe it to the family.'

'I see that what they say about the honesty and integrity of lawyers in the provinces is fully exemplified by you, sir. My card. I look forward to hearing from you.'

As Erik was leaving, he pulled his handkerchief from his coat-tail pocket and wiped his brow, for the sun had beaten down on him through the window during the interview.

When he had gone, lawyer Gobert picked up the square of folded paper which had dropped to the floor as he had taken out his handkerchief.

It was a telegraph message, dated that very morning, giving Verhoven — his card, with a Paris address, described him as a commercial lawyer and broker — advance notice that the Ernst-Martin Mining Company had discovered a mountain of gold in Alaska. It advised him to commend Ernst-Martin stock to his clients before the news was made public on the twenty-third of the month. The share price would rise immediately, perhaps by a factor or ten or twelve. Gobert's hand shook. He asked his clerk the date: it was the twenty-second. Feverishly he scribbled calculations on a sheet of paper. If he mortgaged his house, sold his business, begged and borrowed, he could raise thirty or forty thousand francs. Multiply by ten, by twelve, perhaps fifteen or twenty … There was no time to lose, no time to consult with Marie-Thérèse who, for once, would be forced to admit that he was not the fool she took him for.

He spent the rest of the morning at the bank. He first established that the man Verhoven was what he said he was, a registered commercial lawyer and broker based in Paris. He also learned that Ernst-Martin was a well-known company and was currently heavily involved in exploring for gold in North America. The company was rumoured to be struggling and the market was expecting some kind of announcement. Maître Gobert smiled: he was a man with inside information and not to be fooled by rumours. He realized his assets and then instructed the bank's broker to buy Ernst-Martin stock to the value of the 32,000 francs which he had raised. The figure would have been higher but the speed with which the business had been transacted forced him to accept a lower advance from the bank against the value of his properties than he had hoped for.

What pleased him even more than his astuteness was the thought that Madame Gobert would never be able to sneer at him again.

*

After leaving Gobert to his calculations, Erik sat down at the same table in the same café with the clear view of the lawyer's door. He remained there for an hour or so. He was happy with his morning's work. Yet his enjoyment was clouded by the thought of his mother. He was not surprised, given her poor state of health, to learn that she was dead. Yet he had been more affected by the news than he had anticipated. He had not loved her as he loved Françoise, nor in the way he had adored that other — no, do not think of her! Never think of her! Married at an early age no doubt, to a cruel man — this for sure — and then to have lived under the thumb of a domineering sister-in-law, it was no wonder that she had turned against him as someone to blame for her sufferings. She had not been kind but she had given him life and in return he, though by no fault of his own, had condemned her to a living death. But had she not done as much for him? He had not asked to be born! And when she could have shown him a mother's kindness, she had with undisguised distaste handed him his first mask to cover his shame. Still, he felt guilt for what he had done to her — but no more tenderness than she had ever felt for him.

He paid the waiter and, to shake off his gloom, strolled through the poor parts of the town where he had been a boy. Much was unchanged and he recognised streets where he had begged and doorways in which he had slept. He paused outside the building which had housed the Académie Gortas. It was still a school but it now had a different name, though it still looked grim and was clearly still committed to making boys miserable. He spent the rest of the day touring the country roundabout, trying to trace Françoise. He moved from one parish to the next where he asked priests and sextons for permission to consult their registers. There was no indication that she had married. At the town hall, he looked for the name Dartigoyte in the electoral rolls where, though as a woman she was ineligible to vote, he thought he might find traces of the family name. Again, he drew a blank, though an elderly clerk did recall that some years previously a person of that name — 'interesting name, pre-Norman I should say' — had been involved in the sale of land to the municipality. If Monsieur would care to return the following day, perhaps there would be news.

Next morning, he called at the town hall only to be disappointed: the clerk's memory had misled him. At his bank, he confirmed that his instruction of the previous day had been carried out. Then he made his way to the house in the impasse Bossuet. As he entered through the gate, he removed his eyeglasses and false beard and put them in his hat which he held in his hand. He rang the bell. His aunt, who employed no servants, opened the door herself.

Time had not been kind to her. Her graceless body had grown thinner and even more angular and her face was as brown and wizened as a forgotten apple. The dress which had once been black had turned rusty with age. But she did not flinch when she saw him.

'State your business,' she barked.

'Your welcome, aunt, is as cool as I expected.'

'You are no nephew of mine. I cannot think how you dare show what passes for a face in broad daylight. What do you want here?'

'Let me in, aunt. What would the neighbours say if they saw you speaking to a hobgoblin.'

When she hesitated, he barked, 'Let me in, I said! I will not be denied!'

She led him into a down-at-heel drawing room.

There was no fire in the hearth. Erik was not invited to sit.

'Why are you here? What do you want?' snapped Mme Gobert, folding her arms defiantly

'Only what is mine.'

'And what is that, pray?'

'Principally, my late mother's effects.'

'Effects?' exclaimed Marie-Thérèse with a sneer. 'My sister-in-law left a few sticks of furniture which were vulgar even when she bought them all those years ago, when Louis-Philippe was on the throne. I regret the old King's passing but not the taste of his reign. I would not call my sister-in-law's pieces 'effects': mistakes is a better word. The woman had no taste. Her weakness was for mahogany, overstuffed sofas, floral wall-hangings, and sentimental pictures worth nothing. I tried to sell them but the dealers laughed in my face.'

'Nevertheless, I have come for them.'

'Then you have wasted a journey. Even if you offered a king's ransom, I would not sell them to you!'

Erik looked around the room which was indeed crowded with outmoded Louis-Philippe furniture. It was, as his aunt had said, ugly. But that hardly mattered: it had been *hers*, a link with a time before the world had made him cruel and heartless.

'We shall see what my uncle Gobert has to say.'

'Gobert is a fool ...'

She was interrupted by the arrival of her husband who entered the house crying:

'We are ruined, Madame Gobert! Ruined!'

He flung the door open and stopped dead in his tracks.

'What's this? What business does this homunculus ...'

He stopped when he recognised the silver-topped cane. The words died in his throat and his mouth fell open.

'Ruined?' shrieked Marie-Thérèse. 'What are you talking about? How could we be more ruined than we are already?'

'There is no mountain!'

'What mountain? What have we to do with mountains?'

'The mountain of gold! It was just a rumour!'

'Don't be ridiculous!'

'And Ernst-Martin has gone to the wall! And us with it! It was to be a surprise! Our troubles would be over and we should be restored to our former rank in society ... I tell you, Madame, we are ruined and it is the fault of this ... this ... Verhoven and his damned telegraph!'

'What nonsense is this? This is no Verhoven. Do you not recognise my brother's brat? You must: there cannot be two like him in the world!'

Gobert collapsed into a chair, produced a grubby handkerchief and wiped his brow with it.

'I think I see what has happened, aunt,' said Erik coolly. 'When I was in uncle Gobert's office yesterday, I must have dropped a note. I receive many such notes, nearly all of them offering me ways of making a fortune. I almost invariably ignore them. This one claimed a certain mining company, widely known to be in difficulties, had discovered rich gold deposits in Canada, a proposition so gross that instead of reassuring the market it has brought about the company's collapse. I doubt investors will get five cents in the franc. Did you act on the advice in the note, uncle?'

Gobert nodded dumbly.

'How much?' demanded Marie-Thérèse.

'Thirty thousand.'

'*How much*?' she screeched. 'All we had left in the world?'

'Dear me,' said Erik. 'This is what comes of reading other people's letters.'

'Gobert you are a fool. I always knew it and now you have proved it.'

'One other thing,' Erik went on before she could develop her theme. 'I did not come to Rouen simply to stir old memories, for none of my memories of this place are pleasant. I came looking for investment opportunities. I instructed my bank here concerning the kind of assets I wished to acquire and when I called this morning I discovered that I am now the owner of uncle Gobert's practice and of this house and all its contents. I am here merely to arrange for the removal of my mother's effects which, aunt, are not yours to withhold. The rest will be sold, with the house, by public auction. I want you out of this place today. You have until four o'clock to vacate the premises. I bid you good day.'

Mme Gobert, white with fury, looked at him with hate.

'You would throw your only surviving relative into the street?' she cried. 'Have you no shame? You have cheated us out of the little we have and will cast us into the gutter?'

'No, I have no shame, aunt, nor should you expect me to. Surely you know that Dondedieu blood is much thinner than water. Besides, business is business. Did I force uncle Gobert to throw his money away? I cheated nobody. Ah, I think I hear the removals men now.'

From his hat he took his eyeglasses and false beard.

'But where will we go?' wailed Gobert.

Mme Gobert, her face stony with loathing, turned her back on her husband and, looking Erik directly in the eye, said, 'You do not take after your mother, who never said boo to a goose. You are a true Dondedieu.'

It was as much in the way of family feeling she would ever show him.

As she turned her back on him, Erik added:

'But there is one thing you still have that I want. Give it to me and I will return your property so that you can continue your mean, miserable lives without interruption.'

'What is this thing?' Marie-Thérèse asked.

'When I was eleven, Uncle Gobert fetched me from the place in the country where I had been raised. Tell me where that place is and you shall be restored to your house and livelihood. Moreover, I will pay you handsomely for my mother's effects. Shall we say two thousand francs?'

'Five,' said Marie-Thérèse before her husband could open his mouth.

Erik laughed, admiring her nerve.

'Done!' he said.

His aunt did not look pleased. She was cursing herself for not asking for more.

*

Erik hired a carriage and set off at once. The road to Françoise led him through Mourthe. In the middle of the town, he rapped for the driver to halt. The Charity School was still there, still no doubt making the sons of the deserving poor wretched. The cruel face of M. Mardy swam before his eyes, and he felt Bastingard's breath on the back of his neck. He allowed himself a grim smile. He would be back for them. But now, he had a more important part of his past to revisit.

'Drive on,' he ordered.

They left the town and soon were travelling along a straight road which ran through flat countryside unfamiliar to him. This did not surprise him, for he had never strayed far along the road from Françoise's cottage. But as the carriage rattled across a wooden bridge over a stream, he wondered if it was the one in which Isidore had shown him his face on the day he had stolen his lucky stone and killed his dog with his own a broken pen-knife. He felt the hurt as intensely as he had when he'd found the poor creature's corpse in his secret hideaway.

He was less than a quarter of a mile from the cottage where he had lived for ten years before he knew for sure where he was by the outline of a hill where he had roamed. There was a tree he remembered, though it was larger now, then a curve of the road and the low stone wall he used to sit on …

He was still a hundred yards from the cottage when he told the driver to halt. He got out and looked wonderingly around him. He had a strange sensation that the place had been asleep ever since he had been away and that its sleeping life had been awakened by his return. He felt a strange exultation at the sight of familiar, forgotten things. The outside of the cottage, the neat curtains at the windows, the gate and the wooden fence had not changed. But the garden looked neglected. He walked to the door which stood open.

'Is there anyone at home?' he called.

Inside the room someone stirred. Erik braced himself for the reunion with Françoise. He had a sudden thought: what if she no longer lived there or had changed or was dead? No place really sleeps when people move away and wakes again when they return, for nothing ever stands still. Perhaps Françoise had married and gone away! From the dark interior emerged a person he did not recognise at first. But as she came into the light, there was no mistaking Huguette, Françoise's good friend. She looked at him. Jean did not speak but removed his disguise, for if there was one place on earth where he did not need it, it was here.

'For heaven's sake, look who it is!' she cried in surprise — pleased surprise, not horror or disgust — and turning she called into the house. 'Françoise, here's a visitor for you.' Then beckoning Erik to follow her, she led the way into the little sitting room.

Françoise was lying in a bed which had been brought downstairs for her. She looked much older than her years. Erik had never thought about her age but now he realised that she must only be in her forties. She was thinner, painfully so. Her shoulders looked pinched and her hands seemed too large for the wrists that supported them. Her hair had lost its colour and her face was lined and pale. But it lit up when she saw him.

'Jean! Is it really you?' she said in a weak voice. 'Come here and let me see you.'

She ran a motherly eye over him and approved.

'My, what a fine gentleman you've become.'

She told him her father's inn had been stranded when a new, faster road had taken the traffic three miles to the west of it. It had not burned down. It had died of loneliness. Her father had grown old and on his death had left it to her. She had sold it to a seed merchant who used it for storage. The price he gave her was insufficient to attract a husband and she had gone on living alone in the cottage, supplementing the dwindling sale money with produce from her kitchen garden. It had been a hard life and Erik saw that it had ruined her health.

'You are ill,' he said. 'I shall bring doctors and they will make you well again …'

'We shall see,' Françoise replied and then she asked to hear what had happened to him after the lawyer had come to take him away all those years before.

So Erik told her how he had run away from his mother and the Goberts and travelled with a circus and about some of his adventures in the Orient. He omitted the horrors he had seen and the ordeals he had undergone.

Later, she slept and Huguette told him that there was no hope: Françoise was too far gone.

'She don't eat and when she coughs there's blood. Pink and frothy it is, and her cheeks glow. It's the consumption, a sneaky disease, it creeps up on you when you're not looking. That's why she sent little Léah away.'

He called the driver and gave him a list of medicines and other articles to buy in Mourthe. He was also to bring back a doctor. Then he asked Huguette who little Léah was.

'An orphan girl. Such a sweet child. Françoise took her in when she was left an orphan. Her mother wasn't married and her family wouldn't have anything to do with her. They were all for sending the baby to the nuns. The father ran off too and no one wanted her. So Françoise said she would take her in.'

'It wasn't the first time she'd done it,' said Erik.

'True,' said Huguette with a sigh. 'But it looks like it will be the last,'

The driver brought the doctor back with him. He confirmed Huguette's gloomy prediction.

'She's too far gone,' he told Erik. 'There's nothing I can do for her.'

Erik stayed in the cottage and nursed Françoise until she died. He saw that she was given a proper funeral. Only he and Huguette were present.

But those last days were not unhappy. Huguette brought little Léah to see her adoptive mother from time to time. She was a year and a half old, a fair-haired, a sweet-natured child who smiled at Jean, as unaffected by his looks as Françoise and Huguette had been. Despite the circumstances, Erik would later look back on those weeks as one of the happiest times of his life.

When Françoise asked him to adopt the child and see that she was properly brought up he readily agreed. He could hardly refuse this last request of a dying woman who had done for him what no one else in the world had done: she had taught him the meaning of love. He duly took out papers and officially adopted Léah. He never regarded his duty as a burden. On the contrary, the child delighted him. She was quick and curious and eager and her smile came with dimples.

After the funeral, he lived on at the cottage with Huguette and Léah for a while, revelling in the peace of the place. Every day was a new delight and thoughts of Monsieur Mardy and Bastingard and all those who had persecuted his ugliness receded. What purpose was served by revisiting the past and dwelling on memories of things which could not be undone? He realised that he had been poisoned by misery: self-commiseration had become his only pleasure. He could not forgive nor would he forget. But to waste energy in futile efforts to punish old enemies was to make them live again and let them back into his life. Who would choose to eat gall when a smile from Léah would lighten the darkest day?

So Erik set aside his plans for revenge, left the past to itself and looked to the future. He decided that his next step would be to begin a new life in Paris. But he would not do it alone. He could not be parted from Léah. He unburdened himself to Huguette and said that he was incapable of raising a child by himself. Would she come with him to Paris and look after Léah?

Huguette hesitated. She was frightened by the very thought of Paris. Besides, she was walking out with someone and would have to ask his opinion. The news came as a surprise to Erik.

'Who is the fortunate man?'

'Why, you should know him very well,' said Huguette. 'It's Hippolyte, the man who drives your coach. I shall soon be Madame Folgat. He is a good man, Jean.'

Erik laughed out loud.

'Capital, Huguette! You shall marry your Hippolyte and you will all come to live with me in Paris!'

And so it was arranged.

Chapter 15

When Napoleon III, Emperor of France, decided that Paris, with its still medieval narrow streets and crumbling buildings, was not a fitting advertisement for his 'new' France, he gave Baron Haussmann, the city's Prefect, the task of creating a modern city with wide boulevards, straight avenues and handsome architecture in a style so distinctive that it would startle the world and serve as a fitting monument to his reign. Slums were cleared and light was allowed to shine into the city's heart. A high priority was given to replacing the old Opera House in the rue Lepeletier. It had opened its doors in 1821, long before opera had become the century's most popular form of theatre. Artists deserved less cramped quarters and patrons more elegant surroundings. A prize was offered for the best design. It was won by Charles Garnier, aged just 35. He set to work at once.

A site west of the rue de Richelieu was cleared and work had begun excavating it to a considerable depth, depth being needed to accommodate the unusually large stage which would need scenery fifty feet high to be stored or raised and lowered as required. Moreover, a series of cellars at various levels were needed to house dressing rooms, stage properties, offices and the furnaces and fans required to heat and ventilate the auditorium. Foundations of great strength would be required to support the weight of the building, estimated to be some ten thousand tons. Garnier anticipated that he would have a problem with water, for it was common knowledge that beneath the sandy site ran a subterranean tributary of the Seine which had long since been built over. Installing secure foundations would be his first priority.

'My immediate concern,' he said in his hoarse voice to the muffled figure in green eyeglasses who sat on the opposite side of his desk, 'is that I do not know how much of a problem even a small lake of water will be.'

He paused while he perused a letter on his desk.

'You say in your application, Monsieur Verhoven,' he went on, 'that you have a wide experience of design and construction. But I note that you have no formal qualifications.'

'True, Monsieur. But I have built palaces for Sultans in the Orient …'

'I suspect you had no flooded excavations to contend with in the desert,' said Garnier drily. He had begun the process of recruiting firms of builders, masons, stone-dressers, blacksmiths, plumbers, roofers, joiners, and gas engineers to whom the work of construction would be contracted. Today he was interviewing applicants for the first stage of the operation.

'Since I have seen none of your work, perhaps you would be so good as to give me the benefit of your experience and tell me exactly how you would lay a foundation for a monumental building in waterlogged sandy soil.'

'May I assume that the lake you mention is not a place where water simply collects but has an inlet and outlet which keeps the level more or less stable?'

'Yes.'

Verhoven concentrated on the problem. As Garnier watched, he had a sense of the man's strangeness. It was not simply his appearance, which seemed specifically designed to conceal his identity, but his intensity. Garnier felt it like a physical power. Finally Verhoven began to speak. His voice was calm, precise and unhurried.

'Can the river be stopped or diverted?'

'Out of the question,' growled Garnier impatiently.

'Once the work of excavation has been completed, I should ring the area beneath the proposed building with a double row of wooden piles 20 feet long and about two yards apart driven down until only about eighteen inches showed above the level of the lake which would collect around it. Between this double row of piles, I would pour hydraulic concrete so that the stream would flow round my water-tight wall. The area inside the ring would then be drained and dried out and the concrete ring itself would serve as a footing for the foundations... It would be a costly undertaking.'

'Indeed it would,' said Garnier, 'and a lengthy one.'

He was impressed. The man's ideas were simple and elegant.

'I do believe we are thinking along the same lines, Monsieur Verhoven. Have you the resources, by which I mean the funds, the men, the equipment, to undertake such a task?'

'No, but I doubt if there is any single company in Paris that does. I could find suitable contractors.'

Garnier nodded. He asked further questions, for form's sake rather than to confirm his first impression. Long before he brought the interview of a close, he had made up his mind.

*

When Erik returned to France from Constantinople, he had lived in Paris in a series of hotels. He had deposited the contents of his satchel with a bank, opened an account to draw on for his daily needs and explored the capital he was visiting for the first time. He had been completely won over by the sophistication of its elegant *quartiers* which surpassed in splendour anything he had seen in the Orient. But he was also shocked by the condition of the poor. In time his experiences of Parisian life led him to the view that the wealthy classes were altogether less admirable than their surroundings and that the urban poor were often ignorant and mindlessly violent.

It was in this mood that he had travelled to Rouen to settle old scores. His routing of the Goberts was exhilarating but the satisfaction it gave him was short-lived. His reunion with Françoise and his encounter with Léah blunted his misanthropy and had more lasting effects. In the country, far from the physical and moral squalor of the metropolis, he thawed. His thoughts even led him to consider a less nomadic form of existence. His work for Garnier meant that he would have to live near the site of the new Opera House for some time. But given what he had seen of Paris, he had little enthusiasm for living there.

After some searching, he found a property at Asnières on the northern outskirts. It stood in its own grounds inside a high wall. He brought Léah, Huguette and her new husband Hippolyte to live with him. The arrangement was a success from the start. Huguette acted as housekeeper and looked after Léah while Hippolyte took on the duties of steward and also served as his coachman, leaving Erik free to concentrate on the commission he had been given by Garnier. It was the nearest thing to a regular, family life Erik had ever known and it confirmed the great change in him that had begun when he had been reunited with Françoise.

Aunt Gobert had been wrong: there was more to him than unforgiving Dondedieu blood. Released from the prison of his solitude and his obsession with the wrongs he had suffered, he luxuriated in human warmth. Léah was its centre, its heart. She was a constant source of delight and he doted on her.

He loved her curls, her smile, the things she said. But mostly he loved her because she was not afraid of him, not afraid of anything, because she was blind to his fixed, skeletal grin and burning eyes and pallid, grey skin. One day Erik realised that he was happy.

Each day Hippolyte drove him to the site of the new Opera and drove him back each evening. His days were spent directing his workmen and discussing progress with the other contractors who laboured together under the stern eye of Garnier. An immense hole had appeared where once there had been narrow streets. Then piles were driven into its floor, the hydraulic cement was poured, eight steam pumps emptied out the trapped water and the floor was laid with concrete and made water-tight with bitumen boiled in large cauldrons. Léah was four when the substructure was complete and Erik's participation in the work ended. But he continued to be a familiar figure at the site where he followed successive phases of the construction with interest.

His house at Asnières was a fortress but not a separate planet. Though Erik might choose to ignore his surroundings, his neighbours were only too curious about the mysterious stranger who had settled in their midst. Some had heard on good authority that he was foreign royalty in exile, a Russian prince perhaps or a nabab from India. Others thought he was blind: why else would he wear green eyeglasses? But all agreed he must be rich and rich men always attract the attention of robbers.

One night an attempt was made to burgle the house. The thieves scaled the walls but failed to break in. The damage was slight, being confined to a few scarred shutters. But the incident made Erik feel vulnerable. He was concerned for the safety of Léah and the rest of what he now thought of as his family. But he worried too about his moveable goods on which their style of life depended. He found six trusty men and paid them to guard his family and property.

He did not trust banks and on moving to Asnières had transferred his satchel to a secure room in his new house. The failed burglary made him realise that this arrangement was far from satisfactory and he bent his mind to devising another.

One night, when Paris slept, he drove with Hippolyte to the Opera. The site was deserted except for a watchman who knew them and allowed them inside. They repeated the visit each night for a week, the time it took for Erik to remove a stone-block from the wall of the lowest cellar and replace it with a pivot-mounted trapdoor which gave him access to the empty chamber inside the ring of hydraulic cement beneath. Then he removed the chest of precious stones from the secure room in his house, deposited it in the depths of the Opera and closed the secret door behind him.

Over the next months, there were several other attempts to break in. Though they were foiled by the guards he posted, Erik's fears for his household increased. The sealed chamber beneath the Opera House grew in his mind as the ultimate place of safety where, in an emergency, they would be safe from the depredations of lawless men. There was nowhere more isolated, so secret, so secure. In time, Garnier's contractors completed an inspection tunnel which had an entrance in the rue Scribe, on the western side of the building, and. led down to the underground lake surrounding the foundations. Erik decided that the sealed space inside should be more than a store-room for his gems.

Working at night with Hippolyte's help, he replaced a section of the inner wall above the water level with a swivelling trap door. Then he breached the outer shell with a second trap which opened by means of two levers, one on the inside, the other on the lake side. By using the entrance in the rue Scribe and rowing across the lake to his new double-door, he could now circumvent watchmen by night and workmen by day and was thus free to come and go as he pleased. He began to make the space habitable by ferrying furniture and other necessities to what he began to think of as a refuge in case of an emergency. Gradually he regained his peace of mind and he devoted more and more time to Léah's education.

She was a quick learner, with particular gifts for languages and music. He took her the great Paris International Exhibition. She loved the bright colours and the laughing crowds. Why, it was like Aladdin's Cave, full of surprises. She watched open-mouthed as air-balloons named *Géant* and *Céleste* carried passengers on flights over the exhibition park.

Erik delighted in her and her ways but Huguette, less enthusiastic, finally brought herself to speak out.

'It's not right, Monsieur Jean,' she said, 'it's not good for her to be so educated so young. Living here, never going out, why you've turned her into a young lady without ever having let her be a little girl. There's more to raising children than teaching them to be clever. Girls her age shouldn't always have their noses in a book. She's got to learn how to get on with children her own age who won't always think the way she does or do what she wants them to do. She needs to be contradicted, she's got to learn that she's not best at everything and can't always have her own way. You've got to start telling her "no".'

'You're right, Huguette. I've been foolish. I was a solitary child myself and it never crossed my mind ... You think we should have children from the town to come here and play?'

'Oh it's far too late for that, Monsieur Jean. It would never do. She's a young lady now and needs to be with other children of her own sort.'

'You think shutting her up in a convent would be the answer? You think I should send her away to school?'

The thought of being separated from Léah was so unbearable to both of them, that neither pursued it. But it preyed on Erik's mind until there occurred an event which made such concerns irrelevant.

In July 1870, France went to war with Prussia. Within months, Sedan, the last defence against Bismarck's invading army, was on the point of falling. The mood in Paris had changed from the euphoria of the certain victory over the Germans, which the people had been promised, to anger and then fear at the prospect of defeat. Erik maintained his distance from public affairs and barely kept up with the events reported in the newspapers. But he was not insulated against the new feverish public mood. Rumours spread like wildfire. There were reports that the Prussians had vowed to kill French babies, like Herod of old, that they were just a few miles from the centre of Paris, that they had a new kind of machine-gun which could kill thousands at a time. Spies were found everywhere. Foreigners were attacked by the mob. A sewerman observed disappearing into a manhole in the road had, when he re-emerged, his head blown off by nervous National Guardsmen. And the trouble was not confined to the centre of the city.

One warm night at the start of September, Erik was woken by a voice shouting: 'Fire! Fire!' He could smell smoke and heard running footsteps. He rushed to the open window and saw a glow lighting up the trees and bushes of the gardens. Then there was a thunderous knock at his door and through it Hippolyte urged him to wake up. Erik told him to come in and while he threw on some clothes Hippolyte told him breathlessly, 'The house is on fire, Monsieur Jean. Someone got past the sentries. It's got a terrible hold. Looks like it started in the stables. It's been so dry and there's a wind blowing sparks on to the house itself. It's well alight!'

The firemen had been sent for. Neighbours who had seen the night sky lit up had started arriving, some to look and others to help. Erik raced down the stairs which were lit by angry leaping flames. Once outside, he looked for Léah. He could not see her anywhere. The gardens were full of people. He turned to ask Hippolyte if she was safe, if he'd seen Huguette, but Hippolyte had gone to supervise the fire-fighters who had just arrived. The man next to him turned and horror flooded across his countenance. There had been no time for Erik to hide his bared teeth and those eyes which glowed each side of the nose that was not there, merely two black holes where there should have been nostrils. But there was no time to worry about that now. He ran through the crowds shouting Leah's name while the flames rose higher and higher with a ferocity which made it certain that nothing of the house would remain. Erik wished that he was truly the great Magician of Mazanderan so that he could command the wind to stop and call down a deluge rain to quench the flames. But as he ran, he left terror in his wake, for amid the smoke and glare from the flames, he looked like a gleeful, grinning devil from the lower depths rejoicing in the disaster which had befallen the mysterious stranger who rarely left his house and never did so without his green glasses.

Ignoring the cries of fear and brushing aside the attempts of some to detain this sinister apparition, Erik ran back into the house. The main staircase had started to burn. The wall-hangings were turning brown as though they would burst into flame at any moment. The paint on the pictures hanging on the walls was blistering in the heat. He reached the landing and raced along the corridor to the far end to Léah's room. The door was locked but did not resist his frenzied shoulder charge. The room was burning more fiercely than the corridor and in the light it cast he saw Huguette slumped on the floor. Erik kneeled and shook her. Her mouth and nostrils were black with the smoke she had inhaled and she was already dead. Léah was lying in a nest of bed-linen in which Huguette had wrapped her for safety. Erik seized the water ewer and soaked a blanket which he put over her face and blond hair. Then he gathered her up.

The window offered no way out, for flames from the library below were brushing the panes. Even as Erik looked, one pane cracked, then another, then the whole window blew out. The sudden inrush of air stung the smouldering furniture into vivid, hungry fire. With Léah in his arms, he rushed back along the corridor which was now full of dense, choking smoke. When he reached the landing he saw that the whole staircase was ablaze. Every moment counted. Once the stairs burned away, they would be trapped. Without hesitating, he took them at a run. The first few were strong and bore his weight. But the further he descended, the more fragile they became until he saw that the last few had burned clean through, leaving a dark space. He had no choice but to jump. He landed awkwardly but his momentum kept him upright. With one last effort, he crossed the marble floor, which was littered with fallen, burning timbers, to the door and then he was outside, gulping down fresh, cool, smoke-free air among excited voices.

'He got a little girl out!'

'Get a bucket of water, his clothes is afire!'

'Stand back! Give him air!'

No one recoiled in horror now because Erik's face was blackened, burned, unrecognisable. Among men who also had blackened faces, he did not stand out.

'The little girl's all right! Not even singed!'

Erik sat up. It was true. By wrapping her in bedclothes, Huguette had kept the worst of the fire at bay and the sodden blanket had protected Léah as he had charged along the corridor and down the stairs. A voice at his elbow said:

'What about Huguette, Monsieur Jean?'

His throat too sore to speak, Erik merely shook his head.

'Ah!' said Hippolyte and he turned his head away.

Then another voice, brutal and cruel, said, 'He ain't a hero. He's the pug ugly who started the fire in the first place! I seen him. Give me the shock of my life, he did. He is the ... whatjacallem ... arsonist. I seen him do it!'

The crowd hesitated.

'If you don't believe me,' said the voice, 'take a look at this!'

The owner of the voice was big and the mouth from which it emerged was part hidden by a thick moustache. He seized a bucket of water from a passing firemen and tipped the contents over Erik's head. It washed enough of the smoke-black away to reveal that terrible grinning face.

'There you are! Ever see such a ugly-looking specimen? That there is the face of the arsonist!'

There was a gasp and even strong men took a step back. Now that Erik had been revealed to them in that light, the accusation rang all too true. Here was a monster who looked evil enough for anything. Someone said he'd probably rescued the little girl so he could use her as a sacrifice for some black mass or murder her, drink her blood and eat her heart so that he could live forever! Their mood darkened.

'String him up,' said a voice. 'Save the justices a job!'

But no one wanted to be the first to step forward. Then while the fire continued to consume what was left of the house where he had been happy, Erik stood up slowly and looked calmly at his those who were suddenly his enemies. His eyes burned orange, stoked by his anger at the stupidity of these people, at the mindless destruction that their kind had wrought. His tormentor was right: it was arson and those responsible would pay. He had lost his books, papers and his possessions. They could be replaced. But Huguette was dead, the happiness he had found was going up in smoke and he had been forced into the open where he was a hunted animal at bay.

He bent down, picked up Léah who was frightened by the noise, the angry voices, the heat, the light of the flames, and ran. No one tried to stop him. Once he was clear of the crowd which had been roused by the man with the moustache, no one paid any attention to him. As he reached the gate, Hippolyte emerged from nowhere and fell into step. He said nothing.

Erik led the way down to the river which gleamed dully as it moved silently past the town. There was no one about and no sound here save the call of a hunting owl. When he reached the bank, he laid Léah on the grass verge and left Hippolyte standing protectively over her. He found a large stone and attacked the padlock which secured the iron grill guarding the entrance, at water-level, to a large tunnel. The lock resisted but, such was Erik's rage and frustration, not for long. The clash of rock on metal reverberated and then slowly died away as the iron gate swung open.

The entrance was dimly lit by the light reflected from the river. Erik wrenched an oil lamp from its mooring on the wall and reached for the box of lucifers which was always kept on a ledge under it. He set the lighted lamp on the ground in a yellow pool so bright that it hurt the eyes. Then he went back to Léah and held her close.

'We can't go without Huguette,' said Hippolyte, speaking for the first time. 'I must go back. I'll save her …'

'Come. Old friend,' said Erik gently. 'It's time to leave her. We must go.'

Hippolyte stood stock still for a moment, his face turned towards the glow of the burning house. A tear glinted on his cheek and his lips formed a word: 'Goodbye!' Then he turned and followed Erik who had already entered the tunnel.

A main artery of the Paris sewers on the north side of the river began at the Place de la Concorde and ended nearly four miles away on the bank of the Seine at Asnières. On days when it was open to the public, it was lit by a series of moderator oil lamps like the one Erik had torn from the wall. Paved walkways ran on both sides of the channel and from them tunnels led off to the extensive subways which fed the main watercourse. Holding the lamp aloft with one hand and Léah in the other, Erik led the way.

It took them over an hour to reach the end of the tunnel. There they found their way blocked by another iron grill. Erik gave Léah to Hippolyte to hold and looked around for a tool to smash it open. He found nothing that was fit for his purpose. He entered the first side tunnel he came to and after no more than fifty yards saw an iron ladder fixed into the stone wall which led up to a manhole. He climbed the ladder and carefully lifted the manhole cover an inch, two inches, for he had no wish to have his head blown off. He saw a dimly-lit street lined with dark buildings. There was no sign of life. With a heave of his shoulders, he pushed the metal cover to one side. Then he returned to fetch Hippolyte and Léah. Minutes later, they were outside, walking through the night away from the river towards the site of the Opera on which work had been at a virtual standstill since the start of the War. The exterior walls and roof were complete and the dome rose high above them into the sky..

Erik unlocked the door to the service tunnel in the rue Scribe and, still holding Léah, made straight for the underground lake. The rowing boat was at the small jetty Garnier's men had built for inspection purposes. Hippolyte who had followed unquestioningly looked into the darkness which hid the double shell of the Opera's lowest depths.

'You are right, Monsieur Jean, we'll be safe there' he said.

'Get aboard,' said Erik, 'and hold on to Léah.'

When his passengers were safely in the boat, Erik jumped in after them and with the oar fixed to the stern, propelled them towards the secret door in the outer shell. It yielded to the pressure on the lever. Hippolyte disembarked first. Erik passed Léah to him and then entered the lock himself, closing the trap behind him. He felt in the dark for the lever which opened the second door and stepped into the silent chamber in the bowels of the Opera.

The first lamp he lit did nothing to push back the dense shadows. Though Hippolyte was holding her, Léah began to cry. But as Erik lit more lamps, shapes began to appear, forms which were not strange or unknown to her. Here was a chest which had once stood in the entrance hall of the house at Asnières, there an armchair, a couch, a table which were all familiar and not at all out of place. Léah's stopped crying.

She felt at home.

Chapter 16

The excitement had died down but the smell of smoke still lingered in the air and the great fire remained the main topic of conversation among the drinkers in the Café du Commerce at Asnières. There was a good crowd in, so no one paid particular attention to the man, well-wrapped against the evening chill, who sat alone at a table by the window.

'My nephew's a fireman. According to him, it was deliberate. Arson, he said.'

'The gendarmes were there this afternoon having a good poke round. I saw them. Happened to be passing. It looks fishy to me.'

'Down at the mairie, they're saying they're going to send an inspector from the Prefect's office.'

'They have to do that when there's deaths. No one's seen the master of the house, nor the housekeeper, nor Hippolyte. All missing.'

'They say there was a little girl too.'

'They needn't bother looking for the one who set light to the place,' said a big man with a walrus moustache. 'I could tell them who it was if they only asked. It was the freak.'

'Him you saw with the burning eyes and long fangs and hands like claws?'

'That's him. I keep telling you. I saw him do it. He stuffed kindling in the holes between the firewood stacked against the stable wall. Then he took a handful of straw, put a match to it and up it went.'

'What did he do then?'

The man with the moustache took a pull at his rum, enjoying his moment: 'He sorter cackled and danced while he watched. With that wind, the stables was ablaze in minutes. I never heard horses screaming like that before. It was the smoke. Smoke does that to them. Mad with fear they were. Then sparks set the house alight. Up she went. Whoosh!'

'You're having us on, Auguste. The house was well away before you showed up. I got there before you did. You never saw any such thing. But if you want to point the finger, there's no need to look further than Charlot Bovard. He's had a go at the place more than once but he never got past the shutters. He's out of jail again. They let him out last week. Stands to reason. It was him lit the fire to smoke them out so he could catch them off their guard, get inside and steal what he could get his hands on. But things got out of hand. No, Charlot's your man.'

Then they argued, some saying Charlot was the arsonist, others the freak. Finally they wearied of the subject and got back to the war, for the news was bad. Finally, the landlord pushed his broom about and started closing up. The drinkers drifted away, remembering that they had homes to go to and wives who'd be asking for the wages they'd just spent on rum and absinthe. At the end of the main street, they went their separate ways. The man with the walrus moustache headed towards the river where his shrewish wife and six children lived in a two-roomed boatman's hut.

Suddenly, he couldn't breathe. He clutched his throat and felt a loop of some fine material around his neck, squeezing his adam's apple, closing his air-passages. Within seconds, the blood was pounding in his head which seemed to expand until he thought it would explode. And then the pressure was relaxed and he gulped the night air. The noose tightened again but he could still breathe, with difficulty. He thought he was going to die.

'Where will I find Charlot?' hissed a voice in his ear.

Auguste coughed, his chest heaved. But the noose remained around his neck, holding him up. If it had been removed he would have collapsed.

'Dunno,' he croaked at last.

'That's not the answer I want,' said the voice. 'Try again.'

'Jo-Jo,' said Auguste in a faint whisper.

'The bar by the abattoir?'

Auguste nodded.

'I hope you're right,' said the voice behind his head. 'If not. I'll be back. You know who I am. Don't you?'

Auguste tried to say something but had to settle for a nod of the head.

'I am the face of your worst dreams, the goblin with eyes of fire. Be afraid, Auguste.'

Then the noose was removed and Auguste sagged and fell on the ground.

Chez Jo-Jo was a wineshop on the edge of town, by the river. It stayed open late to cater for the night shift at the municipal slaughterhouse. It was also a notorious hang-out for local criminals. Jo-Jo himself had served five years in the galleys and had no liking for the law. Policemen knew it and gave his bar a wide berth.

It was now around four in the morning. The first of the new day's workers had just begun to arrive for their morning café-calvados. No one afterwards could say exactly when the stranger had arrived. The first they knew of him was when a sharp, impatient voice came from a corner calling for cognac. All eyes turned to look. They saw a muffled figure hunched over his table. It was not easy to tell what size or figure of man he was or what cast of features lurked under his wide-brimmed hat. Jo-Jo brought him a glass of cognac on a tray. His clients watched in silence, waiting to take their lead from him, for Jo-Jo only used a tray for customers he had reason to respect or fear.

The stranger threw a coin on the tray. In the silence, it rang like a tocsin. Jo-Jo picked it up and bit it.

'Don't see many of these in here. I can't accept it. No change,'

'Then keep the change. But bring me the bottle.'

Jo-Jo shrugged, gave a grunt of satisfaction and fetched the bottle. The drinkers at the bar looked at each other with raised eyebrows. One of them emptied his glass and ordered another. He was about thirty with thick curly hair and rough good looks. But his teeth were bad and one cheek was marred by a livid scar.

'Got a better class of customer in tonight, Jo-Jo,' he said loudly. 'Now don't you go putting up your prices or we'll take our business elsewhere.'

His companions sniggered dutifully.

'No you won't,' said Jo-Jo, relighting his pipe. 'Where else would you go, Charlot. Who but me would let you prop up a bar?'

But Charlot gave Jo-Jo a wink, motioned imperceptibly to the man at the corner table and licked his lips. Jo-Jo took his meaning.

The stranger also emptied his glass and refilled it. From his pocket, he took a wallet and began counting its contents. The company could not believe their eyes. Who in his right mind would walk into a notorious thieves' den, throw money around and wave banknotes for all to see?

Leaving the bottle half-empty, the stranger eventually got up and, without a word, walked out through the door. Jo-Jo called after him: '*Merci*, Monsieur! Call again sometime!'

When the laughter had subsided, Charlot drained his glass and fetched the bottle the stranger had left.

'Can't let this go to waste, lads. Come on, drink up. Jo-Jo don't mind, do you Jo-Jo?'

Charlot filled glasses, his own first. When he'd emptied it, he reached for his hat and said he'd just remembered a piece of business he needed to attend to. No one was fooled.

Outside, the new day was beginning to flood the black sky. Charlot looked round him and saw the well-wrapped cognac-drinker heading into the town along the river-bank. He set off in pursuit.

From time to time, his quarry stopped as if looking for directions. Charlot quickly caught up with him but just as he had him in his sights, the man disappeared. Charlot stopped for a moment and then went on, running now. He stopped again at the spot where he had last seen the man. He heard a faint groan. It came from inside the deep shadow of the wall of a house. Reaching for his knife, he crept forward. As his eyes grew accustomed to the darkness, he made out a body lying on the ground. He hesitated a moment, then bent over the man who was breathing noisily. Was he ill? Or drunk? Charlot put his knife away, reached out and patted the man's clothes for the bulge of the wallet or pocket-book he knew was just full of money. Without warning, a hand reached up and grabbed him by the throat. As he staggered back so the recumbent man rose, tightening his grip and almost lifting him off his feet by the neck. Then a fist smashed into his face like a club, splitting his cheek to the bone, then it came again, crushing his nose.

Charlot knew he was going to die. He also knew that it wouldn't be over quickly.

Erik consumed his dish of vengeance hot. It gave himm small satisfaction, though small satisfaction was in fact better than no satisfaction at all.

There was no hue and cry at Asnières. Auguste, unhinged by his experience, stayed well away from the police. Charlot, whose body had floated away down the river, was missed by no one. Besides, France was in turmoil. Within days, the war was humiliatingly lost, the Emperor fled, a new Republic was declared and the Prussians were camped at the gates of the capital.

The great siege of Paris had begun.

*

There was little prospect now that work on the Opera would restart any time soon. But the shell was never deserted for long. In the months that followed, it was used as a military depot, a barracks for the National Guard, a field hospital and a food warehouse. But despite all this activity, no one came near the deepest cellars, for they were too distant, too dark.

Still, Erik took no chances. As a defence against anyone finding the rear entrance from the third cellar, he added a polydiptic chamber constructed in such a way that no intruder could avoid or escape from it. As a gesture of mercy, he added a wrought-iron tree and hung a prepared noose from one of its branches. In Mazanderan he had many times observed trapped men so driven to desperation that a length of rope was a welcome release.

*

But if work on Garnier's great project had stopped, Erik continued to build secret passages and insert trap-doors in floors, ceilings and walls so that the Opera began to turn into a maze of hidden galleries and spy-holes which allowed him to come and go undetected and observe without being observed. He was even able to install a discreet haven in an attic under the eaves where Léah could have the benefit of fresh air and the sunlight all children need to grow up strong and healthy. She was now eleven and Erik was constantly surprised by her poise, grown-up conversation and her already feminine ways. Each day he saw signs that she was turning into a great beauty. In his eyes, she could do no wrong.

He had foreseen the effect a protracted siege would have on a large metropolis. By the end of October, supplies of fuel and food were beginning to grow scarce. When the sheep and cattle which had been driven in to graze in the public parks had been consumed and most of the horses had gone into in the pot, human beings began to look at domestic pets in an entirely new way. The authorities temporarily eased the situation by allowing the animals in the zoo to be slaughtered. But long before elephant steaks and giraffe meat had become unavailable except to the very rich, larks, crows and rats kept the famished population going. But Erik and Hippolyte had bought in a stock of foodstuffs which insulated them against the scarcities suffered by most Parisians, while fresh vegetables came from the beds which Hippolyte cultivated in Léah's play-garden under the roof.

She helped him. She proved to have green fingers and was soon plucking out weeds which he had taught her to recognise. She went exploring, venturing boldly into draughty corridors to see what was around the next corner and climbing up dusty staircases because she was curious to know what was up there. She showed no fear of the dark and never got lost. One evening, she heard Erik, who had gone back to the music Father Verhoven had taught him, play his violin. She said she would like to learn to play too. Erik immediately bought her a half-size instrument. She responded quickly and he was amazed by her rapid progress.

In this way, they lived far beneath the unfinished Opera House unaffected by food shortages, the bombardment which began in the New Year and the intense cold which froze the Seine and killed more Parisians than the shells of the Prussian guns. Trees and fences were chopped down for firewood. But they did not escape the unrest in the streets which threatened to turn into civil war.

There were days when Léah grew restless and strained against her confinement. She was curious about the world outside, on the surface, which she could see from the roof. When it snowed, it looked like fairyland peopled by midgets and she wanted to see it for herself, at first hand. Reluctantly Erik agreed. She put on her best dress and wore her warm coat, with a bright green woollen scarf, and sallied forth with Hippolyte through the door in the empty rue Scribe.

The streets were strangely quiet. There were no carriages, for there were no horses left to pull them, and voices and footsteps were eerily muffled by the snow. On the boulevards, crowds of common people from the poor *quartiers* of the city were hacking at the remaining trees for fuel to heat up their minute supplies of food, the men bearing off whole branches and the aprons and pinafores of the women filled with sweepings and small twigs. The comfortably-off walked quickly by, eyes averted. They had learned to dress in sombre, modest clothes, for anyone wearing anything better was exposed to the risk of arrest for being a Prussian spy or, worse, of being recognised as English. It was not long before Léah's green scarf attracted attention. Brazen women and fearless urchins deserted the trees and wooden hoardings which they had been attacking and turned their attention to this little rich girl and the footman — for that is how Hippolyte's stove-pipe hat and frock-coat labelled him

— who was holding her by the hand. There were jeers and catcalls and the mood of the crowd began to turn ugly.

'That scarf and coat would fetch a price in any pawnshop,' said a voice.

'Ditto his hat,' said another.

Hippolyte hurried Léah away and made for the new Opera House as fast as he could go. The crowd followed but thinned when they remembered the firewood they had cut down and left unsupervised. Hippolyte decided against returning by the door in the rue Scribe, for they would be caught long before they even reached the lake. Instead, he made for the steps of the Opera House which he knew like the back of his hand. Once inside, they could elude the remnant of the angry pack snapping at their heels, lie low and wait until their pursuers gave up the chase.

He made for a door under the great staircase and led Léah down a flight of steps to an undercroft filled with rubble, lengths of timber and blocks of stone. They found a hiding place just as three men burst through the door. Breathing hard, they halted and looked round the cellar.

'Gorn to earth!' the first man said.

'If you'd shut up perhaps we'd hear them.'

They listened.

'Nah,' the third man said. 'We'll never catch them now. Come on, this won't cook my dinner. Best get back to the logging.'

'Don't bother with that,' said the first man. 'Let's just have some of this timber instead. Here, give us a hand.'

They picked up as many planks as they could carry and left. The man who had said nothing stopped at the door and looked back. Had he seen or heard something? Then he too disappeared.

But he was a sly one.

Hippolyte gave the men ten minutes, but they did not return. He stood up and led the way down to the third cellar.

Neither he nor Léah saw or heard the shadowy figure who tracked their every move.

Hippolyte pressed the lever that opened the trapdoor which led into the rear of Erik's subterranean lair. Leah went first and waited. Hippolyte followed, closing the trap behind him. He crawled past her, lowered himself into the darkness of the mirrored chamber and caught her as she dropped down. Almost at once, Erik, alerted by the alarm, opened the secret door, undetectable from the inside, and let them out. Léah flung her arms round his neck.

'I wasn't afraid! And I ran very fast!'

Hippolyte's account was fuller and it filled Erik with alarm at what might have happened.

'You did well to avoid the rue Scribe,' said Erik. 'They would have been on to you for sure.'

'We threw them off the scent, Papa,' cried Léah, her eyes shining.

'She was very brave, Monsieur Jean,' said Hippolyte.

'I'm proud of you, Léah,' said Erik.

It was a quarter of an hour later, when he was alone, that the alarm bell sounded again. Someone had entered the mirrored chamber! Hippolyte had not shaken off his pursuers after all. Erik turned a valve which illuminated the chamber by hidden gas jets. He climbed the ladder which he kept nearby for the purpose and looked through the observation hole. Inside a large, unshaven man of fearsome aspect stood bunching his large fists, ready to fight any of the men he saw around him — until he realised that they were his own reflections. Erik watched for a few minutes. No one else appeared: was the ruffian alone? Erik slid the cover of the spy-hole back across the aperture, replaced the ladder and left his lair through the lock where he moored his row-boat. He followed the now disused gallery which led up from the lakeside beach to the third and lowest cellar. He closed the secret trap which the intruder had left open and then returned by the way he had come. He read to Léah for an hour while, hidden from view, the ruffian beat the walls and screamed himself hoarse in the insulated chamber which grew brighter and hotter until the light burned his eyes and the heat overpowered his senses. No one heard his screams. No one saw him, the next day, reach for the noose. Nor did anyone see Erik remove the body and leave it at the foot of the great staircase where its presence was assumed to be part of the kind of factional conflict which was now becoming increasingly common.

There was nothing Erik would not do to protect Léah.

*

Despite the dangers, Léah's curiosity about the world 'on the surface' was undented. She pestered, she cajoled, she said pretty please until Erik gave in. Sometimes he went with her, but most often she and Hippolyte, now dressed inconspicuously, explored the streets which were quieter after the shelling stopped and the armistice was signed. But tension remained high, for Parisians had lost patience with their leaders who had failed them and showed worrying signs of mounting an insurrection. In March rebels of the Paris Commune asserted their strength and the government fled to Versailles. The civil war many had feared had broken out.

Leah's little forays were cancelled, for the dangers of the lawless streets were now greater than ever. She pleaded and sulked but Erik turned a deaf ear.

The Communards controlled most of the city and took over the major buildings. Garnier's New Opera was occupied by members of the National Guard who used it as a food distribution centre and a field-dressing station for men wounded in their armed struggle against the government. Erik followed these developments during night sorties and by eavesdropping from his secret vantage points in the building itself. He was not unduly concerned. Léah was safe.

But they could not live in complete isolation. The food store was not entirely exhausted but supplies were low and Hippolyte's vegetable garden was exhausted at the end of the long winter. But whenever he or Hippolyte went out, they took care not to draw attention to themselves. But their precautions were insufficient.

The Communards, now in full occupation of the building, soon became aware of how useful the door in the rue Scribe could be as a quick way in. They would go down to the lake and from there climb up the disused gallery to the third cellar which they used for holding prisoners, for storage and as a soldiers' mess. Among them were men who had worked constructing and maintaining the city's sewers. Most were honest patriots, some were not, but they now came into their own. Using their knowledge of subterranean Paris, they led missions to distant parts of the city, some ordered by their chiefs, others undertaken for their own criminal ends. They surprised their targets by appearing out of holes, like rabbits.

Paris was then in the second week of the insurrection. Eric, suitably disguised, had gone out to find out where matters now stood. He returned via the rue Scribe. He walked down to the lake. The rowing boat was there, but it was not as he had left it. There were also multiple footprints in the sandy surface of the beach. He tensed, sensing a threat. But it was too late. Four men emerged from the shadows and surrounded him.

'And what have we got here?' said one, sliding a dark lantern open and shining the beam of Erik's face. He almost dropped it when he saw it.

The others, no less shocked, stepped back a pace. Erik could have shown them fiends and devils, made them throw themselves into the lake, kill each other, anything. But he was curious about the insurrectionists and their intentions. He found that these men who were fighting for a fairer society were less than fraternal. Without warning, a small, wiry man kicked his legs from under him and he fell sprawling on the ground.

'Tie him up,' said the wiry man. 'I want some answers. Who is he? What's this boat for? What's his game? And what's out there in the dark that needs a boat to get to?'

'He's a government man, Georges,' said the man with the lamp, 'a spy. I say we chuck him in the lake.'

'Well?' snarled Georges. 'What have you got to say for yourself?'

'Just doing my rounds, comrades,' said Erik. 'Regular inspection. I report when the water level rises. Could flood the foundations and then there'd be big trouble.'

'Could be,' said a third man. 'Me and Pierrot rowed right round. There's a big structure out there, you can't see it in the dark from here. A big building like this is abound to have foundations and there's a lot of water. If they was breached it would be serious.'

'I got the job because of the way I look,' said Erik meekly. 'It don't matter what a man looks like in the dark ...'

'I still ain't convinced,' said Georges. 'But there's no time to sort this out now. We'll lock him up and have a go at him tomorrow.'

They hauled Erik to his feet, tied his hands behind his back and placed a blindfold over his eyes. They hauled him up the service tunnel to the third cellar. There a dozen or so men were stacking boxes, cleaning their chassepot rifles, sleeping, cooking on camp stoves by the light of lamps and behaving like bandits on the run, though they were communards engaged in a life and death struggle with government forces. Some looked up as he passed and nudged their neighbours who stared in disbelief. Five limestone blocks of the outer cellar wall had been removed and a short passage dug out. The spoil had been stacked neatly on each side of the entrance. It was low and he and his escort were forced to crouch as they entered it. It was no more than a dozen paces long and connected with a tunnel whose existence Erik had never suspected but had obviously been known to the sewer men in Georges' band of insurrectionists. .

Once inside, they turn left and almost immediately halted at a door. Georges unlocked a door, and bundled him through it. By the light of their torch, he got a brief glimpse of his prison. It had been built as a depot for the tools and materials for the men who maintained the network of tunnels of which this one was part. But there was not enough light for him to make out what was kept there now.

'You can cool your heels in there until we're ready for you,' he growled as he turned the key in the lock behind him.

When the sound of their feet had faded into silence, he tried a few steps but soon came up against an obstacle which by touch he decided was square and made of polished wood, perhaps a table. He changed direction but was stopped by something sharp, a jagged edge of metal. He turned round, aligned his wrists behind his back with the sharp edge and began sawing at the rope that bound them until it parted. He rubbed his hands to restore the circulation, removed the blindfold then reached into his pocket and brought out a couple of the lucifers which he, who spent part of each day in the dark, always carried with him. He struck one and found himself in a low chamber filled with a jumble of disparate objects: furniture, curtains, bed linen, porcelain objects, even a pair of carriage wheels, probably booty looted by Georges and his men. Before his match burned out, he saw the glint of several silver candlesticks which looked as though they belonged on an altar: evidently the gang was not above stealing from churches. He struck another match and reached for the nearest candlestick which had a half-burned candle in it. He lit the candle and examined his surroundings.

He had been locked in a low-roofed chamber. There was one exit, a door which had once been solid oak but had, with the passage of time, rotted badly in the damp air. Placing the candlestick on the ground, he lifted his right foot and kicked the timbers. At the third strike, aimed at the lock, the door burst open. He paused, for he had made a great deal of noise. But when the echoes had died away, silence returned. He stepped out into the tunnel and paused. He could hear voices approaching. He shrank back into the doorway. The voices belonged to three men. One held a torch to light the way for the two others who were carrying a fourth who was unconscious and obviously badly injured. Erik let them pass. When silence again filled the tunnel, he returned to the short passage which led back to the third cellar.

He waited for his moment, then stepped out casually. He picked up a peaked workman's cap which one of the rescue party had dropped. He crammed it on his head, found a bucket to carry and made unconcernedly for the service tunnel which took him down to the lake. He was not followed nor did anyone see him get into the boat and rowed away into the darkness.

What fools those men were! To think that they could get the better of him! He had emerged victorious once again, just as he had survived so many times in the Orient! Perhaps he had been born invulnerable. Perhaps it had been given to him to lead a charmed life by special dispensation, as a compensation for his monstrous deformities which would eternally separate him from the company of men.

Erik felt immortal.

There was more than a touch of madness in his exultation

Chapter 17

For as long as he could remember, Erik had relied on himself to combat the dangers of existence. Experience had convinced him that his natural abilities and acquired talents made him equal to all challenges. He was not just a survivor but a conqueror, in his way a new Alexander, for he too had bent Asia to his will. But soon, he would be required to face a test of an entirely different order, one for which he was ill-equipped to deal.

After the Communard uprising was stopped in its tracks and the insurrection strangled at birth, order was brutally restored, and an uneasy peace returned to Paris. Work had resumed on Garnier's building in the autumn of 1871 and life deep beneath it began again at the point where it had been before the War, the Siege and the Commune. With Hippolyte's help, Erik's little kingdom prospered. He installed an organ, for his interest in music had turned into a passion. Music was as clear, logical and pure as mathematics, and as capable of expressing human feelings as the most sensitive heart was of generating them. Léah too was happy. She found innumerable ways of occupying her hands and her mind and every day Erik saw her grow in charm and loveliness. But one day, Hippolyte said, 'Monsieur Jean, beg pardon for raising it, but Mademoiselle Léah won't be a child for much longer. The life she's got here would be all right for a lad, I daresay, but girls are different. There comes a time when they need a feminine hand.'

He was right. Léah was growing fast and would soon be a young woman. Erik had no experience of such things and he bowed to Hippolyte's superior knowledge.

After much deliberation, it was decided that Léah should go to Huguette's married sister who lived in the Latin Quarter. The streets all round had been badly pounded by Prussian shells but the students had now returned and with them the old gaiety. It was a place made for young people.

At first, she spent just a few days away from her home deep under the New Opera, then a whole week occasionally until she was with 'Aunt

Marie-Rose' more than with 'Uncle Polyte' and the man she still called 'Papa'. And it soon became plain that she preferred life 'on the surface' to the restrictive, enforced existence 'under ground'.

Soon Erik was aware that she was changing quickly. She was no longer the sweet, submissive child whose eyes he could open to the wonders of the world.

At first, she told him about everything she had done and seen 'on the surface'. When the novelty wore off, she seemed dissatisfied to be back and eager to return to the Latin Quarter. To show her frustration, she sulked, she flounced. Then there were her outbursts. She was tired of living in a prison, she said. Nothing Erik could say or do placated her. The only way he could put a smile back on her face was to let her spend even more time with Aunt Marie-Rose. If he denied her, she shut herself in her room until she got her way. She became obsessed with her appearance and spent hours in front of her mirror experimenting with her hair and clothes and creams and poses. Erik had expected such behaviour, which he accepted as natural, and steadied himself to weather the storm. But soon, there was worse.

More than once he had to reprimand her for treating Hippolyte as though he were a servant, ordering him to fetch and carry for her and mocking his Norman – and so un-Parisian – turns of phrase. He was also aware that small sums of money went missing, that expensive books or a pretty ornament he had bought for her disappeared from her shelves. She had obviously taken them to sell. Since he gave her more than adequate pocket-money, why did she needed more?

One day, Hippolyte approached him even more diffidently than usual. He said his sister-in-law no longer felt able to welcome Mademoiselle Léah into her home. Various excuses were offered but Erik saw through them and soon got to the truth. Léah, who could be sweetness itself, had developed a cruel, selfish streak. She thought herself grander than poor Marie-Rose whom she treated like a skivvy and expected her to be always at her beck and call. She had also made herself unpopular in the *quartier* by accusing a shop-girl of impertinence and insisting that the girl be dismissed on the spot. She also spent considerably more than the allowance Erik gave her. She had taken to going out alone, secretly, eluding Marie-Rose's watchful eye. On one occasion she had stayed out all night. Marie-Rose suspected that her head had been turned and her vanity flattered by a student or some unsavoury character and that she was heading for a fall. She could no longer cope with such behaviour or be responsible for her.

Erik confronted Léah who did not try to deny any of the charges which had been made against her. He wasn't her father, she said, so what right did he have to tell her how to live her life?

'The right of one who has only your best interests at heart. You are young, Léah...'

She bridled at the word.

'And you are *old!*' she spat back at him. 'Do you think that gives you the right to live my life for me?'

'No, but I know more of the world than you have had time to experience ...'

'But you know nothing of the real world! You live here, like a hermit. You have no idea of what's happening up there, on the surface. Up there, they know how to enjoy life!'

When they argued like this, Léah would storm off in a rage, order Hippolyte to row her across the lake and go back to her friends. Erik no longer knew where she lived, for she never went near Marie-Rose now. He feared the worst. After one violent confrontation, in which wounding words were spoken on both sides and she declared she never wanted to see him again, he followed her. She skipped in high spirits down to the Seine, fully aware of the admiring glances she drew from the men she passed. She crossed the river by the Pont Neuf and vanished into a tavern in the rue Dauphine. From the doorway, he saw her surrounded by students who offered her glasses of wine which she took coquettishly and drank teasingly. Crushed by the sight, Erik turned away. Though he waited until it was dark, Léah did not come out. He entered sat in a corner, sat down and ordered a cognac.

She was not there.

But he learned that the establishment had rooms to rent. Did she live there? Or did she have recourse to its rooms for occasional use? Erik clenched his fists until the knuckles showed white.

She only returned now to what had been her home when she wanted money.

When next she came, Erik took his courage in both hands and told her he knew exactly what sort of life she was leading.

'You've been spying on me! And you've got the nerve to preach to me! You know, Papa,' she said viciously, 'or Monsieur Jean or Erik or whatever your name is, I know your sort. You're the seedy type, oh so prim on top and disgusting underneath, pretending to worry about me and all the time you're after one thing, my so-called honour. Well you needn't worry about it anymore because it's long gone!'

She put her hands on her hips, threw back he head and laughed.

So intense was her derision that Erik flinched as though he had been struck by a whip.

'Anyway,' she went on, 'you never stood a chance in that department because you're a freak. Just because I never threw up my dinner whenever I saw you doesn't mean I didn't notice how hideous, repulsive and evil you are! The girl who looked at you twice would have to be blind!'

There had been a girl, once, and she had loved him with unseeing eyes. And she had been conjured up in his mind by this other, whom he had loved as a man loves a daughter, who still looked like his angel but behaved and spoke like a foul-mouthed harridan. A sacred boundary had been overstepped. He looked at Léah as he had never looked at her before and she was suddenly very afraid. His eyes burned deep into her and her new-found power evaporated in an instant.

'Go,' said Erik. 'There is no more to be said.'

'Give me money!' she said through her fear.

Erik gave her money, a great deal of money.

*

Léah took the roll of banknotes and for a moment regretted that she had gone so far. Had she killed her golden goose? She thought not: she would return and coax and cajole and play on him the way a musician plays on an instrument. She would make him sing to her tune!

She pulled her coat round her, arched her back and faced him. It was a show of defiance designed to restore the balance in her favour. Erik looked at her with dead, cruel eyes and surprised her by saying:

'You have committed the greatest crime of all, my dear. You have killed love. Now go!'

*

From Hippolyte, Erik learned that Léah had finally cut herself off from Marie-Rose and that he had been seen her behaving in a 'forward' way in the Latin Quarter. That was the last he had heard of her. He had asked after her in cafés and her usual haunts but drew a blank until one day he returned saying that Mademoiselle Léah had waylaid him with a message. She needed money.

'She also said there were friends of hers who would like to know that there was a rich, beg pardon, madman living in a lonely place. If you don't pay up, she said, she'll tell them and they will break in. She wasn't herself, Monsieur Jean.'

'Was she well?' asked Erik.

'She looked ill, very pale. And her clothes were not clean, which isn't like her, she was always so neat. There were bruises on her arm. I thought it was mud at first, but no, it was bruises.'

'Did she seem sorry to have run away from us?'

'She talked defiant.'

'You think she's gone to the bad?'

'Perhaps, perhaps not. But it wasn't the Léah I know.'

Obviously Léah's new friends had lost interest once she'd spent the money he'd given her. She might even have fallen into bad company, even into the clutches of a pimp. Either way, it was too late for her. Perdition was her destiny. It was only a matter of time before she ended in the gutter.

'What shall I tell her?'

'Nothing. She has damned herself and there is no helping her.'

Hippolyte paused for a moment, a look of surprise on his face. He had been expecting a kinder answer.

'Very well, Monsieur Jean. I shall tell her nothing. Am I also to give her nothing?'

'Nothing,' said Erik and he returned to his book.

After Léah's departure he had buried himself in his library, believing, like Montaigne, that an hour with a good book will chase away the deepest sorrow. But books had lost their charm. He found it difficult to concentrate. He read whole paragraphs without taking in a word and had to read them again before they made sense. Had he been hasty? No, for his view of Léah's conduct had not changed. But was he not to blame in some way for what she had become? Surely no one could have been kinder, more considerate than he? Yet the fact was that Léah, who was a headstrong child in a woman's body, had rebelled and rejected him and the life he had made for her. But if she was selfish and headstrong, it was because he had made her so. He had smothered her in the wrong kind of love, forced her to walk in his shoes. He had kept her hidden from the world and from people, over-protected her against setbacks and dangers which she had never learned to deal with herself. She was not wholly responsible for what she had become and a good share of the blame for it could be laid squarely at his door.

One thought above all gave him pause: he had failed in the promise he had made to Françoise! What would she have done?

He snapped his book shut and found Hippolyte.

'I shall come with you. I shall give her my answer myself. When and where are you to meet her?'

'This afternoon at five o'clock in the Luxembourg Gardens, near the Medici Fountain. I am glad, Monsieur Jean, that you haven't turned your back on her. She is still a child.'

'We shall see, old friend, if I am wise or weak.'

A military band, all shining brass and handsome uniforms, was playing to a sizeable crowd in the autumn sunshine. Erik wore a full coat with a collar that could be turned up over the ears. His face and head were concealed, as usual, by a false beard, a broad-brimmed hat and his green eyeglasses.

The jaunty martial sound of the band disturbed his thoughts. He gestured to Hippolyte and they moved to a nearby terrace. They leaned on the balcony and looked out on the old Italian Palace, the ornamental *bassin* where a pair of swans glided elegantly, and the strollers who walked past the bowling greens under the mackerel sky of early Autumn. Then, below them and not a dozen yards away, he saw her, her golden hair flowing over her shoulders beneath a pretty bonnet. She sat straight-backed on an iron chair, waiting.

But then he saw that there was a faded, shop-soiled air about her, for the bloom had gone and the sight of her, fallen, diminished, blighted with the shadow of something cheap and tawdry which he did not recognise, made him catch his breath. At that very moment, she looked up. She gave a frightened yelp and leaped to her feet.

'Léah!' cried Erik. 'I have the money! Wait!'

'Keep your money!' she shouted and, gathering up her skirts, she started running towards the rue Medicis, scattering the strollers and overturning tables and chairs.

For an instant, Erik watched paralysed, his mind racing. How could he bear to lose her? Surely there must be a way of winning her round, of coaxing her back? He'd change, he'd listen, give her whatever she wanted, yes, there was still a chance!

He vaulted over the balcony and set off in pursuit. The gap between them narrowed. Léah sped through the gate, out into the busy road and straight under the wheels of a cart loaded with firewood. The cart swerved, collided with a vintner's dray and came to a dead stop, shedding its load of logs. Passers-by screamed. When Erik reached her, she was pinned by the chest under one wheel. The life was being crushed out of her. He ducked under the tailboard of the cart, braced himself and heaved with all his strength. The cart, relieved of most of its load, rose a few inches. Passers-by rushed to help and pulled the broken body free. Erik bent over her.

'Léah!' he Erik, brushing. 'It's all right. I'm here!'

Her face was unmarked but it was deathly pale.

'His fault!' she said weakly, but loud enough for the nearest spectators to hear. 'The freak's fault ... Been after me ... pestering ... He's been trying to ...'

The onlookers were all ears. A law officer arrived on the scene. There was blood now at the corners of her mouth

'Make him...' she groaned, now addressing the onlookers directly, 'make him show his face... you'll see... unmask the devil...'

But the words ended in a choking cough. Her chest heaved but she could not breathe. Yet even as the life faded from her eyes she looked directly at Erik and mouthed: 'I hate you!'

'Poor lamb!' said woman in the crowd.

'She didn't deserve that,' said a man.

'What was that she said about a freak?'

'I dunno, but let's find out. Here, you!'

Erik had been stunned by the venom, the loathing he had seen in Léah's vengeful eyes. He was shaken from his daze as bystanders, with collective courage, surged forward, whipping his hat off, snatching his spectacles from his face which was suddenly bare, a grinning death's head of such spectral horror that the crowd recoiled in revulsion.

The policeman was first to recover. He lunged forward but Erik ducked under his extended arm and broke free. Then he was running. The crowd fell back but a few of the braver men took up the chase.

He sped across the rue de Vaugirard and headed towards the river through a tangle of streets. Gradually, the sounds of pursuit died and he slowed to a walk. He turned up the collar of his coat, held a handkerchief over his mouth and nose and proceeded unnoticed over the Pont Neuf, though he did catch the eye of one man.

He was aged about fifty, of average height, with regular features and an expressive face, dark, melancholy eyes, a neat black beard and lightly tanned skin. He wore a heavy cape and an astrakhan tarbush and followed Erik unhurriedly, at a discreet distance. He did not lose sight of his quarry until Erik disappeared into the New Opera by the door in the rue Scribe. Erik plunged into the welcoming darkness and sat in the rowing boat, waiting for Hippolyte to return. His mind boiled with shock, grief, self-recrimination and misery. Eventually, Hippolyte appeared. His head was bowed and his tread slow and heavy. Erik rowed them to his underground sanctuary and gave him brandy. When Hippolyte was more himself, he said:

'You did well to leave the scene, Monsieur Jean. They wanted your blood...'

'And Léah?'

'Gone to the morgue. I thought you wouldn't want to be involved so I kept silent. No one could put a name to her. So that is where they've put her.'

The morgue was where the authorities took the corpses of unidentified persons: suicides, vagrants who died of exposure in winter and bodies yielded up by the Seine in every month of the year.

Erik could not speak.

'You could go there tomorrow. See her laid out,' said Hippolyte. 'Though perhaps, best not. You might be recognised. But I shall go. I'll pay for her to have a decent funeral. I'll not have her thrown into a pauper's grave like she was rubbish.'

'We shall go together.'

'And afterwards, Monsieur Jean, I shall go back to Normandy. I can't stay here. Not now. There are too many memories. I couldn't bear it. Besides, the family have been wanting me home for some time. My father is failing and my mother can't manage any more. They need me. But I cannot leave Mademoiselle Léah where she is.'

'Then you must go. I shall miss you, old friend. Oh how did it come to this?'

'It wasn't anybody's fault,' said Hippolyte. 'There was badness in the blood. Bred in the bone. I wanted to tell you but Huguette said no. She thought that everyone should have the right to start fresh, without a past to hold them back. Did I do right not telling you?'

'Quite right,' said Erik.

'Her father went to the bad, I knew him. And her mother. She was a good-time girl who died in jail. That's why Françoise took her baby in. Françoise always believed the best of people. Bring them up right and they turn out right, was what she used to say.'

Nor did Erik believe that Leah's fate had been written on her forehead, that nothing he could have done would have changed her destiny.

'No, Hippolyte, it was not pre-ordained that she should end like this. We, and more particularly I, failed both of them,' said Erik bitterly.

'Don't blame yourself, Monsieur Jean. You did your best. It's all any of us can do.'

'When will you leave?'

'As soon as I've been to see her.'

The mortuary in the rue Morgue stood on the eastern bank of the Ile de la Cité, close by the great cathedral of Notre Dame. Outside were displayed a list of physical descriptions and a standing invitation to members of the public to inspect the corpses and put a name to any that they recognised. A crowd of men, women and children had assembled and shuffled past the tall plate glass windows behind which naked, anonymous cadavers, male and female but sexless in death, were laid out for public viewing. Though they were separated from the spectators by the glass, they filled with air with the atmosphere of death. There was a perpetual shocked silence broken only by the scuffing of visitors' footsteps on stone and the trickling sound of the very cold water with which the corpses were constantly washed to delay decomposition.

Erik and Hippolyte stared, appalled, at the rows of grey marble slabs on which the cadavers were arranged. In death they had acquired new, unnatural colours — red, green, yellow, purple — and strange rigidities. On the wall behind them hung rags that had been breeches, petticoats, skirts, jackets and shirts, all displayed as an aid to identification. The drowned were swollen, bellies distended, thighs fat and spongy. The twisted faces of those who had died poisoned by their own hand, still expressed the final agonies they had suffered. The broken remains of victims of accidents showed limbs in impossible poses, sometimes with bones showing through the puffy, swollen, violet skin. There were throats ringed with purple necklaces left by the nooses which had ended desperate lives.

They approached a clerk and enquired the whereabouts of a young woman run over by a cart near the Luxembourg Gardens.

'Accident yesterday, you say?' said the clerk, running a dirty finger down a list. 'Yes. Here we are, just follow me.'

When they stood by Léah's side, he said: 'There we are. That's the one. Run over in the street and crushed. Suicide most like. These girls,' he sighed, 'they get themselves into trouble and they end up in here.'

Léah's hair lay in an ugly damp lump under her head. Her broken body was a livid, unnatural white but dirty brown where the blood had congealed over her ribcage which had been crushed by the cart wheel. But there was blue too, from the bruising. But her face was just as Erik remembered it, before she had ceased being his sweet, his perfect Léah: open, eager, angelic in death.

Hippolyte spun a story about being in Paris to look for a granddaughter who had run away. The clerk tried not to look bored, for he had heard it all before many times. It was always the same story. He wrote down Léah's name and her date and place of birth.

'Nearly sixteen,' said the clerk, shaking his head. 'Shame. Such a pretty kid too.'

He said they should return the next day, after the inquest, for the death certificate.

'Can't issue one before they've decided on cause of death. It's regulations. But you'll need a death certificate for the undertaker. You'll have to make arrangements with him yourselves, gents.'

The next day, Hippolyte packed his bag and slipped out into the rue Scribe on the first stage of his journey home. He had been away for fourteen years.

Léah was buried two days later. There was only one mourner, although a second man, sallow-featured under an astrakhan tarbush, watched from the shelter of an azalea which blazed with bright red autumn leaves.

Chapter 18

After Léah's funeral Erik sat alone in the sumptuous womb he had made for himself in the depths of the Opera. It was as dark and as silent as the earth in which she had been laid. During those first days, he heard echoes of her voice as it had been, innocent and affectionate, before she had grown away from him. But the sound of her voice was only in his head. And now Hippolyte was gone too. He was alone again. From now on he would have no one to talk to but himself. Solitude was not a new experience for him. But he had lost the habit.

Was his gorgeous palace a refuge? Or a place where he went to ground, a bolt-hole in which he hid from the life 'on the surface' which had brought him little joy and a mountain of misery?

He lit all the lamps and flooded his palace with light, even Hippolyte's now empty quarters and Léah's room, which still bore the imprint of her. The salon, as grand as anything the society hostesses of Saint-Germain des Prés could boast, was hung with tapestries and filled with his mother's furniture. He knew it was ugly and belonged to another age, but it had been *hers*. On the walls were paintings but no mirrors. His spacious library was full of voices, but they did not speak for they too were entombed, between the covers of books. He chose one at random and read a paragraph, speaking the words aloud, lending the author his own sonorous voice. For a moment the emptiness retreated. But he did not understand what he read and he returned the volume to its shelf. He sat at the organ. He ran his fingers over the keys and improvised harmonies which expressed and intensified his defeated, anguished mood.

Suddenly he decided to confront his misery, take it by the neck and thrust it back into its hole. He sat at his desk and picked up a pen.

'From this day forth,' he began, 'I shall seek no company but my own. I am full of self. My preoccupations fill up my brain, they are my mania, my only anguish and my sole delight. But I shall purge my mind of them by committing my darkest thoughts to paper. Which is why I now begin this journal …'

In a spidery, spiky hand, he wrote a narrative of Léah's revolt which gave it a distance and smoothed the raw edges of his emotions until he could feel them without being torn apart. Then he slept. When he woke, the first and only sound he heard was the hiss of the jets in the gas lamps. His watch had stopped and Hippolyte had not been there to wind up the clocks as he had done each night for a dozen years. How long had he slept? Was it day or night?

He entered the polydiptic chamber and, with the aid of the ladder he used to reach the spy hole, entered the third cellar through the stone trap. As it swung open, he saw light, a fountain and branches of a tree hanging over the fountain... It was a painted flat, a piece of stage scenery ... For a moment he was stunned. And then he understood.

About a year before, the Salle Lepeletier, home of grand opera for half a century, had been destroyed by fire. The mood of post-war France was truculent and the capital still divided. Some Parisians did not believe that the new republic was a suitable substitute for monarchy while others considered it insufficiently republican. To clear the air and restore 'French gaiety', the government had decided on one measure they hoped would lift the public mood: Garnier was instructed to complete his new Opera House as soon as possible. The work was given a higher priority than rebuilding the Hotel de Ville or the Tuileries, both of which had been reduced to empty shells by the siege and the Communard uprising. The work was now so advanced that the first production to be staged in Paris's new Opera House was in rehearsal. Erik had not entered the building for some time, preoccupied as he was with the problem of Léah. So it came as a surprise to learn that after so many years, the auditorium would be filled with music and the stage with the scenery he was now looking at.

The painted flat partly screened Erik's secret trap door. Even so he made very sure that the coast was clear before emerging into the cellar. There was no one about, no stagehands or watchmen, so that he wondered if it was early morning or late evening. He climbed up two flights of stairs, still without seeing any sign of life. But when he was directly under the stage, he heard voices and snatches of music. He opened another trap and climbed up steps he had built inside the wall. When he reached one of his vantage points, in Box 5 of the grand tier, he found himself looking down on the stage.

An opera was in rehearsal.

But Erik was not the only hidden observer of the scene.

*

One of the last state visitors to the Salle Lepeletier before fire reduced it to rubble had been given a rapturous reception by Parisians. The newspapers were full of the visit to Europe of Nasr El Din, the first by a Shah of Persia. He was shown Versailles, Napoleon's tomb and Franconi's equine circus on the Champs Elysées. He went to the races, attended banquets and took the salute at military parades. He endeared himself to the populace by directing a quiverful of barbed comments against the hated Prussians and by the sheer magnificence of his pomp. He attended a gala performance at the Opera wearing a uniform which dazzled onlookers. Everything about him was gorgeous. Persia fever mounted. Women's fashions and restaurant menus reflected the public fascination with a monarch from the mysterious orient whose wealth was fabled and whose exotic wives were the living embodiment of eastern promise.

Among his numerous retinue was the former daroga of Mazanderan who once had brought the Magician of Nizhny-Novgorod to the Sultana, saved his life by helping him to flee the country and ensured that he would not be pursued by covering up his death by producing a false corpse. After Erik's hurried departure and the incriminating note he had left, the daroga was arrested, stripped of his rank and banished from Mazanderan. He was allowed to reside in obscurity under virtual house arrest in Tehran because he was of royal blood and therefore not to be treated as a common criminal. He was given a small pension on which he was able to live well enough. But when he left Persia and accompanied Shah Nasr El Din to Paris, he seized the opportunity to throw off the restrictions under which he was semi-imprisoned. He lost himself in the capital and remained lost when the Shah left France to return home. His pension continued to be paid, nevertheless, though it did not allow him to live as comfortably in his adopted city as he had in Persia. He had with him his faithful servant, Darius, who administered to his needs in his modest apartment overlooking the Luxembourg Gardens.

It was his custom to stroll through the streets of the capital each afternoon. It was a Parisian habit which he had adopted with enthusiasm, for there was much to see. One autumn day, when the azaleas flamed red in the Luxembourg Gardens – where, to judge by the excitement there had been some sort of street accident – he saw a muffled figure which seemed familiar. It took him only a moment to identify the man, almost a friend, who in his native Persia he had known as the King of Traps and the Prince of Stranglers. He followed and saw him vanish through a door in the rue Scribe. He waited to see if he came out again. After a while, another man, older, with the manner of a servant, also disappeared through the same door into the building which he knew was the New Opera House. When no one emerged, he tried the door. It was locked.

He returned the following day and followed the *feringhee* he had known in Sari and the man's servant to the public morgue. But though he came again the next day and every day for a week, he saw no further sign of his man or the servant.

When Garnier's Opera House opened, the daroga became a regular visitor. He was convinced that Erik was still in the building, which he had taken up residence there, but how that could be or in what part of it he had hidden himself he could not say. It was hardly possible that he had never been seen by some stagehand, carpenter, musician, dancer or any one of many people as they went about their business. With the dogged persistence he had acquired during his policing days, he searched the building from attic to cellars, prowling through corridors and passageways, peering into dark corners, lifting curtains, scrutinising cleaners, ushers and other staff in case one of them was the master of disguise in person.

In time he himself became the object of suspicion, even though. He made no effort to conceal his movements. He was always alone when he was seen but his manner made observers uncomfortable, for he never spoke, never smiled, attended every performance but never gave any sign that he enjoyed or disliked what he saw and heard on stage. Always dressed in the same way, in an astrakhan fez and an enveloping black coat in the long sleeves of which he constantly clenched and unclenched his hands, he patrolled the public foyers and hidden byways of the Opera, hoping for one thing: a clear sighting of the man he had brought to the court of the Sultan-Governor of the province of Mazanderan.

Several times, he caught sight of a shadowy figure moving quietly through a corridor or heard a door closing softly at his back. One hastily snatched glimpse showed the figure wearing an opera hat and full evening dress. And once, as he inspected the third cellar down, where the furnaces were located which heated the building and drove the fans which ventilated it, he caught sight of his quarry and, keeping a safe distance, followed him down the disused service tunnel that led to the lake. When he emerged from the tunnel, his man had disappeared. But a set of footprints led to a simple wooden jetty. There was no boat moored there but in the darkness, he caught the faint splash of oars. Moonlight entered through the shaft of the air vent (he supposed it was the one near the door in the rue Scribe down which he had peered many times), but the gloom was too deep for him to see where the boat was going or who it carried. He explored the beach and found the passage that led up to the door in the rue Scribe. It was locked and he was obliged to retrace his steps to the foyer of the Opera House via the service tunnel. He went straight back to his apartment, for he knew Erik would make no more appearances that night.

He was baffled. He was convinced that he was correct in suspecting that Erik lived in the Opera House. But where? He had examined every inch of the building and found nothing. But the conviction grew that the Master of Traps had built a secret refuge somewhere within its confines where no one would find him.

On one other occasion only did he get a clear sight of an elegant figure in top hat and tails. He followed it to the third level. But this time, instead of walking down the service tunnel to the lake, it disappeared. One moment it was there and the next it was gone. There was only one explanation: Erik's lair could be entered from the lake but also through a hidden back door here in the third cellar down. But though the daroga searched for many hours, he could not find a spring or lever which operated a trap door. Once more he was forced to retreat, frustrated.

But the incident had helped him narrow the location of Erik's lair. Erik's disappearance was a discovery, and it gave him a plan.

For many nights, he stationed himself in an alcove which gave him a clear view of the stairs leading up from the third cellar. One night, just as he was reaching the end of his patience and had begun to tell himself that he was mistaken, that his eyes had been playing tricks on him, that not even Erik could penetrate the mighty foundations of the Opera House, he was rewarded. His eyes, well accustomed to the semi-darkness which was dimly lit by gas lamps, picked out a movement which proved to be an opera hat. It rose and revealed a figure in evening dress mounting the stairs. It passed within six feet of him. The daroga supposed that Erik was about to attend the performance which was shortly to begin. If this was indeed the case, he would be gone for some hours.

When the coast was clear, he left his place of concealment, hurried down the disused tunnel and came to the beach by the underground lake. A small rowing boat was moored at the jetty. He could now put his plan into operation: if the boat was there Erik must have left through his back door and therefore was not at home. It was safe to approach his subterranean lair. Quickly he clambered aboard and began to row.

Enough moonlight again slanted through the air vent to provide illumination for him to steer a straight course. Just as the shore disappeared into the gloom astern, he made out the massive stone wall of the outer shell of the foundations. He knew Erik must also have built a trapdoor here, but he could not detect it, even though he shone the beam of his dark-lantern over a large area of its surface. He assumed the latch or lever would be on the side facing the shore, at the shortest distance from the jetty. But Erik could not be relied on to do the obvious thing. Keeping the stone structure on his left side, the daroga rowed in a circle until he returned to his starting point. He had seen nothing to indicate how Erik came and went through a perfectly blank wall.

He returned to the shore, moored the boat and climbed back up to the auditorium. The performance was over and the audience had moved to the brilliantly-lit foyer which was now full of fashionably dressed women and men in white ties. For most of them, this was the evening's real entertainment: seeing and being seen at the capital's most fashionable social venue. The daroga left, musing on the significance of his latest discovery.

He shared it with Darius who thought for a moment.

'In our country, is it not said that an evil spirit cannot cross a running stream? But, Agha, if a spirit as evil as the Prince of Stranglers has crossed entire oceans, why can he not also walk through walls?'

*

It was not possible that the daroga should remain for long the only person in the Opera House to catch sight of an unexplained presence in its network of rooms, corridors and under-stage spaces. The building was a giant organism which could not function without the constant ministrations of a large staff, headed by the Director, consisting of music masters, dancers, singers, doormen, ushers, stage-managers, scene-shifters, painters, stokers, attendants, even stablemen to look after the horses required for performances of operas such as Meyerbeer's *Le Prophète*... But no one could put a name to the man in the opera-hat and cloak who had been seen moving along passageways, walking down stairs and disappearing around corners. There were numerous sightings. At first people were puzzled. Then the puzzle turned into a mystery and the mystery into an enigma. No one knew who he was or why he was there, and doubt started fears.

But there were more than doubts. Real panic was caused by the discovery of the body of a scene-shifter named Joseph Buquet hanging in the third level down. The men who found him swore they had heard the distant sound of music which could have been a death march. The event served to give credence to the rumour that the Opera House was haunted. Obviously the spectre had put the noose around poor Buquet's neck. Then firemen on a routine inspection of the cellars reported hearing sounds sounded like the low moans of a dying man who they could not locate. A lighting engineer working on the bank of so-called 'organ pipes' which controlled the flow of the gas needed for lighting effects on stage, made a hasty exit through a stage-trap after seeing, or so he claimed, a grinning death's head floating towards him with eyes burning in the dark like twin fires. A cleaner handed in her notice because she had definitely seen a ghost walking along with its head under its arm as she swabbed the corridors on the top floor... And then an alert watchman caught an intruder and, despite his protests, grabbed him by the scruff of the neck and marched him in short order to the Director's office.

The suspect was the daroga who was able to explain that he was Persian and an ardent admirer of the Paris Opera House the like of which did not exist in his country. He was, he said, fascinated by everything about it, from the roofs and attics to the cellars, by the efficient way it was run, by its musical excellence and, not least, its ingenious stage-machinery which he had been examining when the safety officer had mistakenly apprehended him as a person of malicious intent.

Monsieur Vaucorbeil, director of the Opera House, was duly flattered by his oriental compliments and, deciding that the daroga was a distinguished gentlemen and a true opera-lover, took the matter no further, even adding that he was free to explore any part of the building he chose.

The news that an intruder had been caught and that he was perfectly harmless calmed nerves. Even Buquet's death was now plausibly identified as suicide, But the spate of mysterious happenings did not stop.

One morning, the concierge, Madame Giry, a woman of strong character, trenchant views and no imagination, was inspecting the condition of the boxes on the grand tier which had just been cleaned. Without warning, a light, pleasant voice said:

'Madame Giry, I have a task for you …'

Startled, she turned half round to face the speaker on her left, but there was no one there: she was alone in Box 5.

'I want you to take the letter you will find on the shelf under the front arm-rest and give it to the Director. You will also find a ten-franc note under the letter. It is for your trouble.'

The voice was now behind her. She turned round and again found no one. She was not afraid, supposing herself to be the butt of some practical joke, though how a voice could come out of a solid wall she could not say. Still, a prank is just a prank but a ten-franc note is always a ten-franc note. Cool as a cucumber she replied:

'Right you are, sir. And will there be an answer?'

'Certainly. Bring it back here and leave it on the chair.'

Mme Giry, bosom swelling to express her new self-importance, went straight to the Director's office and handed the letter to his assistant who placed it on his desk where Monsieur Vaucorbeil found it later the same day. It was written in red ink, in an ill-formed, spiky hand. It said:

Dear Director,
Over the years, I have watched over Monsieur Garnier's remarkable edifice and your most efficient conduct of its affairs. Thanks to my vigilance, a number of costly accidents have been averted, such as fires I have extinguished before they could get started, and leaking pipes I have made water-tight before they caused a flood. I have given freely of my time but, alas, am no longer able to provide the same level of service. I therefore request that you pay me henceforth, on the first day of every

month, an allowance of 20.000 francs in cash. Believe me, the sum is entirely reasonable.
Madame Giry will act as my courier.
If you do not agree to this arrangement, there will be unpleasant consequences. But it need not come to that.

- The Opera Ghost

Letters from cranks of all kinds were all too familiar to Monsieur Vaucorbeil and his first impulse was to throw this one into his wastepaper bin. But given its threatening tone, he summoned Monsieur Favard, Secretary to the Administrators, who took a firm stand and no reply was sent. Mme Giry was summoned. She told all she knew, which was very little, though she said nothing of the ten-franc note. The head of security was ordered to raise the level of vigilance. And so there the matter remained.

Until one morning, during rehearsals, when a large section of scenery fell from the flies on to the stage, narrowly missing several artists but causing considerable damage. It was discovered that the rope by which it was raised and lowered it had not become worn and frayed: it had been deliberately cut. It was therefore no accident.

That same afternoon, Madame Giry delivered another note.

Dear Director,
I advise you to follow the instructions given in my earlier letter. If not, worse will follow.

- The Opera Ghost

'If you want my opinion, you will ignore this letter too,' said the Opera's head of security. 'It is clearly the work of a disgruntled employee. To respond in any way would be to encourage his malice.'

No reply was sent but somehow the person signing himself 'The Opera Ghost' knew instantly, as if he had been eavesdropping on the conversation, that his new threat was not being taken seriously. For that same night, one of the furnaces in the third cellar exploded, injuring two boilermen. The Director was immediately informed that foul play was suspected.

The next morning, the Director received a fresh note from the 'Opera Ghost'. It was brief. It read simply:

Dear Director, Well?

Within the hour, Mme Giry was despatched with a response agreeing to the conditions stipulated in the original letter. Supposing that a reply would be forthcoming, and that it would be left in the usual place by the malefactor, the head of security mounted guard on Box 5 which he ensured was empty. No one was observed to go in or come out until Mme Giry arrived to see if there was an answer. She reported that the reply had been collected, that she had heard the same voice, though there was no speaker, and that she had found a new letter. The security man could not explain it and Monsieur Vaucorbeil, though a dyed-in-the-wool rationalist, began to feel uneasy. Was there such a thing as a ghost in the Opera House? The letter, in the same red ink and spiky hand, read:

Dear Director,

I am glad that you have seen reason. I will add one further condition for my continuing co-operation: I must be given exclusive use of Box 5 for performances which I shall specify in advance. May I remind you that the first of the month occurs at the end of this week. Mme Giry will serve, as hitherto, as intermediary.

- The Opera Ghost

*

The daroga had told no one of his belief that the Opera House was permanently inhabited by a redoubtable, unforgiving man of fabulous skills and a will of iron. He said nothing out of ingrained caution, for he had lived too long in a country where discretion was essential for survival and a man who wished to die of natural causes in his bed kept his own counsel. But his silence now acted against him. The Director's efforts to hush up recent regrettable events were so successful — the press were told that they were accidents pure and simple and had made little of them — that the daroga, keeping his distance as usual, heard nothing of them, though he would certainly have recognised them as Erik's handiwork. And so, unaware of this escalation of the threat to the workings of the Opera, he continued to observe and patrol.

The very night after the agreement between Monsieur Vaucorbeil and the 'Opera Ghost' was sealed, during a performance of *Carmen*, he began yet another inspection of the spaces under the stage. He took up a position in the dark alcove, and kept watch. His patience was rewarded when he spied the shadowy figure he had been hoping for. It climbed the stairs from the third cellar and made directly for the west wall. There it lit a dark lantern, reached up with one hand and directed its beam on to the stone for a moment. A black hole appeared. The daroga knew it for one of Erik's hidden trapdoors. The figure passed through and the wall closed up again. The daroga crossed to the wall and ran his hands over the area where the dark figure had pressed a spring or pulled a lever. For several moments, he searched in vain. Suddenly he felt a small projection and pressed it. The wall swung open. He stepped into the darkness beyond. The door swung silently shut behind him of its own accord.

He found himself in a tunnel. To his left, he saw the faint glimmer of the dark lantern. He immediately set off in pursuit. The light moved quickly and he was forced to hurry so as not to lose sight of it. This could not be the way into the back entrance to the Wizard's den: they had come too far, the air was too damp and the ground beneath his feet was muddy. Suddenly the light disappeared, cut off no doubt by a bend in the tunnel. He continued to hurry on, but in his haste he stumbled and fell. When he was on his feet again, he had half a suspicion that he had turned half a circle and was facing the direction from which he had come. But in the dark he could not be sure. He felt in his pocket for the candle which, as an inveterate explorer of the dark recesses of the Opera House, he always carried with him. He lit it.

The tunnel was about six feet high and the same wide. The roof and sides were rough-hewn. Saltpetre crystals clung to the walls like dirty snow or strange, sickly blooms. The tunnel was obviously not in regular use. He waited a moment, noting a faint movement of air in the flickering of the flame. He supposed the draught, designed to keep the air in the tunnel fresh, came from an opening on or near the surface. He sighed with relief. All he had to do was head into the flow of the air. Less concerned now about pursuing his quarry than with getting out, he walked on, ignoring smaller side passages which appeared at irregular intervals. He stepped over fallen stones and negotiated heaps of rubble which at times partly blocked his way. Occasionally, the tunnel forked or crossed others at intersections which invariably confronted him with a choice: should he go on making for the source of the draught or try another way? Each time he chose, he scratched a cross on the wall with his knife to mark his route in case he needed to retrace his steps.

The network of tunnels seemed endless and terrifying. He must have walked a mile already in the dark and was still no nearer finding a way out. Nor was there any sign that anyone had come this way recently. Then he heard footsteps and felt cheered until he realised that the sound was the echo of his own shoes on ground that was now harder and drier. Perhaps he had come the wrong way. Had he misread the direction indicated by the candle? Should he have walked with the breeze not in his face but at his back? Was it better to go on or turn and retrace his steps? He sat down on a fallen limestone block to think.

'I'll go back!' he said half aloud.

The words bounced back at him in the silence and seemed to mock his predicament. He stood up and started back the way he had come. His candle was burning low. By its light he picked out the crosses he had etched on the walls. When in doubt, he looked for tell-tale white limestone chips on the tunnel floor. There was no mud now, no more boot marks to show that he had passed this way, but the tunnel here now seemed to be getting damper again. But when he found his way completely blocked by a roof fall, it was obvious that he had taken a wrong turning. And then a drop of water fell from the roof onto his candle and extinguished the flame. He reached in his pocket for another match, but his coat had been soaked during one of his stumbles and all his matches were wet and refused to light.

The daroga was now very frightened. He was suddenly facing the prospect of a lingering death in impenetrable darkness not a hundred feet beneath a city of two million people. Still, if it was written that he should die, then he would not avoid his destiny.

But was his predicament truly the will of God? Or could it be the work of the Magician of Mazanderan who, realizing he was being spied on, had lured him into this tunnel and left him there to die! Perhaps the light he had followed had not vanished around a corner, as he had thought, but had been deliberately extinguished. Erik could have hidden in a side passage while he blundered past towards his doom! The though made him weak at the knees.

Although the fate that is truly inscribed on a man's forehead cannot be resisted, it is a man's duty to defy his enemies and defend his life. Taking his courage in both hands, he stretched out his arms until they found a wall and, feeling his way along it, advanced for two hundred paces, sometimes tripping over fallen debris. The ground turned damp again. Then he stopped. His eyes were now accustomed to the dark and in the blackness he thought he could make out a faint glimmer. There was no way of telling how far away or how strong the light was or even if he was really seeing it. And he certainly would not have seen it if his candle had not been put out. He moved forward. He counted fifty paces. The light was not above his head, not on one side but in the middle of the tunnel, low down, here, under his feet. He knelt and felt planed wood, jointed boards and a rusty iron handle. A trap door! Attacked by the damp air, the boards no longer fitted together tightly and the light was coming through the thin cracks between them. He pulled on the handle. At first, nothing happened. He pulled again with all his strength. The trap groaned, rose an inch, two inches and through the gap the light grew stronger, casting a faint glow over the walls and ceiling of his tunnel.

Below him was a broad passage. At intervals lamps burned in sconces on the wall. In the middle of the tunnel was a narrow canal: he had broken through into part of the capital's network of sewers. He raised the trapdoor to its fullest extent, sat on the edge of its frame and lowered himself into the sewer. He heaved an immense sigh of relief and sent up a prayer to his god. Following the direction of water flowing in the canal, which he supposed would eventually lead to the Seine, he eventually found a ladder of iron hoops fixed to the wall. He climbed the rungs which led to a manhole cover. Moments later, he was breathing the sweet air of a Paris evening.

Chapter 19

From Erik's *Journal*:

July 17, 18— Here is a pretty problem of moral philosophy:

Is conscience absolute?

Or is it modified by space and time?

Consider the following:

If millions perish in an earthquake in a distant land, I will regret their passing but lose no sleep over it.

If a stranger dies outside my door, will I feel more or less closely concerned than if he had died outside my neighbour's door?

Does the conscience of a man who commits a murder trouble him more or less than another murder which he committed thirty years before, in another country?

Surely killing a man, whether by accident or design, will fill the assassin with unease. But how much of this unease is guilt and how much fear of being discovered and punished for his crime? Let us concede, for argument's sake, that his unease is wholly guilt and ask if, having escaped detection for his first murder, he kills again, is his guilt greater or smaller? And if he murders again and again undetected, will not familiarity breed indifference and reduce his guilt on each occasion, until he is able to kill a fellow human being and think no more of it than of swatting a fly?

Habit is such a sly reshaper of hearts and minds!

These musing were prompted by something which happened yesterday, when I entered Box 5 through my secret trap door after the curtain had gone up and the house-lights had dimmed. Imagine my surprise to find a man already ensconced there, in the Box that is exclusively reserved for my personal use! It was not the first time this has happened, for Mme Giry sometimes makes mistakes which habit has taught me to tolerate, for she is a simple soul. I did not fall into a rage against her, nor was I angry with the intruder – a middle-aged, a dumpy little man with a pot-belly – who was entirely blameless. Yet though he was a complete stranger and had not offended me in any way, I took against him instantly. It was an entirely spontaneous, irrational reaction. Without a word, I put my hands round his disgusting, fleshy throat and squeezed. In the light coming from the stage, I saw terror in his staring eyes. After a few moments I released my grip, sat casually in the chair next to him, crossed my legs, and, as if nothing had happened, watched the performance which proved to be mediocre. Apart from the rise and fall of his paunch as he breathed, the man did not move. When the interval arrived, I decided I would not stay for the second half. I got to my feet and left by the way I had come. The man still did not move. This morning, Mme Giry reported that a dead body had been found in Box 5.

I cannot speak for the conscience of others, but I can affirm that in my own case, whether through habit or my nature, my conscience is not absolute but subject to the modifying effects I have described. Of course, by ordinary standards what I did was wrong. But I have killed before and felt – and still feel – no more guilt at having murdered a stranger by heart attack, an action for which I had neither motive nor deliberate volition, than I do for leaving the daroga to die imprisoned by rock, for which I did have a reason.

The two cases are very different. My assault on a perfect stranger was an impulse. For ridding myself of the daroga, I had a motive: to get him off my back. I could not allow him to go on dogging my footsteps, for his infernal prying would eventually have made others curious and encouraged them to hunt me down. But my reaction to both murders has been the same: indifference.

Still, the daroga did once save my life.

But that was twenty years ago and a world away.

Ibid., August 31, 18— The daroga is not dead! I have seen him! Bah! What difference does it make if he lives or dies! Neither he nor his like will penetrate my defences. I am Erik! I am impregnable!'

Ibid., October 3, 18— I count myself fortunate to have devils inside me with which I do battle each day, blessed to have in my inner shadows fiends and tempters to contend with, goblins to tilt at, incubi to dominate until I emerge ecstatic in victory and stand in triumph on the smoking ruins of my hopes, a bright star on a field of black nothingness! My devils bring me no peace! Long may they continue to do so and give me no time to brood!

Ibid., August 13, 18— Why do I continue to write of myself as an empty shell, a man with no human feelings? Is it because I take a morbid pleasure in making myself out to be worse than I am, an insensitive brute and a monster of egoism? Or because my self-esteem was torn to ribbons long ago and I have stopped believing that it can ever be restored? Or because I am simply too tired to shoulder the burden of hope anymore?

Ibid., January 30, 18— A new production of *Le Roi de Lahore* has given me fresh heart. It has shown me that opera is everything. It is love and tragedy and laughter and grief and above all it is music, which is capable of expressing what is beyond the reach of all words except those of the most ethereal poets! Long before Garnier's Palace of Music opened, I attended many performances in the old Salle Lepeletier and elsewhere. I saw and heard many fine tenors and basses, but was always drawn to female voices. Of them, the most unforgettable was the bright, crystal soprano of Christina Nilsson. And with it, such stage presence! Such eyes! The blue of Nordic seas! In comparison, La Galli-Marié, though well enough in the *Carmen* which inaugurated the New Opera House a dozen years or more ago, was stolid.

Recently, after years of neglect, I have begun to train up my own voice again. It has unusual range and moves easily between dramatic tenor and the sweetest *legato*. My motive is its usefulness to my new undertaking: the completion of my own opera, *Don Juan Triumphant*, which will not be performed in my lifetime and probably never after my death. It was begun many years ago and abandoned. I have taken it up again, and with it a requiem. The work of composition is exhilarating, exalting! Inspiration drives out all else. There are times when I go for days without eating or sleeping, such is my absorption in the task. I do nothing but exist inside the world of music and poetry which I am creating!

Ibid., June 14, 18– Will I never be left alone? The daroga, despite the lesson I taught him, continues to patrol the darkest passageways of the theatre, but is no nearer discovering where I hide far from the world. And now an inquisitive scene-shifter has accidentally found his way into the chamber of mirrors. He is there now. I will not save him, for he knows the secret of the trap in the third cellar and would have told it to all the world and thus destroyed my peace and privacy. He is not my concern. He will hang himself in due course with the rope provided on the iron tree. When he is dead, I shall move the body up to the third level. The authorities can make of it what they will.

Ibid., September 9, 18— Today, I have witnessed a miracle! In the *Faust* now in rehearsal, the role of Marguerite is to be sung by La Carlotta, who from what I have heard of her thus far, is not my idea of Faust's beloved. There is a coarseness in her person which is echoed in her voice, especially the lower register. But a new singer is to play Siébel. It is a breeches role and she plays it affectingly enough, but she was born to sing Marguerite! Her voice is capable of expansion and I could help her acquire more notes at the top and the bottom of her compass. She needs help too with her breathing and intonation. Her name is Christine Daaé.

But I run ahead of myself. I have spoken to no human for eight years. Like Crusoe on his island, I have learned to be satisfied with my own company, knowing it to be preferable to the unkindness of strangers. Even if I did not wear the face of the arch fiend, I am unfit now to show myself in public let alone act as her teacher.

Ibid., September 10, 18— It is decided: I *shall* teach her! I have found a way!

*

It was a dark, damp, misty December night when there was a ring at the door of the daroga's apartment in the rue Guénégaud.

Darius entered the daroga's sitting room.

'A gentleman to see you, *Agha*. He would not give his name. He says you have been expecting him.'

'I do indeed know the man, Darius. Show him up and bring brandy. It is a cold night for a man to be out in.'

The daroga had been sitting at his window watching the few late cabs and pedestrians and, in the light shed by the newly installed electric streetlamps, he had seen the shuffling figure approach. He recognised the man instantly. When Darius announced his visitor, he rose and held out his hand. The man was hunched and muffled and leaned heavily on a cane with a silver top. He ignored the daroga's extended hand and slumped into a chair.

'The stairs ...' he gasped as he waited for his breathing to slow enough for him to continue.

The daroga was shocked by the change in him. He had not seen Erik for a month, since the day the drama surrounding Christine Daaé had reached its shattering climax. In that time, the years seemed to have caught up with him. Sustained for so long by the power of will, frustration and rage, he had seemed to defy the passage of time. Surely he could not be as old as he looked, thought the daroga, but he seemed a man whose sun had set and would not rise again.

'You are ill,' he said.

'Dying,' said Erik, accepting the glass of brandy that was offered him. 'I have no appetite. I have no wish to live.'

'What can I do for you?'

'You can nail down my coffin lid by hearing my confession.'

'I am not a priest.'

'No matter. The black deeds I have committed are not sins. They are crimes and they are many. I have done terrible things and terrible things gave been done to me. I do not apologise nor do I complain. But, daroga, few men have been tested as I have been tested. I did what I had to. My life has had no point except survival, and it was not enough. That is what I wish to confess to you who have been to me more a friend than any other man.'

'But ...'

Erik held up one hand.

'I am too weary to hear objections. There was a time when I persuaded myself that I had learned to be indifferent to others and beyond the reach of common humanity. I convinced myself that my obligations to others were cancelled by my expulsion from the human race. I was mad, daroga. But the fit has passed. I will feel easier if I tell you, who were part of it, the story of my return to sanity and my discovery of peace.'

The daroga sat back in his chair in silence and prepared to listen.

'I had lived alone, in the world of my thoughts, my books and my music for so long that I thought I would never have any more to do with the human race But then the miracle happened: last summer, I heard

Christine Daaé sing at an audition! I regularly attended — unseen, of course — auditions at the Opera House and few aspirants measured up to my standards. Her technique was unpolished, but the voice was there! I knew at once what I had to do! I vowed I would make her the greatest voice of the century!

'But how could I, with the face of the Beast, ever approach Christine? My plans seemed to founder before I had begun. But then I remembered an old tunnel which the Communards made use of during the troubles. It ran along the back wall of Christine's dressing-room. Working by night, I designed a system of hollow bricks which functioned as a kind of speaking tube. This allowed me to stand in the tunnel and communicate with her as though I was by her side in her dressing-room. When I spoke to her for the first time, she was more surprised than frightened, then puzzled and soon charmed, for I used my powers of mesmeric suggestion to smooth my way.

She was an amenable subject and did not resist. Guided by my voice alone which without any prompting from me she herself identified with the 'Spirit of Music', she made rapid progress. Within three months, she acquired more high and low notes and improved her flexibility and musicality to such a pitch of excellence that when, as a replacement for La Carlotta who was indisposed (and I confess to having had a hand in bringing about her 'indisposition'), she sang at a gala concert attended by the most fashionable Parisian public and most demanding *cognoscenti*, she was a sensation! The audience was overwhelmed but also amazed. La Daaé had never sung like this before! What had brought about such a transformation?

'Most of her admirers simply accepted it and were grateful. But a few curious spirits attributed it to the Phantom who many believed haunted the Opera House. But not you, daroga. The dogged way you pursued me was proof that you knew the truth. There was no ghost! There was only Erik!'

'Indeed,' said the daroga, 'I never believed that there was such a thing as a 'Phantom' in the Opera House. I knew equally that Christine's metamorphosis had to be the work of the Wizard of Nizhny-Novgorod, the Musician of Mazanderan!'

'But even on the night of the Gala, my moment of triumph turned to ashes. I entered the tunnel to give her my congratulations unseen, as always, through the voice channels I had made. But instead of speaking I was reduced to silence by what I heard. Christine was being helped to recover from a fainting fit, caused as I thought by the excitement of her success. She was being attended by her dresser. But also present was a young man, a childhood friend it seemed, though his words and tone of voice made it clear that he had designs on my pupil. Her reaction was modest and proper but I knew in my heart that she was lost to me.

'Raoul was his name, Raoul de Chagny.

'Fearing I should not be able to control myself if I intervened, I retreated to my haven of peace by the lake. But I knew that my peace had been shattered, that my haven was a delusion: it was no more than a burrow where I would be wretched and my highly-prized solitude would turn into loneliness. For I knew then that I loved Christine, loved her with all my soul!

'She was more than a pupil, mere clay to be modelled into an artist. My head was filled with pictures of her, the way she walked, the blue of her eyes, the sheen of her hair ... Eriknaz ...'

The daroga wondered who Eriknaz was but judged it wiser not to ask.

'... was blind to my ugliness. She loved me for my tenderness, my devotion, my oneness with her. I could think of her now after all these years without hurt and I knew why: what I once felt for Eriknaz I now felt for Christine. It was not passion. I was caught in an irresistible, silken skein of attraction, a compulsion as overpowering as any physical force of nature. It was as if some inflexible law made me gravitate to her. I did my best to strangle my feelings, for they would lead only to certain misery. But how could I resist for long the concentrated essence of womanhood which flowed from her?

'And as my resistance crumbled, so my jealousy grew and it filled me with bitterness.

'I knew that men who become besotted with young women are invariably ridiculous. At first I kept my distance. More, I gave Christine opportunities to be with Raoul so that she could adjudicate freely between him and me. At first, her love of art and loyalty to her 'Angel of Music' kept her on my side. But when she began to resent what she saw as my efforts to control her life, she began to grow away from me. I made it clear that if she persisted in her folly, Raoul's days would be numbered. It was shabby and it was a mistake.

'But though I was determined to keep her for myself, I hesitated to use every weapon in my arsenal. I could have sent Raoul to meet his Maker without compunction and carried Christine off to my impregnable dungeon. But that was not the way. I wanted someone who would come to me willingly, because she loved me for myself! You see how mad I was? Repulsive and self-obsessed, a man so sunk in cynicism could never be a husband for an angel like Christine! For that to happen, I would have needed to hypnotise her, like some oriental fakir, and keep her permanently under my influence, without will or desire or feeling, and that I did not want.

'I denied her nothing and allowed her to be as free as she wished. She used her freedom to meet Raoul on the roof of the Opera House where they thought I would not find them. But I was there – I was always there! – and I overheard her swear to love him for ever and a day. Raoul returned her feelings with interest and promised to spirit her away so that they could live out their days far from me, the ogre who threatened their happiness!

'The rest you know. By now jealousy had made me insane. To have her, there was nothing I would not do, no crime I would not commit!

'Losing patience, I abducted her and took her to my fortress beneath the Opera. Raoul's brother intervened and made a frontal assault from the lake side. He tried my patience too far and I intercepted him and held his head under the water until there was no life in him – you see how far into folly my possessive rage had pushed me? Then you and Raoul broke in through the trap in the third cellar and dropped into the chamber of mirrors. When Christine discovered that I would let her Raoul die if she did not agree to marry me, she capitulated. You too owe your life to her, daroga, to the self-sacrifice a woman made to a madman.

'I had won! I could now play the most exultant passages of my completed opera, *Don Juan Triumphant*!

'But was victory ever so empty? I had achieved by coercion what I could never have obtained through love. I had a promise of marriage extracted under duress! I had placed a ring on her finger! I had struck a bargain with Christine: Raoul's life for her promise to be my wife. But I still did not see what a sordid transaction it was!

'Yet even as I preened before her, revelling in the pomp and pride of success, she looked at me, but not in anger or resentment. A tear formed in her eye and her face said, "Poor Erik!" It was not pity: it was tenderness. Though I knew she could never be more than a friend, I was equally certain that *she loved me, in her way, for myself!* She held my hand for a moment and did not recoil at its clammy touch. She did not see the ghastly face which has always been my evil fortune. And then she did something that not even my own mother did for me …'

He paused. It took a moment before he could trust his voice.

'She kissed me! Here, on the forehead! Of her own free will! She had touched me with her lips! And she did not flinch!

'But I flinched, and more! I dropped my head and sobbed until I thought I would never stop.'

Erik paused, overcome by the memory. In the silence, the daroga said:

'And so Beauty overcame the Beast?'

'Perhaps.'

'Or was it that as an artist, Christine had an instinctive understanding of the human heart, that what she saw was not a Beast at all but a man like any other, vulnerable, with unfulfillable dreams?'

'That may be it, daroga. But however you explain it, that single moment had broken the spell of my insanity. Christine had ended my madness with one kiss and reconnected me with the human race. I stopped being a monster, foul without and foul within, and became a man again.'

After a moment's silence, the daroga said, 'In the east, we make much of a man's destiny which we say is indelibly written in the stars. Perhaps we are wrong, but Fate is sometimes a superb dramatist. Poets and heroes are cut off before they can show feet of clay: death is a dramatic way of preserving them in their glory. Some men's lives are finished works of art and have a beginning, a middle, an end and a meaning. But the fate of common mortals is much more often unlovely, chaotic and vulgar. Most lives are bad theatre, for few of us are cast for the roles we covet. How hard it is to accept that our miseries are pathetic in their insignificance. Heroes lose their kingdoms, their battles, their sanity and their lives. All we can ever lose is our illusions.'

'You are probably right, daroga. But fate was in a cruel, wanton mood when it made me fall in love with Christine. The result was not a tragedy, not even a drama: it was a black comedy, a farce. There was no magic that would turn Erik into a handsome prince. That role had already been given to Raoul.'

'But you forget that I was there, in your fortress beneath the Opera! I saw the change happen. It *was* magic, Erik, it *was* a miracle. I saw you reunite Christine and Raoul and give them both your blessing.'

'When Raoul was fully recovered from his ordeal in the chamber of mirrors, I released them. I even arranged for the cab that collected them so that they might go wherever they liked. They told the driver to take them to the Gare du Nord. There they must have boarded a train. I do not know where they went. But it does not matter now.'

*

After he finished the chronicle of his crimes, Erik sat on for a while, warming himself by the daroga's fire.

By the time he spoke again, the flames had burned low.

'Tonight I destroyed all means of entering the house by the lake, the refuge which I built beneath the Opera where I could live apart. My writings, the manuscripts of my musical compositions, everything I ever achieved which might have made my name live after me is now beyond reach.'

Erik stopped. His long speech had tired him. After a moment, he said, 'But I have one thing to ask of you. Will you see to it that my last wish is respected?'

'What is your wish? What is it you want me to do?'

'I wish you to ensure that nothing further will be heard of my passage on this earth. If my name is ever mentioned, you will say: "There was no such man!" If the gossips say: "There was never a Phantom of the Opera, it was Erik!" you will deny it. If diligent men say: "Let us look for evidence to prove that there was such a man! Perhaps we will find traces, witnesses, manuscripts which will feed our curiosity!" you will mislead them, throw them off the scent, refuse to tell what you know.'

'You may count on me,' said the daroga.

After a while, Erik rose unsteadily to his feet and made for the door.

'Goodbye, Wizard,' said the daroga.

If Erik heard, he did not react. Darius escorted him down the stairs. The daroga stood at his window. The streets were empty now. He heard the outside door open and close. He watched while a hunched figure passed down the rue Guénégaud in the direction of the Seine.

Soon the tapping of his cane on the pavement faded to silence.

*

No more than fifteen minutes later, a man wrapped in an evening cloak hobbled to the middle of the Pont Neuf. There he paused and looked down at the black, velvet water on which the unfriendly light of the street lamps was faithfully reflected. Then using his cane as a support, he hoisted himself on to the parapet, swayed there for a moment and let himself fall.

As the water closed over him and its coldness made him want to gasp, his eye was caught by a movement. It was a white hand. It beckoned to him. It was the hand on the arm of a corpse which had been caught on a submerged projection of the bridge's pontoon. This he knew, but he also knew beyond doubt, beyond reason, that it was the hand of Françoise, kind, gentle Françoise who had loved him unconditionally, *for himself*. He was overcome with relief, with joy, for with her he could be easy and never have to fight the world again. He opened his lips to say that he was coming, but the words were forced back by the eager water which poured hungrily down his throat and filled his lungs. Then his chest was a solid, unresponsive mass. His head threatened to explode, his eyes saw redness, his ears roared, he stopped moving. His limp body touched the river bed then rose to the surface where it floated downstream on the indifferent current, its unseeing eyes staring up at the uncaring stars.

Made in the USA
Columbia, SC
02 November 2020